THE BEST DEFENSE

THE BEST DEFENSE

Praise for LAMBDA Literary Award Finalist Carsen Taite

"Law professor Morgan Bradley and her student Parker Casey are potential love interests, but throw in a high-profile murder trial, and you've got an entertaining book that can be read in one sitting. Taite also practices criminal law, and she weaves her insider knowledge of the criminal justice system into the love story seamlessly and with excellent timing. I find romances lacking when the characters change completely upon falling in love, but this was not the case here. As Morgan and Parker grow closer, their relationship is portrayed faithfully and their personalities do not change dramatically. I look forward to reading more from Taite."—*Curve Magazine*

"Taite is a real-life attorney so the prose jumps off the page with authority and authenticity. [*It Should be a Crime*] is just Taite's second novel, but it's as if she has bookshelves full of bestsellers under her belt. In fact, she manages to make the courtroom more exciting than Judge Judy bursting into flames while delivering a verdict. Like this book, that's something we'd pay to see."—*Gay List Daily*

"Taite, a criminal defense attorney herself, has given her readers a behind the scenes look at what goes on during the days before a trial. Her descriptions of lawyer/client talks, investigations, police procedures, etc. are fascinating. Taite keeps the action moving, her characters clear, and never allows her story to get bogged down in paperwork. *It Should be a Crime* has a fast-moving plot and some extraordinarily hot sex."—*Just About Write*

"Taite's tale of sexual tension is entertaining in itself, but a number of secondary characters…add substantial color to romantic inevitability."—Richard Labonte, *Book Marks*

Visit us at www.boldstrokesbooks.com

By the Author

truelesbianlove.com

It Should Be a Crime

Do Not Disturb

Nothing but the Truth

The Best Defense

THE BEST DEFENSE

by
Carsen Taite

2011

THE BEST DEFENSE
© 2011 By Carsen Taite. All Rights Reserved.

ISBN 10: 1-60282-233-6
ISBN 13: 978-1-60282-233-7

This Trade Paperback Original Is Published By
Bold Strokes Books, Inc.
P.O. Box 249
Valley Falls, NY 12185

First Edition: July 2011

CREDITS
EDITOR: CINDY CRESAP
PRODUCTION DESIGN: SUSAN RAMUNDO
COVER DESIGN BY SHERI (GRAPHICARTIST2020@HOTMAIL.COM)

Acknowledgments

Writing might be a solitary pursuit, but brainstorming, research, editing, and polishing up the final product is a group effort.

Thanks to these very special people for assisting me with their specialized knowledge: John Ambler (private jets), Sharon B. (dead bodies), Mike Bosillo (private investigators), Roselle Graskey (firearms), Vicki Allen and Jean Alston (Harleys), and VK Powell (cop stuff). All of you provided excellent information and advice, and any lingering inaccuracies are my own.

Extra special thanks to my good buddies, VK "Vic" Powell and Sandy Thornton, who carefully read draft after draft, up until the hour the manuscript was due—your insightful advice was invaluable.

A big shout out to the Jewel Lesfic Book Club. Thank you for making me feel like a rock star with every new release. Your support is super motivating.

I am extremely lucky to be a part of the Bold Strokes Books family. I'll always be grateful to Rad for inviting me in, to my editor Cindy Cresap for whipping me into shape, to Stacia Seaman for her attention to detail, to Sheri for her hot cover art, and to all the other folks, Connie, Lori, and everyone else. You make me and BSB look good.

Huge thanks to my wife, Lainey. Don't think I don't notice all the extra things you do to keep our lives running smoothly when I'm in the throes of a deadline. You inspire me to be a better person.

And finally, a big group hug to all the readers who read my books, watch my vlogs, and take the time to let me know you'd like me to keep writing.

Dedication

For Lainey. You're simply the best.

PROLOGUE

"Would you like to take a break, Detective Keaton?"

Skye breathed deeply and shook her head. A break would only prolong the agony. "No thank you, Your Honor. I'm fine."

She wasn't fine. She shook and fumbled through her testimony. She didn't need a mirror to know she was probably also pale. The edges of the room loomed and faded by turns, and she struggled to be present. Trained to deliver tight, simple answers, instead she found herself rambling, her voice trailing off into whispers the jury strained to hear.

The last time Skye felt this nervous was the first time she testified in court. Fresh from the academy, she was called to testify in her first arrest. Her vocabulary consisted entirely of cop speak, and she'd become downright surly under cross-examination. Her lieutenant had pulled her aside and told her to spend a couple of her days off watching seasoned professionals on the witness stand. Skye had quickly learned to adopt a professional, engaging demeanor designed to win more convictions. Over the years, the prosecutors in the District Attorney's office were relieved when they learned she was the lead detective on a case. She could sell even the sketchiest set of facts as grounds for a conviction.

Today was different. Skye was at the center of the case, but this time she was the complaining witness—the victim—not the lead detective. A year earlier, while investigating a case, Skye had been badly beaten, almost killed, by a suspect. Today, that suspect, Theodore Burke, was on trial for the attempted murder.

Ironically, while investigating the murder of Theodore's sister, Skye had done everything she could to pin the death on someone else, the family handyman. When her former partner on the force, Parker Casey, pushed her, Skye had elected to do the right thing, and she came forward with evidence sure to exonerate him. What she hadn't realized was how much of a vested interest Theodore had in the outcome of the case. When the handyman was cleared, Theodore came unglued at the prospect of becoming a suspect himself. Furious at the detective who threatened his security, Theodore Burke, son of an elite Dallas family, broke into Skye's house, tied her up, and beat her. Skye shuddered to think about what he would have done next if Parker hadn't come looking for her and interrupted his crazy scheme. After an unsuccessful attempt to kill them both, Theodore Burke was arrested and charged with attempted murder. Today was Skye's day in court, as well as his.

She flashed back to the dozens of times she had encouraged crime victims to take the stand. *Just tell what happened. Focus on the jury. Don't look at the defendant. He can't hurt you anymore. Your courage will keep future victims safe from harm.* Platitudes and promises, all of which were designed to finish the job she'd started when she had arrested the bad guy. Had she ever cared about the victims as much as she cared about clearing the cases? Did anyone care about her now that she was the victim?

Theodore had sexually abused his sister, Camille, and drove her to commit suicide. Without Camille alive to testify about the abuse, there was no credible evidence to prosecute him for his crimes against her. Plus, Skye's meddling with the crime scene evidence would taint any prosecution for Camille's death. The assault on Skye was the only way the prosecutors would be able to bring Theodore to justice. With her credibility in the tank, would they have even bothered without Parker's testimony to corroborate her account? This trial had nothing to do with avenging her personal harm. She was a means to an end.

Skye stared across the room, breaking her own witness rule, daring Theodore Burke to look her in the eyes. His gaze was steady, mocking even. Skye summoned all her inner strength and fought back the memories of his mad visage and waving gun. She had both physical and emotional scars as evidence of his madness. She would always have them. She couldn't change what had happened, how she had handled it, or what she had done to cause it, but she could do everything in her power to make sure no one else suffered at the hands of Theodore Burke. Skye reached for a cup of water, took a quick drink, then a deep breath. Fortified, she answered every question thrown her way with the professional and engaging manner that had earned her commendations throughout the years.

After what seemed like hours, she finally heard the words, "I have no more questions for this witness." The judge released her and she found herself standing in the hall outside.

"Hey, Skye."

Skye looked up into Parker Casey's eyes. After all they had been through together, more downs than ups, Parker still cared about her. Skye was more embarrassed than appreciative.

"Hey, Casey. They tell you to stick around?"

"No, I'm done."

Skye knew Parker wanted to ask if she was okay, but didn't want to imply she wasn't by even asking. She should be a big girl and acknowledge how she felt, but she didn't want to break down. Not here in the hallway outside the courtroom.

"Want to grab a drink?" Parker asked.

Skye couldn't think of anything that sounded more appealing. A stiff shot of whiskey would be the perfect antidote to whatever she was feeling, but in her experience medicinal drinking was best done alone. "I need to get back to the station. I have some paperwork to clear out," she lied.

"Okay then." Parker looked like she wanted to say something else, but she just shook her head. "If you need anything, you know where to find me."

Skye nodded assent if only to make her old friend go away. Parker was a lawyer now, married to another lawyer. The two women had a thriving practice representing folks like Theodore Burke. Skye had no intention of seeking Parker out for anything. All that had ever bound them together had been severed with the conclusion of this case. As Parker turned and walked away, Skye wondered how much more she could lose.

CHAPTER ONE

I need your badge too."

Skye pulled the shield out of her pocket and placed it on the Deputy Chief's desk alongside her department issued Glock 9mm. She didn't care so much about the gun. She had plenty of those at home. Her detective shield was a different matter. The soft, worn leather holder encased the badge she'd worked hard to earn. Through the years, she kept it shiny. The irony of the shiny badge pinned over her tarnished reputation didn't escape her. She wanted to crack a smart remark, even opened her mouth to do so, but words wouldn't come. She stared at the badge. Shiny, defiant, and no longer hers.

"I'm sorry about this."

Skye looked up. His apology was sincere. She could tell. Chief Henry had been her biggest champion on the force. Even after his own promotions meant he was no longer one above her in the chain of command, he took a special interest in her career. He'd been a second father, a mentor, a teacher. She assumed that was why he took responsibility for relieving her of her duties himself instead of assigning the task to her lieutenant.

She knew coming clean on the Burke case would result in disciplinary action. She had used the guise of justice as an excuse to break the rules numerous times in the past, but each time her actions and the motivations behind them were safely concealed behind the blue veil of her brethren. When she admitted her transgression to a defense attorney, she crossed the line and became an outcast. Although the disposition of the disciplinary action against her had been put on hold while the Burke case was pending, she'd been given two options: resign and maintain her law enforcement certification, or put the department through a protracted termination proceeding and be stripped of all that she had worked to earn. It wasn't much of a choice.

She shrugged. The chief might be sorry, but it didn't change anything. His loss was short-lived. He would find another young cop to groom, someone to whom he could teach all his well-honed shortcuts. Someone who would crave his admiration and respect so much that he or she would shove the rules aside in favor of meting out real justice, quick and sure. Her replacement would be one of many waiting in the wings. She sincerely hoped that person would benefit more from breaking the rules than she had.

She shook his hand and left his office. The walk through the corridors was interminably long. The halls were lined with offices of the powerful elite in the Dallas Police Department. Chief Henry had chosen headquarters for their final meeting instead of her precinct, probably out of respect for her privacy. Here, there would be less of an audience of her peers to watch her dishonorable exit from a career distinguished by high profile arrests and solid convictions. What he probably hadn't counted on was that this particular walk of shame led to a sharp sense of loneliness. Neither her partner nor any of the other detectives from her squad were there to commiserate with her, pat her on the back, mourn her loss as one they could easily have experienced themselves. She was a pariah now. She'd broken the code, but the real transgression had been revealing her shortcomings to a defense attorney. The enemy. Having allowed the other side to glimpse a flaw in the mechanics of law enforcement, she'd never be welcome on the right side of law and order again.

Skye strode from the building, refusing to betray any embarrassment in her carriage. She walked through tall glass doors and crossed the street, counting the seconds until she could get on her bike and ride away.

"Skye! Hey, over here."

She looked in the direction of the voice, spotting her partner standing on the side of the building she'd just left. *Former partner.* She stood in place while he walked toward her, huffing at the exertion.

"You okay?"

She nodded. She wasn't. She might never be, but she wasn't going to talk about it.

"Are you coming back to the station?"

His subtle way of asking if she'd been fired almost amused her. "No, Ed. I'm never coming back to the station."

"I'm sorry."

Everyone was sorry. *Well, everyone should stick it. I'm the one who should get to be sorry, but instead everyone wants to say it first and have me reply with platitudes: it's okay; I'll be fine; don't worry about me. Well, fuck that.*

Skye didn't speak.

"Do you want to grab a drink?"

She did. She wanted to hold on to a big, tall glass of whiskey with both hands. She wanted to feel the burn as it crossed her lips and coursed down her throat, searing a path to her gut. She craved the slow, building buzz of warmth simmering in her belly and rising up until her ears reddened and her thoughts floated out of her head. She'd get what she wanted, but she didn't need company.

"No, thanks."

"Okay."

Ed Peterson didn't move. He seemed rooted in place, as unable to move as he was to come up with something appropriate to say to the partner who had taught him the ropes. She may be leaving the force while he continued to ascend the ranks, but their roles would never be reversed. She walked toward her bike and signaled for him to follow. Once there, she reached into one of the saddlebags, shoved aside the contents she'd hastily packed when she'd emptied her locker earlier, and pulled out a revolver. Ed looked around wildly, obviously afraid they were being observed. She ignored his frenzy. She didn't care who saw them.

She didn't recall where she'd gotten this particular handgun. It was a thirty-eight, common enough, though not the preferred weapon on the street. As a throw down, the gun would serve its purpose. Reliable, easy to fire. Skye could count on it to do in a pinch. Now Ed could. She wondered if he ever would, but not enough to discuss it with him. Instead, she said, "It can't be traced. Save it for a special occasion." He would either understand or he wouldn't. He was no longer her responsibility. She shoved it toward him, grip first. He stared into her eyes as if to divine her intent, but Skye didn't give him anything. Finally, he took the gun from her grasp and placed it in his jacket. Wisely, he didn't offer thanks.

Skye unlocked and pulled her personal weapon, a Sig P228 9mm from the special compartment inside the saddlebag and slid it into her shoulder holster, where her duty Glock had been. She'd always preferred the Sig, but the missing Glock left a big hole. The gun, the badge, the rank, the camaraderie—the list of things now lost to her was long, and the emptiness ran deep. Filling the space was an insurmountable task. She'd never shied away from the impossible before, but now…Now, all she wanted was a drink, a strong, deep glass of forgetting to wash away her memories and aspirations.

She threw her leg over the seat and started the Harley's engine. Ed shouted over the noise. "See you around?"

Skye didn't bother shouting her response. "I doubt it."

Her first stop after leaving police headquarters was the nearest liquor store. She sat in the parking lot and contemplated how many bottles would fit in the bags on her bike alongside all the property she'd cleared out of her locker at the station. Not enough.

She considered her options and ruled out a stop at home to make room for a liquor run. Instead, she roared out of the lot and steered her bike in the direction of Oak Lawn. She may not want company, but strangers didn't count. A short trip later, she parked in one of the several empty spots in front of Sue Ellen's. It was just after five o'clock. She stowed her helmet and shook out her shoulder length hair.

As she walked toward the bar, she noticed a few groups of women on the patio. Outdoor heaters took the edge off the crisp fall evening. It was the perfect weather for sitting outside. As Skye unzipped her jacket she remembered two things: she was packing, and she wasn't allowed to take her gun into a bar anymore. Like most law enforcement officers, Skye had a concealed handgun license. Losing her job didn't take that away from her, but only cops with CHLs were allowed to carry just about anywhere. For regular citizens, like she was now, there were limits. Liquor stores and bars, the two places she'd wanted to be tonight, were both on the list of forbidden places. Resigned to her new status, she strode back to her bike and subtly placed her weapon in the locked compartment inside the saddlebag.

Moments later, she was seated at the downstairs bar with a cold mug of beer and a shot of Bushmills. Skye wasn't alone, but a lesbian bar seemed the safest place to be, since the likelihood she'd encounter any of her police brethren was slim. She'd always taken special care not to let her orientation become an issue on the job, and it was a relief to sit in a bar with women holding hands, kissing, and dancing in each other's arms, without the slightest worry she might be seen.

The androgynous bartender deftly poured Skye's drinks, then offered to assist her with anything else she needed. Skye didn't respond to the remark, but filed it away for future use. Right now, all she cared about was the dulling promise of the alcohol in front of her. She drank swiftly to fulfill her end of the bargain.

"I can't possibly dance after that ten course food festival you and Nick whipped up. It's my birthday. Just let me sit on this nice barstool and watch you lovebirds sway to the music. That's my wish." Aimee Howard slid into the nearest seat and dared her friends to drag her away. This was the first dateless birthday party she could remember, but the choice had been hers.

"Fine, but let me at least get you a drink." Mackenzie Lewis, Aimee's best friend, stood waiting for her order. Aimee pushed her playfully away. "You've been waiting on me all night." Aimee called out to Mackenzie's lover, "Dr. Wagner! Oh, Dr. Wagner!"

Jordan Wagner strode over to Aimee's perch and inclined her head. "Yes, Birthday Mistress?"

"A Cosmo for me and one of whatever my friend slash personal chef here is having. Oh, and do get something for yourself."

Aimee's tone was teasing. She, Mac, and Jordan had been friends since college when, while attending UT in Austin, they all discovered they had several things in common including the fact they were all from Dallas, and they were all lesbians. They became fast friends and, recently, Jordan and Mac had become lovers.

But Aimee was still holding out for the love of her life. She'd engaged in what her friends had nicknamed serial monogamy for years. Her friends teased that she kept a moving company on retainer to escort the flavor of the month into and out of her home. Aimee protested, but she had to admit she was generous at the onset and often displeased with the end result. Her wealth and status was a definite handicap when it came to finding a mate who loved her more than the trappings that accompanied her devotion. After years of perpetually picking the wrong women, she seemed doomed to let the swell of first date lust sweep away any trace of skepticism.

Just last week, Aimee had turned out the latest woman allowed to grace her home after she learned the fiend was gathering material for a book about the adult lives of children of Dallas socialites. Aimee thought the idea behind the book was thoroughly unengaging and unlikely to be picked up for publication, but Aimee wasn't keen on the idea of her lover going through her mail and trash looking for tidbits that might be interesting to her readers. She took swift action and hired movers to send the woman packing.

Following this latest relationship crumble, her circle of friends were determined she wasn't going to spend her birthday alone, and they had rallied to show her a great time. Another couple in the group, Meaghan and Haley, were her designated drivers. After they picked her up at her home in Highland Park, the evening started at MacKenzie's East Dallas restaurant, the Lakeside Grill, with a tasting menu personally prepared by Mac's chef, Nick Walters. After dinner, Jordan insisted they adjourn to Sue Ellen's to dance off dinner. Aimee dreaded this part of the evening. Dancing usually meant pairing off. Even though it was her big night, she was the fifth wheel, despite the obvious efforts of the other two couples to include her in her own celebration.

Jordan placed her Cosmo on the bar alongside another for Mac. She grabbed Mac and Aimee and pulled them both toward the dance floor. "Remember in college? The three of us used to dance together all the time. Come on, let's show 'em what we got." Jordan's magnetism was difficult to resist. Aimee reached for her drink, toasted the air, and drank half of it down. *What the hell. It's my birthday.*

❖

Skye lost count of how many drinks she'd consumed. At some point she stopped ordering the beer back, and concentrated on whiskey as her drug of choice. Her dealer, the bartender, seemed happy to keep them coming. Each new glass was delivered with an increasingly heavy side dose of attention, a brush against her hand, a whispered comment, a knowing smile. Skye wasn't sure whether the bartender was motivated by the prospect of dollars in the tip jar or a chance to get in her pants, and she didn't care. In her current state, Skye was likely to give her anything she wanted. Sex would be just another drug to soothe her pain.

It must be late, she thought. The bar was crowded and most of the women were well on the way to inebriation. Skye noticed a good-looking group of women on her left. She wasn't sure how long they had been there, but it was obvious they all knew each other well. They were older than many of the patrons, and they carried the look of professional success in their classy wardrobes. A sporty blonde was pressed up against a tall, dashing redhead. A couple. Another couple, nursing Perrier, watched them indulgently as if they had been the matchmakers.

The last woman in the group was the one who caught Skye's attention, a voluptuous blonde. Her hair was perfectly coiffed and framed her face in well-tamed waves. Despite her strong buzz, Skye could tell her lapis blue eyes held just a hint of sadness behind the twinkle she put on for the crowd. Her body was full-figure perfect, every curve rounded out her designer dress with promises of pleasure beneath, except for the neckline, which did more than promise. Low-cut lines displayed perfect cleavage, and for a brief moment, Skye imagined herself running her tongue down the side of one breast and back up the other as she explored the valleys of this woman's offering. She flicked a glance at the blonde's hands, perfectly manicured French nails. Her tiny feet were encased in tall pumps, with slight openings for her painted toes to peep through. Her makeup was flawless, and her diamond jewelry shone bright. Everything about her spoke expensive, high-class socialite. She was the antithesis to Skye's rough, windblown look.

Skye shrugged. She had no business lusting after picture-perfect divas. Raised with five brothers, she was pure tomboy. While she might appreciate girly beauty from a distance, she didn't understand it. Why would anyone go to all the trouble of layering over the attributes they were born with? This woman's body spoke volumes about her natural beauty. Skye was willing to bet she was even more gorgeous when the makeup, hair products, and jewels were stripped away.

As if she could hear Skye's thoughts, the blonde turned away from her friends and looked in Skye's direction. Skye maintained her focus until the blonde locked eyes with her. She had no idea what her own expression spoke, but the blonde's look was curious, her lips turned up in a playful smile. Still, something lurked beneath the smile. A hint of loneliness?

Skye knew that feeling, even pretended she liked it. Was the blonde pretending too? Skye wasn't fooled by the entourage. Sometimes a crowd only accentuated the isolation. She stared at the blonde, unable, unwilling to break the connection.

She considered going to her, asking her to dance, but after countless drinks, she wasn't sure she could even walk. She resigned herself to merely returning the smile, an invitation for the woman to approach her instead. Would she? The events of the day had shattered Skye's confidence more than she cared to admit. Her pals on the force called her cocky, but she knew the other not as nice words they used behind her back.

Maybe the combination of sex and alcohol was the perfect plan to take the edge off. She shrugged away the foreboding sense this encounter would lead to more. The blonde started toward her, and Skye broke their connection for a moment to take a drink. She looked back in time to see her plan unravel in a sequence of brief scenes. The tall redhead tapped the blonde on the shoulder. The blonde stopped moving and looked back. The redhead introduced her to a beautiful dark-haired woman who, like the blonde, sported a cocktail dress and all the appropriate accessories. The women shook hands. Skye could imagine the conversation, led by the redhead. *Meet this nice woman. She's like you. Much better for you than the rogue across the room. No need for you to slum it with her, when you can go out with someone in your same social class.*

The connection broken, Skye swiveled back to her drink. As she pulled the whiskey toward her, the bartender tapped the glass. "Another Bushmills, or are you ready to call it a night? My shift's over now." Her penetrating stare conveyed an invitation.

Skye couldn't help herself. She shot a look at the curvy blonde across the room before turning her attention back to the bartender. She read the full extent of the offer in her eyes. Drink or sex? The choice was hers. She was tired of making choices. Justice or truth? Quit or be fired? Be a cop or be...? She drained the last drops from the glass in front of her and pushed it toward the bartender.

"Why don't you choose for me?"

"Damn, where is she?" Aimee didn't try to hide her frustration. *It's my birthday, after all.* She had finally summoned up the courage to approach the hot blonde at the bar, when Jordan interrupted to introduce her to one of her friends. Cynthia Hanley had a cause to pitch and was hopeful Aimee might toss some of the famous Howard fortune her way. Jordan had already contributed to the cause and was helping Cynthia line up additional donors. Aimee listened politely for a couple minutes before encouraging Cynthia to contact her office and schedule an appointment to make a full presentation. She'd barely heard a word she said. Instead, she'd been focused on scouting out the striking blonde at the bar. She looked around but didn't see her anywhere.

Mac waved a hand in front of her face, breaking her intense visual search. "Who are you looking for?"

"I saw this woman at the bar."

"And?"

"I'm not sure. I think she was asking me to dance or something."

"You talked to her?" Mac placed a hand on Aimee's forehead and lifted her Cosmo from her hand. "Honey, are you feeling okay? You've been with us all night. I think I would've noticed if a woman asked you to dance."

"It was more of a silent invitation. I could feel the request from across the room." Aimee knew she sounded crazy the minute the words tumbled out, but she couldn't deny the magnetic pull she'd felt when the woman had smiled her way. Now she felt a vacuum. She was certain the woman was no longer in the bar.

Mac continued to seek out the stranger. "What did she look like?"

"Long, windblown blond hair, lean body, but muscular. Dressed in worn jeans, tight black T-shirt, black leather boots." Aimee surveyed Mac's appearance. "Actually, she was an edgy version of you."

"Wow. You sure got a lot of detail from across the room."

"There was a connection. I can't explain it, but the air between us crackled." She laughed. "I know you probably think I'm crazy. She was totally not my usual type, but she was totally hot. And now she's gone. I can feel it."

Mac slid an arm around her waist. "I'm sorry." Then, as if Aimee's earlier remark had just penetrated, she asked, "What do you mean, totally not your type?"

Aimee smiled. "Wondered when you were going to snap. Face it, Mackenzie, you athletic babes are too much for a sedate gal like me to handle. I can guarantee she hits the gym first thing every day. I don't need some chick who's going to wake me up in the morning for anything other than to serve me breakfast in bed."

"Breakfast?"

Aimee shared a wicked grin with her. "Okay, well, I would consider waking up early for something besides breakfast. Maybe if we wait here until then, she'll come back."

CHAPTER TWO

S kye rolled over onto an empty whiskey bottle. She extricated the intruder and chucked it onto a clump of dirty laundry growing by the side of her bed. She rubbed her eyes and tried to focus on the bright green numbers of her bedside clock. Twelve eighteen, likely p.m. since the sun glared, accusingly, through her window blinds. She wasn't entirely sure what day it was, not that it mattered. She thought about rolling back over. She'd probably sleep better now that she wasn't lying on a hunk of glass, but a rolling in her gut urged her out of bed.

The path to the bathroom was strewn with the detritus of her chaotic life. Who knew drinking and fucking could wreak such havoc? The revelation was especially surprising since all the fucking had taken place elsewhere. Lord knew she couldn't bring women back here to screw. She might lose them in the clutter. In the last three weeks since she'd been dismissed from the job, she'd gone home with a different woman every night. Despite herself, she'd kept a vigilant watch for the blonde, but she didn't see her again. Finally tired of the knowing looks from the bartender at Sue's, she started trolling other bars to find new prospects. The bartender would gladly soothe her pain, again and again, but Skye wasn't interested in forming even the pretext of a relationship. No double dipping.

No matter whom she went home with, she managed to make it back to her place before dawn. Sitting in the dark, she drank to fill the empty spots in her soul, to quell the fear of being alone, to silence the memories of her assault at the hands of Theodore Burke in this very room. The alcohol only worked to reduce her waking fears to nightmares, lulling her into sleep before the piercing pictures of her experience sent her screaming back awake. She was stuck in the cycle, but she didn't know how to break it. Her attempts consisted of more alcohol, more strangers stroking her to oblivion. Both remedies worked temporarily, but she had yet to find the permanent fix. Looking around the room, she realized she wasn't going to find it here.

When the phone rang, she was tempted to chuck it across the room. There was no one she wanted to talk to. She glanced at her message machine. The display read "memory full." She couldn't remember the last time she'd checked it. She conceded it might be time to ease back into the real world and lifted the handset.

"Yeah."

"Skye, is that you?"

Oh shit. Skye straightened at the sound of her mother's voice, and arranged the covers on her bed, embarrassed at having been caught in such a mess. *She can't see you.* The thought didn't change her behavior. From a very early age, Skye learned to believe in her mother's strong sixth sense based on many occasions she had witnessed the power in action.

"Hi, Mom." She cleared her throat to dismiss the creak of speaking the first few words of the day.

"Did I wake you?"

"No, I'm awake." Mostly true, she decided.

"We've been worried about you. We're having a late lunch. Get cleaned up and come on over."

Skye looked in the mirror. Her hair was smashed flat against her head, and the bags under her eyes bore witness to days of fitful sleep. Her only clothing, a T-shirt, was streaked with whiskey stains. A shower alone wasn't going to make her presentable, but her mother's invitation wasn't a request, it was a command.

"Sure. I'll be right over."

The shower did its part to wake her up, but Skye rooted around in the kitchen for coffee to take her the rest of the way. An exhaustive search turned up enough grounds for a small pot, but no filters. Not to be deterred, Skye shoved a paper towel in the coffee maker, and moments later, shuddered her way through a cup of the rough brew.

Later at the gas station, her problems weren't so easily solved. The gas gauge on her bike registered at near empty and both of her credit cards were declined at the pump. She flashed back to the numerous times she'd used her cards at the bar lately and guessed she'd spent more on alcohol than she'd realized. A thorough search of her pockets turned up a scattered assortment of bills and coins, totaling ten dollars and forty-seven cents.

On the ride over, Skye wondered who would be at lunch. She'd finally figured out it was Sunday when she saw the bulky edition of the paper for sale at the convenience store where she'd purchased her fuel. When she was growing up, Sunday afternoon dinner represented the most important meal of the week. Everyone was expected to attend, dressed for a formal meal. Skye surveyed her attire. Levi's, black T-shirt, and heavy black leather boots. Well, at least she was dressed. Hopefully, her mother would understand her current circumstances had diverted her attention from adherence to social graces.

Her father answered the door. Stuart Keaton, retired assistant chief of police, was a formidable man. When Skye was growing up, her father's career was at its peak, and she'd always thought of him as a cop first, then a father. She dreaded his reaction to her separation from the force. Chief Keaton thought that the job was a calling. She figured he would think she wasn't worthy of the badge and, by association, not worthy of his respect.

Nothing about his expression or demeanor betrayed his feelings, but his words told her everything she needed to know. "Hey, girl, your mother is in the kitchen with the wives. Why don't you go help her get the meal ready? I'll be outside with your brothers. We'll talk later."

Never in the thirty-five years she'd been alive had her parents ever treated her differently than their five sons. They'd expected her to excel at sports, suppress tears when injured, and become a decorated cop. Just like her brothers. Her mother cooked and cleaned, with the assistance of a part-time housekeeper, and never had Skye been expected to perform "womanly" domestic duties. Mowing the lawn, changing oil in the cars, landscaping preparation—those were the only tasks she was expected to do around the house. Her dismissal to the kitchen was a strong message about her new rank in the household structure.

Her mother's greeting was completely different. Large spoon in one hand and potholder in the other, she closed the distance to give her a fierce hug. Skye fought the tears that threatened to appear as her mother held her close. When she finally pulled away, her mother tilted her chin and looked intently at her face.

"You're not sleeping."

Understatement. Skye was just grateful her mom didn't mention the puffiness that accompanied the dark circles under her eyes. She knew her mom wasn't so naïve that she wouldn't realize Skye had been medicating with alcohol, but she didn't want to discuss it. Their family rules were firmly in place—no direct discussion of uncomfortable topics, even here in the kitchen with "the wives." Her brothers' wives were supportive, feminine, and obedient. No way was Skye going to discuss her circumstances with any of them. Her father and brothers were a different matter, and Skye wondered how her family of cops would make it through an entire meal without mentioning the topic of her dismissal from the department. She wouldn't have to wait long to find out.

"A good meal will make you feel better."

"I'm sure it will." Skye gestured toward the stove. "What can I do to help?"

"Sit. Keep me company." Her mother pointed to the large oak table in her vast kitchen. Clearly, her ideas about Skye's role in the family hadn't changed. She placed a large glass of iced tea on the table and urged her to drink.

"Mom, I'm sorry I haven't called." Skye felt like a heel in the face of her mother's kindness. "I've been going through a lot lately."

"Hush. You'll get through this. You're a good woman, Skye." She leaned close to her and whispered in her ear. "You don't need a badge to prove it."

The words were exactly what she needed to hear, even if she didn't believe them. She knew her father and brothers would strongly disagree. As if she could read Skye's mind, her mother added, "They'll come around. Don't you worry."

Coming around didn't take the form Skye expected. After everyone's plates were full, her father tapped a knife against his tea glass to command everyone's attention. All eyes turned his way.

"I have a couple of things to say, and then this subject will be closed forever." His steady gaze in her direction signaled to Skye that "this subject" was her termination from the force. Perfect. She braced herself for his public airing of her dirty laundry.

"The official record states Skye resigned from the force. Her personnel jacket shows only a lengthy term of commendable service. I will not tolerate anyone implying she was anything other than a decorated, honorable law enforcement officer. Should anyone imply otherwise, I expect you, as her brothers, to display loyalty. Skye has retired to pursue other interests. End of story." One by one, he scrutinized her brothers' faces. "Do I make myself clear?" They each nodded in turn.

His next comment was directed to Skye. "My old partner, Ernie Lavatos, runs a security company. It's good work. He'll provide you with a car and uniform. You'll have to work shifts, but it's good work," he repeated as if to convince himself.

Skye fought to contain the shudder the words "security company" evoked. She hadn't worn a uniform in years and the thought of donning heavy polyester clothes was almost as distasteful as the moniker "rent-a-cop." Sure, she might get a shiny new badge, but she wouldn't be allowed to carry a firearm to back it up. She kept her eyes focused on her father to avoid the sympathetic expressions of her brothers.

Her father ignored her silence and her brothers' barely concealed reactions and continued. "I'll give you his number after dinner. He's expecting you to call tomorrow. You can start work tomorrow night."

She knew by his tone, he expected her to accept the work without question. If she did, she would spend her nights tooling around mostly vacant parking lots in a four-door box-shaped car instead of picking up women in bars. Skye flashed to the spare change in her pocket. Forty-seven cents remained after her trip to the gas station. She figured she could scrounge another ten bucks from loose change in her apartment, but she wouldn't be picking up too many women with that kind of dough. She wouldn't be doing much else either. Resigned to her fate, Skye hoped the job site wasn't farther away than the ten bucks' worth of fuel in her tank could reach.

CHAPTER THREE

Aimee loved Monday mornings as much as someone could love something she barely noticed. While the rest of the world scurried around, frantically transitioning into work mode, she usually made a point of sleeping in. After all, as a successful real estate broker, leisurely weekends were rare. Her boutique real estate firm was at the top of the list in the more exclusive areas of the city such that even with a business partner and four other agents working for her, Aimee remained as busy as any of them. Most of her clients had known her for years and didn't want to place their trust in anyone else. Born into a long line of brokers and developers, real estate was in her blood, and she took special pride in helping her clients manage the sale and acquisition of unique residences. Often, Monday morning, when everyone else's focus turned back to their own careers instead of acquiring or divesting themselves of a home, was the only time she could guarantee to be completely her own. Even Elsa, her housekeeper, had the day off.

Actually, this past weekend had been fairly slow. As the holidays approached, everyone seemed more focused on shopping for presents than homes. The lull in business zapped any touch of guilt she might have for sleeping the morning away.

The sharp ringing of the phone bit into her sleepy haze. Aimee considered ignoring the caller, but after three rings she was already half awake. If she didn't do something to interrupt the noise, she'd have no chance at revisiting la-la land.

"Hello," she grumbled. It was her home phone. She didn't have to act happy.

"Aimee?" The voice on the other end was barely a whisper.

"Yeah, who's this?"

"It's Tom. I have to make this fast. They don't know I'm here yet."

Aimee sat up and scratched her head. Tom was her business partner. What she didn't know was who "they" were?

"You're going to have to make more sense than that. I was sound asleep when you called. Oh, and speak up. I can barely hear you."

He continued, still in a whisper. "A whole team of cops just descended on the office. I've never seen anything like it. There must be a dozen of them. They have a warrant and they're picking the place apart. I ducked into the storeroom when I heard them so I could call you. Based on what I've heard, they're looking for—"

Silence. Aimee shook the phone. "Tom? Hey, Tom? Are you there?" Nothing. She hung up and redialed his number.

"You've reached the voice mailbox of Tom Glannon. I'm not available to take your call right now—" Aimee hung up without listening to the rest. Next, she dialed the main office number. Three rings in, she jumped at the sound of loud banging. It took a minute before she realized the banging was coming from downstairs, not her phone line.

What the hell? She hung up and ran toward the front stairwell. Most of the time, Aimee loved her spacious home. Days like today, she hated living in a six thousand square foot three-story all by herself. She paused at the first floor landing and peered out the tops of the tall, arched windows. The street was lined with rows of dark sedans and SUVs, none of which were the Mercedes Benzes, Lexuses, and Range Rovers like she was used to seeing in her Highland Park neighborhood. Aimee spotted a cluster of uniformed men with guns dash toward the side of her house. Although she had almost no direct contact with law enforcement, Aimee had seen enough episodes of *Criminal Minds* to know a herd of some kind of cops was in the neighborhood to take down someone important.

Suddenly, she connected Tom's phone call, the raid at her office, and the insistent pounding on her front door. The battalion of officers amassing outside was here for her. Instantly, she went from voyeur to hunted.

Glancing down, she wondered if her short cut negligee would buy her any leniency. The shouts of, "Federal Agents, open the door!" foreclosed any thoughts she had about changing into something more modest. Surely, once they realized they had the wrong place, she could crawl back into bed and pretend this whole experience was just a bad dream.

"I'm coming," she called out, but the sound of her voice was lost against the loud boom of the battering ram that felled her reclaimed oak wood door flat into the foyer. The stained glass windowpane in the door shattered. Before Aimee could properly mourn her loss, a sea of agents in black flak jackets stormed into the entryway, and shoved their big black guns in her direction.

"On your knees! Hands on your head! Now!"

Aimee dropped to her knees immediately. *So much for the negligee.* Her levity faded fast as she felt cold, biting metal encircle her wrists. She was certain this was all a huge mistake, but she was on her knees, restrained, with nasty looking guns pointed in her direction and a circle of men in black sporting an alphabet soup of initials on their vests and jackets. Whatever the mistake was, it wasn't going to just go away. She struggled to think of something she could say or do to stop this home invasion and secure her release. Bits and pieces of television shows played through her mind. Finally, she found a common thread.

"Do you have a warrant?"

"Yes."

The tall man standing over her uttered only the one word. Apparently, she was supposed to accept it as the final say. He was entirely in black except for broad white letters on his vest. This one read ATF. Aimee searched her mind. Alcohol, Tobacco, and Firearms. He had that last one down. He was holding a huge black gun and wore a shoulder holster with its twin. Aimee didn't see any evidence of a neatly folded paper warrant, the kind detectives shoved in the hands of defendants as they entered their homes. *Should he show it to me? Don't I get to see exactly what it says? When do I get my phone call? Am I even under arrest?* Her television references were a mixed bag when it came to answering these questions. Aimee decided the best way to get an answer was to ask a question straight out.

"What the hell are you looking for?"

The man didn't respond, but Aimee heard a single word echoing through the halls of her home: "Clear!" In a few minutes, she was surrounded by at least a half dozen more armed men, ICE, FBI, and more ATF. One of them nodded his head at her and two others yanked her to her feet and walked her down the stairs. They seated her at the head of her formal dining table and filled in the remaining chairs. The one who had nodded removed her cuffs.

"Where is she?"

Aimee scrunched her brow for a moment, then the pieces began to click into place. They were looking for her good-for-nothing ex. *Writing a book, my ass. I bet she was up to some nefarious fraud scheme.* Whatever it was had to be horrible enough to merit a federal raid with a battering ram and a full arsenal. She would gladly give up the tramp. In fact, she was certain the moving company receipt contained the tramp's new address.

"I'm going to need to look for her address, but I'll be happy to help. She moved out a few weeks ago. I'm sure her new address is on the mover's receipt."

"She's not working for you anymore?"

Aimee was confused. Tramp had never worked for her. She'd never worked at all unless you called pretending to write a book working. Aimee remembered Tom's phone call. Federal agents were at her office. Something was off, and she was back to thinking the whole thing was a big mistake.

"Who are you talking about?"

The men seated around the table exchanged glances, and then the one obviously in charge leaned forward and tossed a set of papers in front of her. "Nicole Howard. Your niece."

Before Aimee could process his statement, questions came fast from several directions.

"When was the last time you saw Nicole?"

"Just before her midterms, uh, a few weeks ago. She came by the first weekend before heading out of town."

"Where was she going?"

"I think she was headed to Vegas for the weekend."

"You don't know?"

"I don't remember. She was only here a couple of hours before her flight."

"Why is this address listed as her residence?"

Aimee considered the question before answering. Nicole's dad, Aimee's brother Neil, had been transferred to Europe during Nicole's first year of college. In order to maintain her resident status, Nicole lived with Aimee during breaks and vacations, though this past year her stops at Aimee's home on the way to various travel destinations were brief. The last time she'd seen Nicole, she'd been downright surly and they had had a fight, though about what Aimee couldn't quite recall. Aimee wasn't sure if Nicole's representation that she lived with her constituted some kind of crime, but she was pretty sure these badasses weren't here to arrest Nicki on a tuition violation.

"Her parents live in Europe. She was already enrolled at UT Austin when they moved, so she uses my address as a home base."

"And she worked for you?"

Ah, that's why they were at the office. "For a few weeks last summer."

The main questioner nodded, but his eyes betrayed he thought she was lying. Aimee started to protest, but decided to take a different tack, and ask some questions of her own. "What do you want with Nicole?"

"I'm afraid that's confidential."

"Can you at least tell me what you think she's done to merit such a show?"

"I'm afraid I can't tell you anything. Security reasons."

"Really?" Aimee could feel her voice rise along with her temper. This guy wasn't afraid of anything, and she was annoyed at this attitude. "You can bust down my front door and manhandle me, but when it comes to answering a simple question you're 'afraid'? Whatever." She folded her arms and resolved these bullies would get no more information from her.

They got the message. As a group, they stood and strode from the room. The leader turned back to deliver a final message. "We're going to find Nicole. If you see or hear from her, tell her to turn herself in. Any assistance you provide her in evading our efforts will constitute a federal crime, a felony, on your part. You've been warned."

Aimee spent the entire day soothing ruffled feathers, including her own. Once they were satisfied she didn't have Nicole locked away in some secret compartment in her home or office, the federal agents left as quickly as they had arrived. She learned only one thing about their investigation—they were consumed with finding Nicole. The papers the agent had given her didn't help. It appeared to be a search warrant, but the two sheets of paper didn't contain any useful information. She had no clue why this crowd was so intent on finding Nicole.

The minute they left, Aimee made three calls. First order of business—door repair. Her second call was to Tom. She told him the raid was all a big mistake and she apologized for the inconvenience. He was unflappable. He assured her not to worry. The action at the office had happened early enough that none of their clients was on the premises at the time, and he'd already calmed down the few employees who were on site. Aimee breathed a sigh of relief although she knew word was certain to get around.

Her third call was to her attorney, Rudy Harrison. Rudy handled exclusively real estate and business matters, but he promised he would make some calls and see what he could find out. She had done all she could for now, but since it was now eleven, her morning's sleep was ruined. It was, however, almost time for lunch. She had no appetite, but she did have a destination in mind. Before she left, she placed one more call. Nicki's number was programmed in her cell.

"The number you've dialed is no longer a working number. If you believe you've reached this message in error, please check the number and dial again."

❖

When the food came, Aimee decided she was hungry after all.

"I think stress is best cured with cheese." She bit into a toasty grilled cheese sandwich.

Mac leaned over and snatched a sweet potato fry from Aimee's plate. "Or something fried." She munched on the fry and asked, "What are you going to do?"

While they were waiting on lunch, Aimee had highlighted her horrific morning to Mac. The whole experience had seemed surreal, especially as she relayed the details while sitting on the beautiful patio of Mac's restaurant, the Lakeside Grill, nestled against White Rock Lake. With bright shirted cyclists and a striking city skyline in the background, Aimee told Mac about the intense morning raid of both her home and office.

"I don't have a clue. I called Neil on the way over here. God love him, but since they moved to Europe, he and Nicki haven't talked that much. He said he hears from her when her rent and tuition payments are due. He asked me to see what I could find out about whatever's gotten the FBI all worked up."

"I'm surprised she hasn't tried to contact you."

"I'm not. Last time I saw her she barely said two words. She dropped in, left her laundry for Elsa, and took off for the airport with some guy once her clothes were washed and folded. I tried to ask her about school, but she made some comment about how she was doing the best she could in that elitist liberal environment."

"Seriously? Little Nicki? I thought she loved Austin, and for crying out loud, she was talking to her gay aunt. Liberal environment? Whatever."

"I gotta tell you, Mac, I feel sad. I used to be her favorite relative, but since this semester started, I feel like she only reaches out when she needs something."

"I understand. Now back to my original question. What are you going to do?"

"I told Neil I would do something. He offered to come back, but I told him to wait. I've always been closer to Nicki than her parents have, and if I can get hold of her, I'm sure I can find out what's going on. She may have been acting like a brat lately, but I have to believe it's just a phase.

"I was hoping Rudy would have called me back by now." Aimee glanced around and leaned in close. "I know you'll probably think I'm imagining things, but I swear someone's watching my place. When I left this morning, I saw a florist van parked on my street. It was there when the feds left and still in the same place over an hour later. Unless someone on my street is having a wedding at their house on a Monday, I can't imagine any other reason for that van to be there that long."

Mac placed her hand over Aimee's. "Well, whether it means anything or not, you'll feel better when you get this sorted out. Are you sure Rudy can help? He's a great guy, but he's not going to have a clue about where to start."

Aimee remembered Rudy had done the legal work when Mac purchased the property for her restaurant. "I know. I guess I was thinking he might know someone who would."

"Good thought." Mac scrunched her brow. "Hey, I have an idea. What about that attorney you dated last year?"

"Morgan Bradley? She wasn't someone I dated, she was my client."

"Date, client. Fine line for you. Let's just say the way you described how she looked, she sounded more like a date than a client. Anyway, doesn't she practice criminal defense?"

"Yes, she does, with her wife." Aimee waved a hand at Mac's raised eyebrows. "They're in practice together. I can't believe I didn't think of them."

"You must have blocked her from your datebook when she got married."

"She was never in my datebook. We went out once, on a setup, and she spent the whole time brooding over the hunk she wound up marrying. I'd hate her for it, but having met Parker, I can hardly blame her. Morgan Bradley has impeccable taste. I helped them buy a house last Christmas."

"Sounds like she owes you a little professional courtesy."

"Oh, she paid me well, but you're right. I'll give her a call after lunch." She slapped away Mac's hand as it inched toward her fries again. "Don't you own this place? Can't you get someone to bring you your own order?"

"Yours taste better."

Aimee smiled for the first time that day. "That's what all the girls say."

❖

Skye placed the paper bag containing her brand new uniform on the bar next to her wallet. The clock positioned above the neatly lined rows of liquor bottles read seven p.m. She had three hours before her first shift. She chided herself for volunteering to fill in for another employee who had called in sick. She'd been up early that morning to comply with her father's request. Ernie Lavasos was a likeable guy, and from the looks of things, he ran a fairly professional outfit, which she expected from a retired cop. But nothing could change the fact that the uniform in the bag beside her was a costume. When she wore it, she would only be playing the role of a cop, but she'd never be one again.

The bartender with whom Skye had started her tailspin leaned toward her. "Haven't seen you in a while."

Skye hadn't had the heart or the energy to return to Sue's or go anywhere else last night after she'd finally escaped her parents' house. She didn't have the money either, and while she could usually count on her looks to get a few drinks purchased by prospective partners, she decided a good night's sleep was the wiser choice. Alone and sober, she hadn't slept any better than when she drank and fucked her way into oblivion. She peered back at the bartender, whose name she'd forgotten, and wondered what this woman, who had witnessed her exploits, must think of her.

"Everyone needs a night off now and then."

"Need something to do tonight?"

"I'm good. Starting a new job." The moment the words left her mouth, Skye regretted them. She had no desire to discuss this necessary, but unwelcome, career move.

"Tomorrow?"

"Tonight."

"Need a drink to fortify you?" The question carried only the slightest tinge of judgment.

Skye's sight drifted toward the beautiful beckoning bottles. *Just one drink to take the edge off.* She would have an easier time struggling into the polyester wannabe cop outfit with a single shot. Besides, her assignment was to keep guard over a car dealership. No one was going to sneak a hunk of metal past her, no matter how many drinks she had. One was nothing. One was necessary. She scrounged in her pocket and pulled out four dollar bills. Enough for a beer and a tip. She'd rather have a stiff shot of whiskey, but she'd have to wait on a paycheck to be able to afford what she really wanted. The irony of her situation struck her cold: work a job you don't like to make money to buy the things you do. She'd spent her life working a job she loved, and having the things she wanted. The sacrifice was disheartening.

"It's on me."

Skye lit up. She could have what she wanted after all. She looked deep into the bartender's eyes. There she saw the true price of the choice beverage and chose not to make another sacrifice. She slid the bills across the bar. "Thanks, but I got it. Beer. Draft. Keep the change."

She nursed the beer which became ridiculously warm by the time she had to leave. She waited until the bartender was busy with a group on the other side of the bar, then she slid off her stool and skirted the edge of the dance floor to the restroom. She was thankful all the stalls had doors and she had a jacket to disguise the ugly navy outfit. She made a quick exit, not even stopping to check herself in the mirror before she left.

Striding out the door, she popped a stick of gum. One drink was a mistake. It made her breath smell and induced the craving for another.

The ride across town was quick and clear. Monday night traffic was virtually nonexistent, and she was able to outmaneuver the few cars that got in her way. As she sped down the road, with the wind whipping her jacket, she wondered why she was in such a hurry to arrive at a job she was destined to hate.

She cut the engine as she approached the car lot and guided it quietly toward the gate. She didn't want to startle the guard she was there to relieve, but she was mildly curious about whether he was vigilant enough to detect her approach. She slid off the seat, kicked the well-oiled stand into place, locked the bike, and pocketed the key. She glanced to her left, then at the ground, before carefully choosing her steps. She found a low spot on the fence and vaulted over. Within seconds, she spotted the guard she was there to relieve. He leaned back in a chair on the showroom floor, watching the news on the big screen plasma TV hanging on the wall. Some security.

Skye considered surprising him. They weren't supposed to carry firearms, but her Sig was tucked under her jacket and, though she doubted Mr. Lazy had considered doing the same, she decided not to risk being shot. She approached the showroom door and pushed the buzzer.

He took a good five minutes to get to the door, likely taking time to remove any evidence of his sloth on duty. He opened the door about five inches and peered through. Skye initiated introductions.

"Keaton." She stuck out her hand. "I'm your relief."

His handshake was firm. "Ron Denny. You're early."

She offered half a smile with her explanation. "My first day."

He looked her over. "You on the job?" Lots of cops worked security part-time for extra money. Skye never had. Her father always said extra hours spent doing easy guard duty dulled good cop instincts. *Guess he figures I don't need those instincts anymore.*

"Used to be."

"You're carrying."

Skye knew it was a guess, but a good one. She did a little sizing up of her own. Her first impression told her this guy was likely a career wannabe. He wore the misshapen uniform like a second skin, and he was comfortable enough on the job to risk getting caught using his client's business like his own personal living room. Despite these conclusions, his sharp two-minute assessment of her had her rethinking her initial impressions.

"Is that a problem?" She waited for him to point out it was against the rules.

"Not for me."

At least he wasn't a hypocrite. "Good." She gestured toward the inside of the showroom. "Wanna show me around?"

"Sure." He shifted his belt, hitched his pants, and led the way to a bank of monitors. "Not much to this place. They aren't worried about theft as much as vandalism. Vandals usually travel in packs, so they're pretty easy to spot on the cameras. I do a walk-through every hour."

Skye held back a yawn as she thought about how boring the next ten hours were going to be. No wonder he watched TV.

"Did you bring a meal?"

She shook her head. She hadn't thought about not being able to leave the premises to grab a bite to eat.

"You're not the first one that didn't think about it the first night. I've got a cooler my wife packed for me. I'll leave you a sandwich or two. Let's walk the perimeter together then I'll take off."

He led the way, and as Skye hurried to keep up, she chided herself. Ron was a good guy and she had no business making snap decisions about his work ethic based on a few minutes of observation. She wouldn't want anyone treating her to the same level of scrutiny based on her behavior the past few weeks. She had a lot to learn.

CHAPTER FOUR

Her shift ended two hours ago, but Skye couldn't even think about sleep. She was keyed up, restless, and starving. The sandwich Ron had left was long since digested. An exhaustive search of her apartment yielded nine bucks and some change, but no food. She could grab fast food, or she could do the smart thing and buy a few staples to get her through the week. The idea of grocery shopping made her shudder. She rode up Cedar Springs, the scene of her many assignations over the past two weeks, and pulled her bike into a parking space in front of Hunky's, a popular hamburger joint. She remembered she was wearing her gun and Hunky's sold alcohol, which meant she couldn't take her gun in the restaurant. She was in a high traffic area and there was no way she could take off her jacket and stow her weapon without raising an alarm. She missed her cop privileges.

As she contemplated her next move, a vehicle pulled in next to her. She heard a gasp and turned toward the sound. She was facing a beautiful blonde, stepping out of a huge late model Lexus SUV. The woman's coral suit was a blend of sharp tailoring and soft curves, and her blouse dipped low to reveal ample cleavage. Skye experienced a tinge of recognition. She knew this woman, but she couldn't place her. She edged closer, drawn to the frank attraction telegraphed in her eyes.

"Well, we finally meet." The woman thrust a hand in Skye's direction. It hung in the air for a moment before Skye recovered her manners.

"Uh, hello."

"My name's Aimee Howard. What's yours?"

Skye wasn't a stranger to women trying to pick her up, but this situation was different somehow. This woman acted like Skye should know who she was, if not her name. She searched her mind for a memory, desperate to connect. Skye knew lack of sleep was affecting her ability to comprehend. Hazy images teased her, but when she tried to pin them down, they danced away.

"Would you care to join me for lunch?"

"Lunch?"

The woman, Aimee, looked puzzled, then tried a different tact. "Or dinner? Oh, hell, who needs a meal? Why don't we just run away together?"

Aimee's last question was punctuated with a playful smile, and Skye instantly remembered. Despite the intervening weeks of booze-filled nights and the parade of naked women, she was certain the woman standing in front of her was the beautiful blonde who'd captured her eye from across the bar the night of her resignation. Up close, in the sober light of day, Aimee Howard was more of a knockout than she remembered, in an every-detail-is-perfect kind of way. She didn't have a lithe model body, but otherwise she looked as if she were ready for a photo shoot from her obviously expensive suit to her perfectly matched accessories. But her allure ran deeper than her looks. Her easy smile signaled genuine interest, her teasing tone was irresistible. Skye drew closer, until an inner voice mocked—*she's totally out of your league.*

The thought jogged her memory again. She recalled Aimee headed her way before her friend intervened and introduced her to a more suitable hook-up. Skye had seen plenty of women like this in her time on the force. Rich socialites. They spent their time and money on the finer things in life—spa treatments, three martini lunches, and shopping jaunts at Northpark Mall. She may not bring a woman like Skye around her friends, but she'd slum with an ex-cop for a lunchtime quickie. Well, Skye thought, this ex-cop is too tired and too depressed to be some spoiled socialite's afternoon delight. Time to set the record straight.

"Actually, I was headed out."

"Oh, I thought I saw you pull up just now." Disappointment damped the expensive smile.

Skye shrugged. Aimee could cheer herself up with a pricey bauble. "I have to be somewhere." Lame, but her exhaustion precluded a better excuse. She threw a leg over her bike, turned the key, and pressed the starter. Speaking over the loud noise, Aimee offered one last chance for her to change her mind. "Why don't I give you a ride? I have air conditioning."

Patronizing. That sealed it. "You have air conditioning. I have fresh air." She pulled on her helmet. "Enjoy your day of leisure. I'm sure you think you deserve it."

Aimee watched her peel out. She was completely baffled and utterly embarrassed. She didn't make a habit out of picking up women, but she was certain the blonde on the bike was the same woman who was sending her come-hither looks at the bar. The same woman who disappeared when she finally decided to act on her impulses. The moment the woman removed her helmet to reveal tousled blond waves, she knew she better act fast before the woman got away again. The direct approach had been a miserable failure. Beneath her professional exterior lurked a daredevil college student who wanted to fire up the Lexus and chase her down if only to confront her about her remarks. *Day of leisure indeed.* She didn't know what the hell she was talking about or who the hell she was dealing with. *Good riddance.*

On the heels of her kiss-off came a dose of reality. *Who are you kidding? You want to run your hands through her wild hair and shimmy her out of her tight jeans.* The desire surprised her as much today as it did the night of her birthday. At least then, she could write up the unusual attraction to a few too many Cosmos and regret over another year celebrating singlehood. Today, in full sunlight, she had no plausible explanation for the magnetic pull of the Harley riding, rough-around-the-edges woman who obviously hadn't given her a single thought since they'd exchanged glances two weeks ago. She may have a penchant for picking the wrong women, but her choices at least walked the walk of the upper crust in order to get what they wanted. She doubted the blonde who'd just peeled out altered anything for anyone. Aimee was intrigued, but concluded the woman's abrupt exit was for the best. She was beyond rude, and Aimee's week had started off badly enough without adding a surly stranger to the mix.

❖

Aimee pulled a bottle of water off the tray in the middle of the conference table and twisted the cap. "Nice office."

"Thanks." Morgan flashed a big smile at her law partner and wife, Parker Casey. "We had fun putting it all together."

"Congratulations on the new office, but most of all, congratulations on your wedding." Aimee's well-wishes were sincere. Morgan Bradley, gorgeous, hot shot defense attorney was a perfect catch, but from the moment Aimee met her she could tell Morgan was preoccupied by the call of another. When Morgan and Parker finally broke through the barriers that kept them apart, Aimee was as happy as anyone to see their relationship become solid. She'd helped them with their first joint home purchase and was genuinely happy for them when she received a wedding announcement in the mail a few weeks ago.

"Thank you. We had a fantastic time in Vancouver, just us. We're having a big reception for all our friends and family in a few weeks at our house. We hope you'll join us."

"I wouldn't miss it."

Parker cleared her throat, and Morgan took the hint. "Enough about us. I filled Parker in with the details you gave me over the phone, but I'd like to go over a few things. First off, did the agents take anything from either your home or office?"

Aimee handed over the papers the agent had left behind. "They didn't take anything from the office, but my business partner, Tom, said they spent a lot of time on the computers. I don't know if they downloaded anything while they were there."

Morgan interjected. "That's not the way they usually operate. They may look at files while they're there, but if they wanted something off the hard drive, they would just load up all your equipment and haul it off."

"That's exactly what they did at my house. They took a desktop and two laptops. One of them has all my current client information. I have backups of most of it at the office, but not all. How long do you think they'll keep them?"

"I'll call the agent and find out what their timeline is for checking out the data. If they're just looking for leads to find Nicole, then they'll probably process the hard drives quickly, but if they seized the computers as potential evidence of a crime, then you won't be seeing them until this case is disposed of." Morgan ran a finger down the page in front of her. "I see they listed a number of guns. Are those yours?"

"Yes, they are. They're properly registered and I have a permit to carry a handgun." Aimee's tone dared Morgan to comment. All she got was a wide smile.

"I had no idea you were a firearm aficionado. We'll have to go to the range together sometime."

Who knew? Aimee filed the information under the heading, Don't Make Assumptions, which instantly conjured an image of the woman from the bar. Aimee had been certain the woman was interested in her, both the night of her birthday and earlier today, but she'd been way off base. *Boy, was I. I couldn't even get her to give up her name.*

Parker reviewed the papers. "One of the items listed here is 'letters.' Any idea what that means?"

"They took a small stack of letters and cards. Nicki used to send me short notes on a regular basis."

"Anything special about them? Did she reveal any state secrets in between birthday wishes?"

"Not a one. Actually, her notes were fairly boring. I think she wrote me once a week her first semester of school to avoid homework." Aimee smiled at the memory of Nicki's voluminous correspondence. "If freshman woes are illegal, then they hauled away enough evidence to send her to prison for sure."

Morgan returned the smile. "Why don't you start by giving me some background on Nicole?"

"Sure. Her full name is Nicole Lassiter Howard. We call her Nicki. She's twenty-one, in her senior year at my alma mater, UT." She referenced the University of Texas.

"Good student?"

"She was her first two years. Now? I don't know. You know how some kids become more liberal when they go to college? Nicki's been just the opposite. The guy she's dating has a Sarah Palin sticker on his car. I saw it last time she came to town."

"Anything else make you think Austin's hippy attitude hasn't rubbed off on her?"

Aimee smiled. Austin was home to the largest public school in the state, the University of Texas and the city's motto was "Keep Austin Weird." She'd attended the school, not just because it was one of the best in the country, but as a way to escape her own conservative upbringing in Highland Park. She met Mac and Jordan, her best friends, while at school, and found the courage to come out in the accepting atmosphere of the college town.

"Not a chance. If anything, after a couple of years there, she developed a sudden allergic reaction to tolerance. We were very close growing up. I was her favorite aunt and I could do no wrong."

"And now?"

"I don't know how to describe it. Things changed this semester. She still calls me when she needs something, but we don't really talk anymore. I don't know any of her friends, what classes she's taking, or what she does for fun. I feel more like a parent than a permissive aunt. Most of our conversations dead end when she starts talking conservative nonsense."

"Well, drugs are probably out as a reason the feds would be looking for her," Parker said. "Rabid conservative doesn't fit the drug dealer profile. What can you tell us about her boyfriend?"

"Not much. I think his name's Earl. Sorry, I wish I'd paid more attention. I call him TB, in my head anyway." At Parker's puzzled look, she added, "Tea Bagger. He spouts a lot of the same ideas all those crazy Tea Party activists are fond of. At least, I think he does since Nicki quotes him every time we talk. My experience with him is limited to seeing him sitting in his car, honking his horn for Nicki to leave the house. Do you think she's in trouble because of him?"

Morgan took up the thread. "Hard to tell." She pointed at the papers Aimee brought to the meeting. "The search warrants don't contain any detail about why they think your home or office would contain any evidence related to Nicki, and I can't really tell what they were looking for based on the few items they took. In order to get the search warrant, someone had to swear out an affidavit to a judge. That affidavit is what we need to determine where this investigation is headed. I think we should make a few phone calls and see what we can find out. I'll give you a call as soon as we have a better idea of what we're facing." She stood as if to signal the end of their meeting.

Aimee remained seated. She pulled a checkbook out of her oversized Birkin bag. "How much of a retainer do you need?"

Morgan and Parker exchanged a look. Morgan answered. "Why don't you let us figure out what we're facing before we get into specifics?"

Aimee snatched a pen from the table and started writing. "I think you two are great, but my house was invaded by a fleet of storm troopers looking for a girl who weighs less than some dogs. I was handcuffed and harassed. My place of business was raided, and I'm certain once word gets out, a few choice clients will never darken my door again. A few phone calls aren't going to make this go away. Nicki's going to need the best defense you can muster, and I'm willing to pay for it. I may not be her favorite aunt, and she may not be my favorite niece, but those bastards really pissed me off." She punctuated her last remark with a loud rip, tearing off a check and setting it on the table. She was satisfied the fifty thousand dollar investment would yield quick results. "This should be enough to get things started. I trust you'll call me when you find something out?"

❖

After Aimee left, Morgan lifted the check and handed it to Parker whose eyes doubled in size.

"That's a lot of zeros. I worked for years as a cop before I brought home that kind of money in a year."

Morgan laughed and snatched it back. "It's not ours yet. We have to earn it."

"Suggestions about where to start? If this were a Dallas County case, I'd just go get a copy of the affidavit from the judge who signed it."

"I imagine the affidavit supporting the warrant is under seal and won't be public until they arrest Nicole. The feds hate tipping defendants off about the reasons they're coming for them. Of course, they don't mind signaling their arrival by storming into a residential home with enough personnel to invade a small country." Morgan furrowed her brow. "We should probably start by calling the agent who signed the warrant. I imagine he'll be glad to pawn us off on the Assistant US Attorney who's investigating this case."

"As long as we're going to start with the cops, I may as well make the call."

"Good plan. See what you can find out, then I'll give the AUSA a shout."

"They're not going to want to give up much unless we're ready to turn her in."

"I know, but hedge on that point." Morgan looked Parker in the eyes. "Sorry. Someday I'll remember that you already know what you're doing."

Parker knew Morgan's instruction had more to do with the fact Parker used to be a cop, one of "them," rather than a concern about her experience as a lawyer. Parker's separation from the force had been the result of betrayal by her family in blue, but she still believed most cops were honest, hard-working individuals. "I can bluff as well as they can and I'm happy to do it. Believe me?"

Morgan glanced around the room. Satisfied they were alone, she leaned in and kissed Parker. "I'm sorry, sweetheart. I know you know what you're doing. Forgive me?"

Parker didn't perform a similar check before pulling Morgan into her arms. "No forgiveness necessary. We each have our strengths and we'll learn from each other. Right, Professor?"

"Absolutely. Now get me some information."

❖

As she strode out of the office, Aimee glanced at her watch. Three o'clock. Mac would be at the Lakeside, but she'd already taken up a few hours of her time the day before with Nicole's problems. She wasn't far from her parents' house. Maybe she should stop by there and see if they'd heard from their granddaughter lately. Her brother said Nicki didn't keep in touch with them. In fact, he'd insisted she not tell them what was going on, but Aimee figured the quickest way to solve this mess was to find Nicki. She may as well start with the rest of the family.

She left the Oak Lawn neighborhood, home to Dallas's gayborhood, and drove to the elite town of Highland Park. Nestled within the city of Dallas, Highland Park was a fully incorporated town with its own police force, courts, and school system. The residents wanted the convenience of the big city without giving up the ability to ensure their landlocked island was run exactly to their specifications. Aimee had grown up here and spent every waking moment plotting escape. College in Austin provided exactly the escape she needed, but the primary lesson she'd learned in school was that the endless possibilities of her mind was all the escape she needed. Following graduation, she took possession of her massive trust account and proceeded to work among the conservative elite as an out lesbian, taking their money and donating generous portions to gay and lesbian causes.

The year before, she completed her transition back to the city of her childhood when she moved into the Tudor home she inherited from her grandmother's estate. Her home was modest compared to her parents' palatial mansion. Complete with servants' quarters, a theater, and a bowling lane, the Howard estate was a tribute to all the excess money could buy. Growing up in this insular community,

Aimee hadn't realized most families didn't have servants, let alone the ability to perfect their bowling game without leaving the house. She could only hope that the advent of the Internet meant that kids growing up here now had a greater appreciation of their wealth in relation to the income of the average American.

She pulled her Lexus SUV into the large circular drive spanning the front of the mansion. On evenings when her parents entertained, teams of valets stood waiting to whisk high dollar sports and luxury vehicles to safe parking on the back half of the property. Today, Aimee parked on her own. She left her car at a rebellious angle.

Regina Marie answered the door. She'd worked for the family as long as Aimee could remember. "Aimee, fancy you dropping by in the middle of the day. Your mother and father will be pleased to see you."

Aimee smiled, joining in the lie. Mr. and Mrs. Howard were happy to speak about their lovely daughter and her successful real estate business over cocktails with friends, but they weren't fond of up close and personal interaction with her. They acted as if homosexuality was catching. She had learned to ignore their distaste for discussion about anything that had to do with her personal life. She avoided interaction with her parents, but when she was with them she refused to avoid the details of her life, however uncomfortable personal talk made either them or her.

She gave Regina a hug and plunged into the reason for her visit. "Have you heard from Nicki lately?"

"Let me think." She tapped a finger against her forehead. "I believe she called here to speak to Mr. Howard about a week ago."

"Did he happen to mention what she wanted?"

"No, ma'am."

"Okay, well, I guess I'll go talk to him." Aimee had hoped maybe she could shortcut a confrontation with her father, but she resigned herself to checking with the source. As she walked toward his study, Regina tapped her on the shoulder.

"He didn't mention anything, but I happened to hear a thing or two."

Aimee offered a conspiratorial smile. "Oh you did, did you?"

"It's time for my afternoon break. Why don't you meet me in the kitchen? I'll make you a cup of coffee and we'll chat."

"Perfect."

A few minutes later, Aimee nursed a steaming cup of coffee and listened to Regina's version of the half of the conversation she had heard.

"I could tell Nicki wanted to make a withdrawal from her trust account. He resisted at first, but then caved in like he always does when his grandbabies ask for something. Mr. Howard took down some bank information. He repeated back a bunch of numbers to make sure he got it right."

Aimee reached over and grasped Regina's forearm. "This is between you and me. I don't care if you were listening to his conversation with a paper cup against the study door. Nicki's in some kind of trouble, and I need to know everything I can if I'm going to help her out of it." Aimee told Regina a toned down version of her visit from the feds. She knew the loyal family servant might grab a shotgun and go after them herself if she knew how the feds had treated one of her charges.

"I think you should know a couple of men came by here earlier today. Your father invited them into his study, but they were gone again within minutes. Only thing I heard was 'you can contact my lawyer.' And last week wasn't the first time Nicki called here asking about her money. She might say hello to Mrs. Howard, but mostly she talks to your father. I think she wanted the money for some charity."

"What made you think that?"

"Your father doodles when he's on the phone. I happened to see the slip of paper he wrote the wiring instructions on and it had the name of some federation or coalition, or something like that. I don't recall exactly what it said, but I got the impression that's where the money was going."

"Kind of odd for a college student to be begging for money for someone other than herself, isn't it?" Aimee's question was rhetorical. She remembered her college days. Her trust fund took care of tuition and other basic living expenses, but her father had been stingy about doling out money for extras since she'd chosen a public school, albeit one of the best in the country.

"I stopped trying to figure out people a long time ago."

Aimee nodded at Regina's sage advice. She finished her coffee and stood. "Your company and delicious coffee were exactly what I needed. I'd leave on a good note, but I suppose I should pay my respects or I'll never hear the end of it."

Her mother's suite was on the third floor. Aimee knocked on the door and waited for an invitation into the inner sanctum. Evelyn Howard answered the door dressed in a smart Chanel suit. Vintage.

Aimee was wealthy in her own right, even without the trust account her grandmother had funded. She loved the freedom associated with wealth, the primary aspect being she didn't have to suck up to her parents, but as she eyed the fine lines of the perfect designer suit, she allowed it wouldn't kill her to be polite for a chance at first dibs on the wardrobe. She leaned in and kissed her mother lightly on the cheek.

"Hello, Mother."

If Evelyn was surprised to see her, she hid the emotion well. She accepted the embrace, then smoothed nonexistent wrinkles in her suit. "Hello, dear. What brings you to the house in the middle of the week?"

"I had an errand nearby. I haven't seen you in a while. I apologize for the timing—it looks like you're on your way out." Aimee knew better than to lead with the calamity surrounding Nicole's disappearance. She wasn't too old to be scolded for not observing social graces. One mustn't rush into a story, especially if it involved scandal.

"I have a moment. I'm headed to the League tea." Evelyn's gaze swept over Aimee. "If you'd like to join me, we might be able to find something suitable for you to wear."

Aimee suppressed a laugh. The Chanel collection might be worth a hug and a kiss now and then, but suffering through a stuffy ladies' tea? The conversation about the various charities each of the privileged women worked would quickly devolve into gossip. Aimee had no desire to watch a group of entitled ladies eat their own.

Besides, she looked fine the way she was. Her own suit might not be couture, but it was the height of fashion, and it fit. An accomplished tailor would have to work for hours for her to fit into her rail-thin mother's garments.

Her mother never made overt references to Aimee's figure. That would be too gauche, but she did act as if finding clothes to fit Aimee's full figure were a plebeian chore. Aimee decided long ago her mother was secretly jealous of her curves, but the reference still had the power to sting. *That settles it. I'll buy my own Chanel collection at auction.* "Thank you for the invitation, but I need to speak with Dad. Give my regards to everyone." Aimee left before her mother could respond.

Her father's study was a floor below. Aimee was surprised he was home in the middle of the week. Gordon Howard maintained a palatial corner office at Howard Enterprises on the top floor of Thanksgiving Tower in downtown Dallas. Here at the mansion, his study was more sedate, but still substantial. As a child, Aimee had loved this room with its floor to ceiling bookshelves loaded with beautiful leather bound books. After being scolded for cracking the spine on one of the classics, she learned the volumes were for display purposes only. What a waste.

The lower shelves featured Gordon's wall of fame, interspersed with the unread books. Aimee shuddered at the thought of her father shaking hands with Dubya and Dick Cheney, but the evidence was there for all to see. *Hey, Dad, do you and Dick ever talk about how in the hell two major conservative wanks ended up with lesbian daughters? Dick's probably okay with it since his daughter's not a real lesbian. Does he console you for winding up with the real thing?*

Gordon Howard was dressed for the office. His expensive pinstripe suit spoke authority. Aimee heard it loud and clear. She took a deep breath and crossed the threshold into his seat of power.

"Hi, Dad. Working at home today?" Aimee knew he preferred a more formal address, like "Father," and that was precisely the reason she rebelled.

"Aimee. How nice of you to drop by. Taking a break from your little business adventure?"

Aimee didn't let him get to her. She was used to his disparagement of her thriving brokerage. His disdain had nothing to do with chauvinism. His rancor had to do with the fact she wasn't using her expertise for his direct benefit. If Aimee had taken a position of power in one of his many companies, he would have been a proud papa, but after years spent growing up in the stifling, conservative atmosphere, she would never place herself back under his thumb.

"Actually, I had business in the neighborhood." It wasn't really a lie. Her first order of business was finding out what had happened to get Nicki in deep with the feds. She worked out a few lead-ins to the question she really wanted to ask before plunging in.

"Have you talked to Nicki lately?"

"Nicole? Why do you ask?"

"Have you?"

"I talk to all my grandchildren. If you had some, I would talk to them as well."

"Maybe I'll surprise you with some one day." Aimee didn't take time to enjoy his pained expression. He knew her well enough to know her statement didn't mean she was headed back to heteroville. "Dad, Nicki's missing. If you've talked to her recently, maybe you have some information that might help us find her."

"Are you certain she's missing? I just spoke with her last week."

"What did you talk about?"

"Have you abandoned your little real estate venture to become a private eye? Why don't you let your brother worry about Nicki? I'm certain she's fine."

"I'm certain she's not." Aimee wasn't sure why she felt compelled to hold back her encounter with the feds. She sensed her dad's early morning visitors had something to do with Nicki, but if he wasn't going to disclose to her, she wasn't inclined to tip her hand. Besides, her brother would kill her if he knew she was ratting Nicki out to their strict father. Typical of her family to ignore the unpleasantness of a potential scandal.

"Well, I don't know why you would think that. She's been seeing that nice boy. Maybe she's with him."

Sarah Palin sticker equals nice boy. Lesbian equals bad daughter. Such distinctions were easy in her father's world. Aimee wasn't giving up that easily. "What did you talk about when she called?" Her persistence paid off.

"Random things. She called to tell me about her school, her activities, her boyfriend."

"And you gave her money?"

"What if I did? It's her money, I'm merely the trustee. I should deny her what's rightfully hers?"

Aimee sighed at his tone. He'd had a different attitude when it came to doling out her own trust account, but she didn't feel like arguing the point. She realized she wasn't going to get any additional information out of him. "No, Dad."

"You know if you need anything, all you have to do is ask. Do you need money, dear?"

He knew she didn't. He may pretend to have no interest in her business ventures, but she suspected he watched her entrepreneurial adventures closely, whether with pride or resentment, she couldn't tell. She tried not to care what he thought, but she couldn't help the tiny tinge of hope that he might acknowledge her success rather than pretend it didn't exist. Years of experience told her protesting his assumptions wouldn't buy his recognition. Her answer was short, simple, and mostly true. "I'm fine."

CHAPTER FIVE

Morgan stood in the doorway to Parker's office. Parker was bent over several sets of books laid open on her desk. Her charcoal jacket hung on the back of her chair and the sleeves of her once crisp royal blue shirt were rolled to the elbows. Morgan resisted a strong urge to cross the distance between them and push back the unruly strand of dark black hair curling its way across her face. Instead, she cleared her throat.

Parker tore her gaze away from her books. "Trying to sort out jury instructions for the Eldridge case. Some law professor I know taught me to work on the jury charge at the beginning of the case. She said if I knew what the prosecutor had to prove, I would be able to construct a perfect outline for my defense."

"Oh, she did, did she? Did she also mention how important food is to keep your brain fueled?" She strode over and tapped on the open books. "Shut this down by six. I'm taking you to dinner."

"Dinner sounds great."

"Any luck on Nicole Howard?" Morgan asked.

"I made some calls, but I haven't learned anything yet. I talked to the case agent, Davis Landers. He's ATF. He conducted the raid at Aimee's house. He said the team at Aimee's office was led by ATF, but FBI and ICE agents were on scene. Apparently, whatever this is, it's a joint task force investigation and the case is out of the Western District."

"Interesting. They've been teaming up a lot lately on Homeland Security investigations."

"He mentioned that as well, but that was his only hint. He gave me the standard line about how we could bring her in, and they would be happy to tell us more about the investigation at that time. Or we could just ask our client if we want to know why she's in trouble. Of course, I didn't let on we can't ask her anything because we don't know where the hell she is."

"You get any other information?"

"Not much. What I did manage to get was all vague, and pretty much standard fare. 'She's in a lot of trouble.' 'The sooner she comes in the better for her.' 'They believe she has vital information that she could use to bargain a better deal.' 'She's in danger.'"

Morgan had worked enough federal cases to know how the game was played. Prosecutors didn't deal in the abstract. They wanted a defendant in custody before they would even talk about a plea agreement, and even then the plea agreement didn't define the terms of the sentence, it only set the boundaries. Ultimately, a judge would use a two-volume text full of guideline computations to determine how much time a defendant would serve, and since the plea bargain would stipulate there was no right of appeal, you were stuck with the result. The best hope a federal defendant had of making sure the guideline computation was as low as possible was to rat out everyone they knew who might have committed a crime. The greater the "cooperation," the lower the sentence.

"Did he at least tell you which Assistant U.S. Attorney is working the case?"

"He did. Her name is Lily Berek."

"Really?"

"You know her?"

"I went to law school with her. I haven't spoken to her in years. She clerked for a federal judge after law school and then started at the U.S. Attorney's office as a junior prosecutor. I didn't realize she was still there. She was super smart. She must be in a pretty powerful position by now. If she's working on this case personally, that doesn't bode well for Nicole."

"Were you friends?"

"Pretty much, but like I said, I haven't talked to her in years. Not since I moved away." A few years after graduation, Morgan, having quickly developed a stellar reputation as a litigator, was offered a position with a national firm and she moved to D.C. to join their Washington office.

"She'll take your call, right? Old law school buddy, back in town."

"I'm sure she would."

"Call her now. I'm curious."

The number for the United States Attorney's office for the Western District of Texas was programmed in their office phone. When the call connected, she asked the receptionist to put her through to Lily Berek. She repeated the request to Lily's secretary, the fact that she had to push through two layers signaled Lily had achieved status at the office.

"I'm an old friend. Just calling to catch up with her." Morgan didn't feel like explaining the real reason for her call to layer number two.

"Hi, Lily, it's Morgan Bradley. Do you remember me?" Morgan nodded at Parker and waved her hand in circles to indicate Lily was rambling about the past. She responded with a few tidbits about her legal career over the years, including the fact she was back in Dallas and had started a new practice.

"And that brings me to the other reason I called. I've been hired to represent a person of interest to your office. Nicole Howard."

Parker watched impatiently for the next few moments as Morgan made cryptic notes on a napkin and murmured vague responses. Lily was doing all the talking. After a few minutes, Morgan told Lily she would convey this information to her client and let her know what she would like to do. Then she hung up the phone.

"What happened?"

"I got the same line you did from Agent Landers. Serious case, dangerous people, cooperate now or else. She's hot on this case, and she really, really wants to get her hands on Nicole now. She let loose the ATF's involvement isn't just because of illegal firearms and she made a couple of veiled references to the Oklahoma City bombing. From the way she was talking, I think it's definitely some kind of Homeland Security case, but nowadays everything is. That's the only way they can get the level of funding they want to bankroll these large task force operations."

"Oklahoma City? Seriously? Looks like we need to find Nicole before the feds if we want to have any leverage."

"My thought exactly. If they find her first, she gets no credit for turning herself in. She's probably still in Austin, or at least in the area. Should we try and find an investigator down there?"

"We could, but I'd rather use someone we know, especially if she's hanging with a dangerous crowd. Too bad Jake's swamped." She referred to Jake Simmons, the private investigator whose services they used when he wasn't busy working with his primary firm. "I have an idea," Parker offered hesitantly. "I know a sharp detective who has recently become unemployed."

"'Become unemployed'? Sounds complicated."

"It is. A little. I'm talking about Skye Keaton." Parker held her breath, waiting for Morgan's reaction. She didn't wait long, and her response was exactly what she'd expected.

"No way."

"Seriously, Morgan, I've been thinking about this since last week when we had to hire that wannabe P.I. instead of Jake to serve the subpoenas on the Donohue case. Skye needs work and we need a good investigator. This is the perfect way to try out the relationship, see if it works for us."

"Last time I saw Skye, some prosecutor was extolling her virtues as a decorated homicide detective. What changed?"

"Dallas PD did to her what they did to me. They threw her under the bus when she no longer fit in."

Morgan felt the heat of her anger redden her face. She didn't even try to control her rising voice. "Not the same. At all. You were set up to take the fall for a bad shooting. She set herself up by skirting the constitution one too many times. And, as I recall, she was a key figure in your departure from the force." Morgan didn't bother mentioning the other, more personally painful factor. In betraying Parker, Skye had not only burned a professional partnership, but a personal one as well. While Morgan was thankful Parker's painful past drove her to pursue law school, a decision that ultimately led to their relationship, she wasn't as forgiving as Parker was when it came to Skye's transgressions. "Oh, and another thing. We can't use an investigator who lacks credibility. How will she hold up under cross-examination? Is she even licensed?"

"She needs a break. We need to find a missing girl. All she has to do is find Nicole—she doesn't need a license to look for a missing person. She's not investigating this case. Once we negotiate her surrender, we can get Jake to dig deeper into the investigation. Skye won't have to testify. You have to admit, we have a much better chance of finding Nicole with a recently employed police detective looking for her. Some of these yahoos posing as private investigators haven't worked a real case in decades. They wouldn't know where to find a good deli, let alone a college student. Besides, how hard can it be? I figure she'll locate Nicole in two days, tops."

Morgan looked deep into Parker's eyes. Her probing search yielded only a strong desire to help a friend. She couldn't deny Parker the opportunity to do for someone else what none of her cop brotherhood had done for her.

"Okay, bring her on board if she wants the work, but let her know it's only temporary. No substantive work—just find Nicole. After all, how hard can it be to find a college student?"

❖

Skye yawned again. She'd been struggling to stay awake for the past hour. Not a good sign since she had ten hours left to go on her shift. Time to walk the property or wind up dozing in front of the plasma TV.

The fleet of SUVs parked on the lot reminded her of her strange encounter with Aimee Howard that afternoon. She knew she had acted like a jerk. If she could have a do-over, she would have handled the situation more gracefully, but she would have denied Aimee's advances nonetheless. Her manners may have been atrocious, but her assessment was spot on. Aimee may dabble in blue collar, but

Skye was done with dabbling. No more medicating with a liquor bottle, no more strangers in her bed. The force of the attraction she felt would only spell trouble for both of them. Besides, if Aimee could see her in this silly uniform, she would be spared the trouble of dousing the chemistry between them.

Skye went onto full alert at the rumble of the approaching car. The sound stopped just outside the gate. She glanced at her watch. Ten thirty p.m. No chance the driver was there to look at a car this time of night, but what were the odds something exciting might actually happen at the car lot on a Tuesday night? She heard a car door open and slam shut. A single set of footsteps walked the fence line, headed in Skye's direction. She drew her gun and dropped out of sight. Within seconds, she saw a tall, lean figure wearing a ball cap testing the locked gate.

"Lot's closed," Skye called out. She watched the figure turn toward the direction of her voice. Despite the shadows, she could make out enough of the form to tell the late night visitor was a woman.

"Skye, is that you?"

She knew that voice. She thought she'd heard it for the last time a few weeks ago. Skye holstered her weapon and stepped into the light. "Parker? What the hell are you doing here?"

"Better question is what the hell are you doing here?" Parker looked her up and down. Skye could tell she was holding back a remark about her uniform.

"What are you looking at?"

Parker glanced away. "Nothing. Chill. Are you supposed to be carrying?"

"I have a license. You on the job?" She came off sullen and defensive, but she didn't care. She was embarrassed for Parker to see her here, working hard to keep a car lot safe.

Parker held up a hand, palm up. "Truce. I didn't come here to give you a hard time. Let me in so we can talk?"

Skye's curiosity trumped her embarrassment. She unlocked the gate and led Parker to the showroom. They settled into expensive leather chairs.

Parker spoke first. "Nice place you have here, but last time I saw you, you were on the job, the state's star witness against Teddy Burke. What happened?"

"You know the drill, I was given a choice. Turn in my shield or have it taken from me. I chose the easy way out." *Because I'm not brave like you.*

"Don't beat yourself up. We all do what we have to do to survive."

Skye acknowledged Parker's generosity with a simple nod. "If you didn't come to talk to me about the job, why are you here?" Her question was devoid of tone this time.

"I'm here to offer you a job."

"In case you hadn't noticed, I have a job." Skye waved her arm. "Pretty cush don't you think?" She didn't try to hide the sarcasm this time.

"How'd you end up here?"

"My dad. Assistant Chief Keaton may have retired, but he's still trying to direct my life. If I can't be a cop, I can be a pseudo cop."

"I remember your father well. You get a lot of grief about resigning?"

"Yep, the passive aggressive kind. Suddenly, I'm only good enough to hang with the women folk."

"Ready to get back to some real detective work?"

"Did you come here tonight to lead me on? I thought you were married now."

Parker smiled. "I am. Can you believe it?"

"You're lucky to have her. She's smart, hot, and she's obviously crazy about you."

"Yeah, yeah. You're just jealous."

"Maybe I am. Can you blame me?" Skye wondered if Parker knew what she was really jealous of. She changed the subject. "How did you know where to find me?"

"I asked around. I used to be a detective too, you know. I ran into Sean and he told me you were here."

Skye sighed at the mention of her brother. "You already knew I wasn't on the job."

"Yeah, I guess I did."

"Sucks."

"Yep. It won't forever. Trust me."

Skye was already tired of talking about her dismal past and uncertain future. "Why are you really here?"

"I told you, to offer you a job."

"Doing what?"

"What you do best. Investigating. We need a good investigator. You need"—Parker paused and waved her hand at the car lot— "Well, you need something other than this. Am I right?"

Skye looked down at her ill-fitting polyester uniform with the embroidered appliqué. Lavasos Security Specialists. She couldn't feel less like a specialist, dressed like a geek, strolling a car lot all hours of the night. Parker's offer, vague as it was, sounded perfect. Skye only had one hesitation.

"What about your wife? What does she think about this?"

"Honestly? She has mixed feelings. Look, we have one urgent assignment and it should be a snap for you. Do a great job and she'll come around."

She held back asking Parker how it felt to have to answer for her decisions. Truth was she envied Morgan and Parker's closeness even as she'd written off the possibility of the same for herself.

Skye looked at her watch. Ten more hours of boredom. Whatever work Parker had for her couldn't possibly be worse than babysitting luxury vehicles, but it might be temporary. This job was a sure thing. If she stayed on, she could work her way up to the day shift. Maybe someday, she would be a supervisor, driving from site to site to make sure her employees stayed awake on the job. Suddenly, an image of her aging self, dressed in the same blue-black polyester, day after day, year after year, flashed before her eyes. Temporary challenge beat permanent boredom any day of the week.

"I can start in ten hours."

CHAPTER SIX

"M s. Howard, the call you were expecting is on line one."
Aimee resisted the urge to remind the receptionist not
to call her "Ms. Howard." Her regular receptionist was on her
extended honeymoon and Natalie was filling in during her absence.
Aimee picked up the phone, punched the line, and injected her voice
with all the drippy sweetness she could muster. "Mrs. Donaldson,
how are you doing this fine morning?" She listened to the expected
harangue, interjecting calm, but firm, admonitions when the tiny
spaces allowed. "The size of the crack in the pool isn't the issue...
The prior foundation work must be included on the report...I
understand the water leak preceded your ownership of the home,
but since it hasn't been repaired, we have to disclose it."

Aimee had fought with the eighty-year-old woman since the
day she'd listed her house for sale. Beatrice Donaldson acted like
she was one meal away from a homeless shelter, but Aimee knew
better. Not only was she the widow of one of the richest oilmen
in the state, she had amassed her own fortune from a cosmetics
business specializing in personal, in-home sales. Even at the ripe
age of eighty, she still made occasional trips to the large office
building that housed her booming enterprise. And she hung on to
every penny she made as if it were her ticket to heaven.

Beatrice insisted her house was worth way more than Aimee
did, and she steadfastly refused to provide all the information
required on the seller's disclosure. Beatrice was used to having

her way, but Aimee stood her ground. She told Mrs. Donaldson to complete the form with the correct information or take her listing elsewhere. She knew Beatrice would comply. Aimee's agency was the best at moving these unique, high-end mansions, and Aimee also had the added luxury of not needing the income from her business. She respected that many of her employees did, and she wouldn't do anything to jeopardize the business, but clients like Mrs. Donaldson didn't think that through. As much as she loved having her own business, on days like today, Aimee wondered if she should scale back her lifestyle and make do with her trust account. Maybe she needed to take a break. As she listened to Mrs. Donaldson drone on, she seriously considered the idea. Tom and the rest of the team were well qualified to handle even her pickiest clients.

When she finally finished the call, Aimee buzzed the receptionist. She needed a break. "Natalie, please hold my calls for the next hour. Tell anyone who calls I'm in a meeting and I will call them back before lunch. If it's urgent, give it to Tom."

"Even the woman holding on line two?"

Aimee sighed. "Who's on line two?"

"Some lawyer. Margo Bradford."

Aimee pretended to bang her head on the desk. The faux release burned off some of her frustration. "Do you mean Morgan Bradley?"

"I'm sure she said Bradford."

Yes, I'm sure the woman has no idea how to pronounce her own name. "Put her through. And ask Tom to come into my office. Now."

Aimee took a deep breath. "Hi, Morgan, it's Aimee." She listened while Morgan briefly explained she and Parker had made some calls about Nicole's case. They didn't have a lot to go on, but they suggested a meeting to discuss strategy. Was she free this afternoon?

Tom entered the room and started to duck back out when he saw she was on the phone. Aimee signaled for him to come back in, then focused on the call. "I can be at your office at four if that works...Perfect."

Aimee clicked off the line and turned her attention to Tom. "Sorry, that was the attorney I hired to represent Nicole, Morgan Bradley."

"Has she turned up yet?"

"No, and until she does, there's not much we can do for her. Morgan wants to see me again this afternoon. Apparently, they have a plan to try and find Nicole. I'm sorry this is taking my attention away from the business."

Tom waved away her concern. "Don't worry about it. There's nothing going on the rest of us can't handle." He paused and grinned. "Well, except no one wants to deal with Mrs. Donaldson."

"Don't worry. I'll handle her if you don't mind picking up the rest of my slack."

"No worries. Do what you need to do to help Nicki out."

❖

A few hours later, Aimee sank into a seat in the conference room at Bradley & Casey Law Firm and faced Morgan and Parker. "I don't understand why they wouldn't give you any information. Did you tell them you've been hired to represent Nicole?"

Morgan responded. "We did. Neither the prosecutor nor the case agents have to tell us anything until they have Nicole in custody. They told us enough to let us know that whatever she's involved in is extremely serious, and whoever she is with has access to illegal firearms and other potentially more dangerous weapons."

Aimee opened her mouth to ask more questions, but shut it once the gravity of Morgan's words sunk in. Nicki was in deep trouble. "What will happen once they find her?"

Once she's arrested, they have to bring her before a judge to be arraigned, have the charges read to her. Often the case agents or prosecutor will give us information in advance of an arrest, but I get the impression they don't want to tip their hand because it might risk her going into hiding."

"Why did they come to my house?"

"You can be sure they've already checked her place in Austin, and when they didn't find her there, they started making their way down the list of likely places. Your house is listed as her permanent address. They also know her parents are out of the country."

"If they know all that, why can't they find her?"

"Good question. It might be something as simple as she's staying with a friend, maybe the boyfriend you mentioned. Yours and her parents' addresses are contained in her files at the university. Maybe they only checked the easy places first. Rest assured, they will work their way down the list of possibilities. They will eventually find her. With a federal warrant, her activities will be limited. I think our strategy at this point is to find her first. If we turn her in versus them arresting her, we have more leverage to negotiate on her behalf."

The approach sounded reasonable. "Okay, what's the next step?"

"We propose hiring a private investigator to send to Austin and see if they can find Nicole or determine where she is. Once we have a lead on her location, we propose that you, along with one of us talk to her about turning herself in. Ultimately, it's her decision, but we can help explain to her why it's to her advantage to face these charges, whatever they are, head on."

"Is there some reason I shouldn't drive down there myself and see if I can find her?"

Parker took up the conversation. "We don't know if she's aware the feds are after her, but chances are good she knows something is up. Would it be natural for you to show up looking for her?"

Aimee shook her head. "No, I helped her move in and I visit occasionally, but I don't show up unannounced."

"Then I"—she glanced at Morgan who nodded—"we, think it's best if the person looking for her is skilled in doing so surreptitiously. We don't want to scare her off before we can reason with her."

Aimee nodded. She wasn't convinced a real life gumshoe was necessary, but then again she didn't have any experience with finding fugitives. "Can your investigator find out anything about the pending charges?"

"Probably not," Morgan answered. "The information about the charges is locked up tight. Parker and I have both tried to get the case agent and the prosecutor to tip their hand, without success. In my experience, when the authorities are this tight-lipped, it means they still have at least a few unapprehended persons they're trying to locate, and a court order sealing the arrest warrant. I think our best strategy is to find Nicole before they do."

"Fair enough." Aimee pulled out her checkbook. "I'm willing to pay whatever it takes. I have only one condition. I want to meet the investigator."

Morgan nodded. "We figured you would. She should be here in about five minutes. Oh, and if it's okay with you, we can pay her fee and expenses from the retainer you already paid. We'll send you a bill if we need you to replenish the funds."

The only thing Aimee heard was "she." As much as she hated to admit it, she had automatically assumed the investigator would be a burly man, maybe even one who wore a fedora and smoked cigars. She chided herself for the stereotype, and fiddled with small talk until the female dick arrived.

Skye had to admit she was excited. Since Parker's visit the night before, she hadn't been able to think of anything but the prospect of quitting the security job. Even though she'd only been on the job for two days, the idea of not being tethered to the car lot for twelve solid hours was exhilarating. So exhilarating, she could handle whatever anger her father might dish out when he found out she'd ditched the job he'd gotten her. Surely he wouldn't be angry long. A private investigator may not be the same as a police detective, but it was definitely a rung up from security guard.

She parked her bike and removed her helmet, taking a moment to check her appearance in the side mirror. Sans silly uniform, she looked like a detective again in her crisp white shirt and black leather jacket. She spent a moment finger combing her hair into an acceptable muss before taking a deep breath and pushing through the lobby doors. The well-appointed offices of Bradley & Casey reinforced her excitement about the prospect of working someplace more respectable than a car lot. She declined the receptionist's offer of a bottled water or cappuccino, and settled back into the arms of a plush leather chair. As she listened to the receptionist announce her arrival over the intercom, she felt important, confident, essential. Feelings she hadn't experienced in a very long time.

"Hey, Skye." Parker shook her hand, then spoke to the receptionist. "I'm going to duck into my office with Ms. Keaton for a minute before heading back to the conference room." She turned back to Skye, indicating she should follow.

After leading them in, Parker stood just inside the door, indicating they wouldn't be there long. "Thanks for coming."

"Pretty sure it's you doing me the favor here."

"This client is a friend of Morgan's. She's our realtor."

"I get it. Keep the client happy." Another thought popped into Skye's head. "Are we doing this case as a favor?" She knew Parker would understand what she meant.

"We're going the extra mile, but she's paying for it. Quick heads up about the case: her niece is in trouble with the feds. We don't know what for and we won't find out until we turn her in. We need you to find her."

"She on the run?"

"Don't know. She may not have a clue about the charges. She's a student at UT. You'll need to go down there and pinpoint her location. Once you know where she is, call us and we'll take it from there."

"Sounds pretty simple to me." Skye felt a prick of disappointment. "When this is done, do I beg back the job I just quit?"

"Get this assignment done, quick and easy, and we'll have plenty more work for you."

Skye glanced around Parker's office. "Nice digs."

"We're doing pretty well."

Skye followed Parker to the conference room, her confidence soaring. She was back in the game. No more polyester clothes, scraping for lunch money. The minute this assignment was complete, she would get her official PI license, and start clawing her way back to a respectable career.

Her confidence drained when she entered the conference room and saw the curvy socialite from the day before. A jolt of arousal mixed with incredulity. Was this some kind of joke? Yesterday she propositions her on the street and today she just happens to have a meeting at the same law firm where Skye is going to work? *Meeting at the law firm, wait a minute, is she the client?* Skye shot a questioning look at Parker, but only caught her back. She was momentarily saved from having to face Aimee by Morgan who was up out of her chair, headed her way.

"Skye, good to see you."

The tone was right, but years as a detective made Skye fluent in body language. Morgan was reluctant about hiring her. She would have to prove her worth, and she wouldn't get a second chance for redemption. She started by delivering a firm handshake and strong eye contact. "Good to see you too." She meant it. During the Burke case she'd developed a healthy dose of respect for Morgan Bradley as an attorney. Parker's obvious love for her meant she was an upstanding person as well. Parker's standards were high. If she loved Morgan enough to join her in business as well as marriage, Morgan was indeed an amazing woman.

"Skye, I'd like you to meet Aimee Howard."

She turned toward Aimee, eyes lowered, unsure how to act. Should she point out they had met before? They hadn't really. Their near encounter in the bar and the run-in on the street hardly constituted a meeting. She knew Aimee's name, but she hadn't introduced herself. She raised her head to face her, but was saved the trouble of having the first word.

"*This* is the woman who's going to find Nicki?" Aimee's words were directed at Parker and Morgan.

"This is Skye Keaton," Parker replied. "She's a former homicide detective with Dallas PD. She has the perfect qualifications to locate a missing person, and we think she will be able to find Nicki in a quiet and efficient manner."

"Is there a particular reason she no longer works for the Dallas police department?" Aimee's tone implied knowledge of the answer.

"I resigned." Skye, tired of being discussed, decided to remind them she was standing right there in the room. She didn't, however, feel the need to explain herself.

Aimee nodded, but the look in her eyes told Skye the subject would come up again. She turned to Morgan. "Are you sure we don't need a *real* investigator to find Nicole. I can afford for you to hire the best."

Skye held the reins of her temper tightly. Where did the bimbo get off? Real investigator, my ass. She wanted to unleash a torrent of angry retorts, but she didn't want to harm her newly repaired relationship with Parker. She chose the only other option she could think of and walked to the door. The hand on her arm stopping her wasn't the one she expected.

"Wait." Morgan's request was gentle but firm. "Why don't we all have a seat and talk about the situation."

Skye couldn't help but obey the quiet authority. She observed Parker as she mouthed a quick "thanks" to Morgan out of Aimee's view, and wondered if Parker was ever able to deny her wife anything. Morgan's magnetism zapped even her own rebellious impulses. She took a seat at the large table, as far away from Aimee Howard as she could get.

"Now, let's talk." Morgan turned to Aimee. "The private investigator we regularly use also does work for another firm, and they are currently in trial and need him to be in town and available for the next week. You would have no reason to know this, but an attorney's relationship with a private investigator is like a relationship between a patient and doctor. We're all pretty picky about who we trust to keep information confidential and to get results. Our cases often rise and fall on the strength of small but critical facts.

"Here's the situation. We need to find Nicki, and we need to find her quickly and discreetly. I could spend a ton of your money to hire someone who looks great on paper to get the job done, or I could hire Skye, who I know has the skills necessary to find Nicole. I choose Skye. It all boils down to one issue. Do you trust me?"

As Aimee nodded her head, Skye concentrated on fighting back the rising blush she could feel creeping up her neck. She never expected to feel loyalty for a defense attorney, but after Morgan's speech, she would walk a plank for her. As for Aimee Howard, well, she would put her in her place as soon as she could.

❖

Aimee figured Morgan deserved her deference. After all, her stellar reputation was built on a stack of real life courtroom wins. If Morgan trusted Skye, Aimee would go along, but she didn't have to like it. Seriously, what kind of detective was she if she barely remembered locking eyes with her just a couple of weeks ago?

Aimee had to admit she was embarrassed Skye didn't remember her. The silly, sinking feeling she'd felt the night of her birthday slithered back into her consciousness. Aging, single lesbian. Can't keep a relationship going. *What a catch.* No wonder Skye had disappeared before Aimee could approach. She probably caught the scent of failure and made a quick getaway.

Apparently, she didn't mind being around a loser if the loser was paying her salary. To be fair, Skye sat at the table, cool and calm, like she couldn't care less if Aimee hired her. She looked decidedly different today than either time Aimee had seen her before. She was more tailored, polished. The crisp in her shirt signaled she cared about her appearance, despite her more casual jeans and heavy black boots. Aimee wondered if Skye had ridden her Harley to the law office. Her windblown hair suggested she had. But what really got Aimee going were her dove gray eyes. The soft color was a surprisingly gentle setting for the sharp looks Skye shot her way.

"Does Nicole have a room at your house or is the address purely for school purposes?" Skye asked.

Aimee heard the implication and chose to ignore it. Lots of students used other relatives' addresses to get in-state tuition. She wasn't going to let someone on her payroll judge her. Besides, she donated tons of money to support her alma mater. Since she was never going to have children of her own, she may as well reap some benefit from her charity. "She stays in the guest room when she visits. She keeps a few things there so I suppose you could call it her room. I'm sure the federal agents thoroughly searched all the bedrooms."

"I'd prefer to check them out myself. Why don't I meet you at your house this evening? I can take a look around and get a list of names and numbers for folks I should contact in Austin. I'll leave in the morning."

Aimee hesitated. She didn't want another stranger in her home. *She's on your side.* The reminder didn't alleviate the anxiety she felt, anxiety rooted in her own insecurities rather than protection of her personal space. Either she was going to have to trust Morgan, and by extension Skye, or find another attorney and start over. She pulled a business card from her purse and scrawled her home address on the back before shoving it in Skye's direction. "Come by at seven."

CHAPTER SEVEN

Immediately after she left Parker's office, Skye went to the bank and deposited the healthy check she'd been given to work on the case. Parker told her to let them know if she needed more for expenses. Then she spent the next couple of hours packing a small bag for the trip south and cleaning her two favorite handguns. She figured one or two days would be enough to get the job done, but she needed to look respectable enough that people would actually talk to her in her quest to locate the wayward Nicole. Space was an issue. She didn't have a lot of storage room on her bike. She finally decided on a couple shirts and an extra pair of jeans. She didn't need to dress up too much. After all, most of her interactions would probably be with college students. She rolled the sparse arrangement of clothing and placed it along with her guns into a small duffle and left it by her door, ready to be strapped onto her bike in the morning.

Skye rumbled up Aimee's drive at six fifty-five, feeling decidedly out of place on her big, loud Harley. As she waited for Aimee to answer the door, she checked her appearance in the glass pane set in the tall oak door. Her fingers were trying to arrange her hair into a respectable style when the door swung wide, and immediately Skye wondered if she had the wrong house. She addressed the short, plump woman. "I'm looking for Aimee Howard."

"Ms. Keaton?" At Skye's nod, the woman motioned her in. "Ms. Howard is expecting you." Skye chided herself. She should have expected Aimee wouldn't answer the door herself. Judging by the neighborhood, she was likely to run into even more servants lurking in the halls.

Servant One led her to a room a few steps from the foyer and told her to have a seat while she fetched Ms. Howard.

She didn't sit. Instead, she chose to roam the room and practice her snooping skills. On two of the walls, bookshelves rose from floor to ceiling. Brick lined the exposed wall with a painting scattered here and there. Skye focused on a particularly large canvas. She supposed the painting would be considered abstract because that's what she always heard it called when you couldn't for the life of you tell what the artist had in mind. Lots of color, slung from a short distance. Probably a druggie. Oh well, better painting in a studio than out selling crack on the streets.

"That's one of my favorites."

Of course it is. Skye fixed an appropriately appreciative expression on her face before she turned to greet her new employer.

"You like Richter's work?" Aimee asked.

"I'm not much of an art critic." Skye kept her tone careful and controlled.

"I see."

Two little words with a ton of meaning. Skye chided herself. She was going to have to be more careful. This woman was sharper than she originally thought. It was almost as if she could read her thoughts. Since her current thoughts included the observation that Aimee was the finest piece of art in the room, it was time to change the subject to suit her own comfort level. "I'd like to start by looking at Nicole's room."

"Follow me then. It's upstairs." Aimee gestured for Skye to follow. "Did you see anyone watching the house when you pulled up?"

The lady had a lively imagination. "No, no sign of surveillance. Why? Do you suspect you're being watched?"

"I'm pretty damned sure I am. Maybe they took a break for the evening."

Skye nodded. She didn't think the feds would waste time staking out her place. Stakeouts cost tons of money and weren't used as often as television and movies made it seem. She decided it couldn't hurt to indulge her client a bit. "I'll look around when I leave and let you know if there's some reason to be concerned."

They didn't speak again as they walked to the third floor of the spacious home. Skye knew she should take advantage of every moment to find out what she could about Nicole, but Aimee's commanding presence and sex appeal robbed her of words. She chose instead to use her observational, rather than interrogational skills.

The house was well kept and professionally decorated. She may not recognize the art on the walls, but she could tell it was expensive and probably original. She wondered if Aimee picked it out herself or if the decorator was the culprit.

"Which rooms did they search?"

"All of them, I assume."

"You didn't watch them?"

"I was handcuffed. Not exactly free to roam about the premises."

Aimee's pained expression signaled that despite her flippant tone, the experience was beyond unpleasant. She imagined it had been Aimee's first negative encounter with anyone in law enforcement. Aimee Howard was the type of woman whose call would be taken by the upper echelon of the Highland Park police department. To have her home invaded by federal authorities would have been a jarring invasion to Aimee's protective bubble of privilege.

Skye did a rapid reassessment of her initial impression. Aimee must have given the feds a hell of a time. They would've known fairly quickly she wasn't the suspect, meaning there was no need to restrain her unless she was trying to block the search. *Wildcat.* Skye tried to imagine the well-coiffed Aimee Howard locked in a struggle with a team of gun-toting federal agents. She probably broke at least one nail, wrinkled her stylish outfit, and maybe even smeared her makeup before she'd wound up with her hands bound behind her back.

Skye shook her head to clear the image that was fast bringing her to arousal. She focused on the way Aimee looked now. Too perfect to touch. Well, looks were definitely deceiving in this case.

Aimee couldn't decide if she liked the way Skye's penetrating stare made her feel. Exposed, vulnerable. She'd had enough of those particular feelings this week. "Is there a reason you're staring at me?" Part of her sensed Skye wasn't looking at her so much as looking through her. *What does she see?* Whatever it was, the vision captured her attention completely. Just like Aimee had wanted to capture her attention a couple of weeks ago and then again yesterday on the street. Not anymore. Skye Keaton might be splendid eye candy, but she had yet to show any other traits of interest.

"Do you live here alone?" The question seemed more personal than professional, and despite the change in subject, Aimee felt even more exposed. "I would have expected Morgan and Parker to fill you in on any details you need in order to find Nicki."

"Is there a reason you don't want to answer my questions?"

"Efficiency. Aren't I paying you by the hour?" Aimee didn't want to admit she was more annoyed at the nature of the question than the fact Skye was asking questions at all. "It's not my fault you didn't get the background you needed."

Skye visibly bristled. "You're paying me to do my job. How I do it is my decision, based on years of experience."

Aimee knew Skye was right, but she was angry, the kind of anger born out of embarrassment. The feeling shamed her, but she didn't have to let her actions shame her more. Skye obviously hadn't felt the same jolt she had in their brief connection at the bar. Aimee realized she was clinging to a tenuous connection that didn't exist. She stifled her anger. "You're right. I'm sorry. Why don't you take a look around Nicole's room and anywhere else you want? I'll wait downstairs. When you're done, I'll answer any questions you have."

Skye wasn't sure what to make of Aimee's sudden change in attitude. She nodded her agreement, but her natural tendency toward cynicism kept her guard in place.

The guest room where Nicole stayed was as impeccably decorated as the rest of the house. Skye found it hard to believe a college student had ever lived in this room. The only visible traces of Nicole were a few pieces of clothing hanging in the spacious walk-in closet. A pair of jeans and two shirts. Skye recognized the bold white stitching on the jeans as those of an expensive brand. The shirts were colorful, but plain Banana Republic T-shirts. Nicole had money to spend on clothes. She had enough money to spend on clothes that this pair of jeans wasn't a coveted piece of clothing, left as it was at her aunt's house in a completely different town than where she lived.

Skye searched the pockets and found a crumpled charge receipt. The date was cut off, but she determined the purchase was fairly recent since the paper was still crisp and the ink wasn't faded. Freedom Army-Navy Store, Austin. The receipt wasn't itemized, but it reflected a cash transaction for a little over three hundred dollars. Pretty steep for salvage store accessories to go with her trendy clothes. It might mean nothing, but it was a place to start. Stupid feds. If they'd found it, they would've taken it with them, securely tucked in a glassine bag. Skye reminded herself to get a copy of the list of things they had taken following their search of the house and Aimee's office.

The rest of her search revealed nothing of interest. When she joined Aimee downstairs, she was surprised to find her in the kitchen.

Aimee gestured at a generous spread. "I haven't had dinner. How about you?"

Skye hadn't. She didn't have a lick of groceries at her house and, though now she was flush with cash, she hadn't purchased anything since she was headed out of town in the morning. For the second time that evening, she considered the tenuous line she walked. A meal was hardly a significant personal event.

"Food sounds great. Thanks." At Aimee's urging, she grabbed a plate and filled it with an array of delicious looking food. They settled into chairs.

Skye took her first bite at the exact moment Aimee announced, "No one else lives here."

Skye swallowed roughly. "Pardon?"

"You asked if I live here alone."

"I see." Skye feigned indifference, but filed the information away for future inspection.

"What about you?"

"Me?"

"Yes, you. Tell me more about yourself. Besides the fact you were a detective for the Dallas PD."

"Like what do you want to know?" Skye's hunger clouded her usual caution. She dug into her food as if she hadn't eaten in days.

"Like what do you do for fun?"

Skye stopped mid bite. Aimee's expression was playful, teasing. Personal and professional boundaries might blur when it came to the questions she asked Aimee, but the demarcation was sharp and solid in the other direction. She had no intention of revealing anything to do with her personal life to Aimee or anyone else, especially not when the dangerous crackle of attraction threatened to distract her from her only chance at a respectable job.

If the circumstances were different, she would consider showing, rather than telling Aimee the answer to her question, but she needed this work. Not for the money, but for the boost to her confidence. She didn't have a clue what Aimee was up to, but she wasn't going to risk this job, so this socialite could slum it for the evening.

Skye pushed her plate away and stood. "It's getting late. I plan to leave early in the morning. I need you to make a list of all of Nicole's friends in Austin, including her boyfriend and any other guys she dated. Include their contact information if you have it. Get the list along with anything else you think might be helpful to Morgan or Parker. I'll stay in touch with them while I'm in Austin."

Aimee stiffened, but Skye ignored an impulse to soften her impersonal good-bye. Better to make it clear now that their only interactions would be for the purpose of finding Nicki. When the job was over, their lives would intersect no more. Skye left quickly to emphasize the point.

❖

Skye waited until nine a.m. to hit the road in order to avoid the rush hour commute. The drive would take three hours, not accounting for any traffic, and the route along I-35 was notorious for random construction projects that shut the road down often for miles at a time. At least the weather was good. Not a cloud in sight.

Despite her preparations the day before, she still had a couple of stops to make before she left town. The first had come up when she called Parker to discuss their mutual client.

"What's her story, anyway?"

"What are you talking about?"

"One minute she acts like I'm not competent to find Nicki, the next she's coming on to me."

"Coming on to you? Seriously, Skye."

"You don't believe me? You don't think I'm good enough?" Skye felt silly for the words the moment they left her mouth. It wasn't like she cared either way. But she did. The assumption, real or imagined, she wasn't the right type for Aimee or any other respectable woman ate at her insides.

"Now you're talking trash. If I didn't think you were top-notch, I wouldn't have hired you for this gig."

"Yeah, right, because finding a college student is so damn difficult you had to have the best. Sure you're not just tossing me a bone, Casey?"

"You're welcome to throw it back if you want. I can get someone else to find Nicole if you're not interested."

"Look, let's take this back a notch. I'm sorry. This whole private eye thing is weird. I'm not used to having someone looking over my shoulder. I'll get over it. Anyway, the real reason I called was to see if I could come by and pick up that information Aimee sent over."

"Sure, you can come by, but why don't I just e-mail that stuff to you?"

"I'm not taking my laptop. No room on the bike."

"Seriously, Skye, you still don't have a car?"

Skye's steadfast refusal to purchase any mode of transportation with more than two wheels was a source of constant needling from friends and family. Most claimed she did it so she never had to cart anyone around. She always replied with an offer to share the ride, which all but her late night pickups declined. She preferred the maneuverability of her Harley.

"You still driving that old junker you call vintage?" Her comment was designed to elicit a defensive yelp, and she wasn't disappointed. Parker's '68 Mustang was always in need of just one more little repair to keep it roadworthy.

"Yes, but I'm married to a woman whose car actually runs."

"My Harley runs just fine."

"Speaking of twentieth century, can't you get e-mail on your phone?"

"I did, on the one I had on the job. I turned it in along with every other piece of city property in my possession when I was shown the door. I'm talking to you on my stripped down, phone calls only cell phone."

"I can tell you right now, your Neanderthal method of communication isn't going to work. Morgan and I are in court so much, it's easier to reach us by text or e-mail. Come by the office. I think Morgan's old iPhone is still around here. You can take it and get it activated before you leave town."

A leash. Skye chose not to speak the words because she wanted this job, but the thought of being on the end of anyone else's instant access made her ill. "Yeah, okay. I'll come by."

"Oh, and just so you know, Aimee went out with Morgan once."

"Your point?"

"I don't have one. Not really. Well, maybe I just wanted to point out that you may not be her type."

"Like I couldn't figure that out for myself. Guess you think you're hot shit because Morgan picked you over her."

"No, but I do think I'm lucky."

I could use a little luck, Skye thought as she burned up highway miles on her way to Austin. She was making good time, and she should hit the university campus by one o'clock, despite her late start. As she approached Exit 353, she debated whether she should pull off and grab a snack at the famous Czech Stop Bakery. The growl in her belly made the decision easy. She reasoned a snack now would mean she could show up ready to work without stopping again for lunch. Besides, even over the low roar of her bike's engine, she had heard the ringing of the stupid phone

Parker made her carry. She should check and see if it was anything important.

Her inbox contained two messages. She didn't recognize either return address. The e-mails were listed in the order received. First on the list:

> *I realize you're probably already on the road, but please call me as soon as you arrive in Austin. I've had some ideas I'm sure will be helpful to you in your search for Nicole. I'll be waiting for your call.*
>
> *Aimee*

Seriously? How did she get my e-mail address? Please don't let her have my phone number. The last thing I need is some client micromanaging my every move. She remembered she had another e-mail to check.

> *Skye,*
>
> *Aimee called shortly after you left. She said she had some information for you so I gave her your contact info. I hope you don't mind, but it just seemed easier for her to get in touch with you directly. Have a good trip.*
>
> *Parker*

Of course I mind. Skye powered down the phone and shoved it in the tank storage leather pouch on the bike, determined to finish her early lunch in peace. Parker had given her the list of Nicki's contacts in Austin this morning. If Ms. Aimee Howard had additional important information to share, she could send it to her in an e-mail. Skye punctuated the thought with a large bite of Czech pastry. The sweet yeast sang against the tart apricot filling and soothed away any lingering frustrations about her pushy client. A couple of kolaches later, she was speeding toward Austin, with no interruptions in sight.

❖

The week was practically gone and Aimee resolved she would get some work done in order to have something to show for it. After she e-mailed Skye, she called an impromptu meeting at the office. Over lunch, she discussed the status of any pending contracts with her team. Each of her agents was a shareholder in her boutique firm and business meetings were the norm in their office. It was a unique arrangement in the real estate world, but Aimee wanted to build the business for all more than just herself. Today, her concern was doing whatever she could to return some sense of normalcy to the office after the invasion at the beginning of the week.

When the meeting was over, she stopped by Natalie's desk.

"Yes, Ms. Howard?"

Aimee resisted the urge to admonish her to use her first name. She was only here for a couple more weeks. She couldn't possibly drive her crazy in two weeks time. "Any calls?"

"No, Ms. Howard, no calls."

"Okay. Let me know if Skye Keaton calls. Interrupt me if you have to."

In her office, Aimee checked her computer for an e-mail from Skye. The clock in the corner read two p.m. Skye should be in Austin by now. Parker said she had an iPhone, all set up with e-mail service. Surely Skye had gotten her request for contact by now. She rapped her fingers on her desk. Aimee picked up the phone, then replaced it in the cradle. She should let Skye do her job. She'd probably only been in Austin for a couple hours at the most. She wanted to tell her about Nicole's recent contact with her father and her request for money.

If that's all you wanted to tell her, you could have put it in the e-mail. Aimee didn't want to admit it, but she knew why she'd asked Skye to call. She wanted a connection she couldn't get from exchanging typed text. Skye Keaton was an enigma and she wanted to cut through the mystery. She looked like she was in her mid thirties, and she'd worked her way up through the ranks at DPD to become a detective. Aimee was no expert, but she watched plenty of cop shows. Cops who made it to detective were the kind who stuck with the work, no matter what. Why had Skye quit? Maybe she'd been hurt on duty and retired rather than take a boring desk job. She sure didn't look like she had any injuries or health problems. On the contrary, she looked fantastically fit. Maybe she hadn't quit voluntarily. Aimee pushed the thought away. Morgan and Parker wouldn't have hired a fired Dallas cop to look for Nicki. Would they?

Aimee opened her Internet browser and Googled Skye Keaton. Dozens of entries appeared, most detailing testimony in murder cases. The top, most recent entry drew Aimee's eye.

> *This afternoon, Dallas PD Homicide Detective Skye Keaton took the stand in the trial of Theodore Burke. Burke was on trial for attempted murder of a police officer. Detective Keaton is no stranger to the witness stand, having testified at dozens of trials during her tenure on the force, but today she is the state's key witness because of her role as victim, rather than lead investigator in the case.*

Aimee clicked on the link and read the rest of the story. She was familiar with the Burke family. Her parents' mansion was only a few blocks from the Burke estate, and she remembered the blazing headlines last year when the youngest member of the family, Camille Burke, was found dead in her room at the mansion with a gunshot wound to the head. Morgan, along with a group of law students including Parker, had represented the man police arrested for the crime, but the investigation revealed police had arrested the wrong man. Camille had actually committed suicide to escape the abuse of her older brother, Teddy. Teddy, in turn, went to extra pains to cover up his own crimes, but when the police drew close, he attempted to kill the detective who found him out. Aimee was amazed to learn that detective was Skye Keaton.

She glanced at the date on the headline. Teddy Burke's trial ended just a few weeks ago. The article indicated Skye was still an active member of DPD at the time she testified. If Skye had quit the force, she'd done so right after the trial. Aimee's mind raced with speculation about Skye's reasons for leaving her job. Maybe she couldn't handle the stress anymore. After all, she had a close brush with death. After years on the force, had this been the first time she'd been in danger? She thought about calling Morgan to get her questions answered, but decided against it. She didn't want Morgan to think she didn't trust her judgment, especially when it seemed there must be some strange connection between Skye and Morgan's law firm. It was pretty odd that they would all be working on the same side after having been engaged in a legal battle mere months before.

No, she wouldn't ask Morgan about Skye's background, but she would get some answers. Aimee was not without connections. She located an old directory and turned the pages until she found a familiar entry. As she dialed the number, she let her mind wander to the many questions she had about Skye while ignoring the primary query: Why was she so interested in the past of a woman she barely knew?

Chapter Eight

"Single room. Ground floor. Near the front if you have it."
Skye waited patiently for the middle aged, Middle Eastern man to locate a key. She paid cash, in advance, for two nights. The man smiled as he accepted the familiar currency. This wasn't a "we need your credit card for amenities kind of place." Any extras would be purchased from a coin-operated vending machine, and all the room furnishings were likely bolted down.

The sign out front read simply MOTEL, perfect for keeping a low profile. She wasn't exactly sure why she cared. All she had to do was find the girl and then go home. She had plenty of money for expenses. Maybe she should have stayed at some cool hotel downtown where she would be in walking distance to nice restaurants with white tablecloths and real silver. The kind of places Aimee Howard was used to. She pictured the voluptuous blonde seated across from her, leaning forward to offer Skye a particularly tasty morsel. From her fingers.

Skye shook her head. She wasn't here to lounge and eat, and she certainly wasn't here to daydream sexy thoughts. Especially if those thoughts involved bossy Aimee Howard. She had a job to do. When she turned in her receipts, would Aimee appreciate how frugal Skye had been with her money? She doubted it.

Skye was in the room only long enough to use the restroom and stow her duffle. Her first stop was Nicole's apartment near campus. She had been surprised to learn the college student had her own place. She knew Nicole could afford it, or at least her parents could, but she imagined the rich child of socialites would be banded with a group of other like females in a sorority house or some other such horrid place.

The apartment complex was plush and enormous. She had Nicole's apartment number, but it still took her a good ten minutes of driving around to find the correct building. Hardly anyone was around. Good. She didn't want to be interrupted.

She knocked on the apartment door, idly wondering if she could keep the retainer if Nicole appeared at the door, ready to turn herself in. She didn't wonder long before she decided no one was going to answer. After glancing around to make sure she wasn't being observed, Skye reached into her boot and extracted a slim leather case. Her father had given her the set of lock picks when she graduated from the academy.

"You're a smart girl, but you lack brute force your brothers possess. There'll be some doors you can't get open under your own physical power. Use these when you can't find another way around."

Even then the leather case was butter smooth with wear. Skye suspected the picks had been in the family for a while. She treated them like an heirloom, but she used them liberally. She'd found plenty of occasions that didn't offer another way around. She'd taught herself and her skill was advanced. She never spoke to her father about the gift beyond a simple "thank you" the day it was offered, but she knew Chief Keaton would be proud of her prowess.

The lock popped, and Skye drew her weapon before pushing the door in. As she crossed the threshold, she assumed a Weaver stance, sweeping left, then right, more concerned about safety than scaring anyone who might be inside. She kept up the maneuvers as she walked through the spacious apartment until she determined all the rooms were clear. Nicole was nowhere in sight, but a single sheet of paper, containing a vaguely worded list of seized items—laptop, DVDs, letters—gracing the kitchen counter told her the feds had already swept the place. Skye placed her Sig back in the holster and she concentrated on finding clues the feds had missed.

Perhaps because she was hungry again, she started with the fridge. The contents consisted of a scattered bunch of fast food condiments. The only item resembling real food was a pint-sized carton of milk. She checked the expiration date and shuddered when she saw it was two weeks past. Clue number one. Skye pulled a small flip cover notebook from her back pocket and scrawled the date. The rest of the kitchen was sparsely stocked with a random set of plates, pots and pans, a box of Cheerios, and a picnic style set of salt and pepper shakers.

Skye moved next to the only bedroom. The double bed was made. Skye sniffed the air. Musty. The small walk-in closet was stuffed with clothes, similar in style to the few pieces in her room at Aimee's house. Skye was willing to bet Nicole spent more on clothes in a month than her own rent. If Nicole had taken as much with her as she left behind, that number would probably be double.

The top shelf of the closet held a full set of expensive, brand name luggage, seven pieces in various sizes. Skye checked the bathroom next. The counter and cabinet were full of products likely purchased at stores like Neiman Marcus. The shower caddy was stocked with shampoo, conditioner, body soap, and a loofah. The only out of place items were a cheap can of men's shaving cream and a bar of Irish Spring. What she saw throughout the apartment confirmed her suspicions. Nicole hadn't planned an extended trip. Skye needed to figure out when she'd last been seen.

She pulled the Army-Navy store receipt from her back pocket. *Freedom.* Interesting name. Maybe she should swing by there and see if they remembered Nicole shopping in their store. First stop though would be to check in with the apartment manager.

The suite of business offices was plush. Not a starving student in sight. A man was seated at the desk, while a sharply dressed woman stood strategically by the entry. She was the first to speak.

"Can I help you find your next home here at The Winds at Willow Lake?"

Skye grinned at the Stepford impersonation. She was pretty sure the lake the woman referred to was the pond located in the middle of the property. She glanced at the man seated at the desk.

She probably had a better chance of getting valuable intel from him, but it might be harder to come by. She touched the woman's elbow and steered her to the other side of the room, careful to keep her voice low. "Actually, I live in Dallas, but I could use your help with something very important." Skye fixed her features to convey the importance of her impending request. The woman squinted back at her, as if by squeezing her eyes tightly she could keep whatever information she was about to learn from falling out.

"My sister lives here. You may know her. Nicole Howard. Apartment fourteen twenty?" Skye figured she looked enough like Nicole to pass as a sibling.

The woman nodded her head slowly. "Yes. I do." She lowered her voice. "You know federal agents were here searching her apartment?"

"I do. Our attorneys say it was a big mistake, and they're sorting it out. I'm sure it was very troubling for Nicole. I remember how hard it is to be in college, miles away from your family." Skye lied. A couple of years at the community college around the corner from her house was her only experience with post high school education. All she'd ever wanted to be was a cop, like her dad and brothers. Well, that ship had sailed.

She turned her focus back to the task at hand. "I don't want her to know I was checking up on her, but I did want to make sure she has everything she needs." Skye leaned in to whisper a series of questions. "Have you seen her lately? Does she look okay? Losing weight, gaining weight? Is her rent paid?" She rocked back on her heels and waited for the woman to answer whatever she chose.

"Come to think of it, I haven't seen her in a while." She paused. "Her rent's all paid up through the end of the semester. I think your parents wired the money at the beginning of the school year." She appeared disconcerted, as if she wasn't holding up her end of the bargain in this information exchange. Then Skye saw a light bulb go off. "She does have some mail. Her box was overflowing and the postman started delivering it directly to the office." She paused, as if reflecting.

Skye waited through the beats of silence, hoping, hoping.

"Would you like to collect it for her?"

Bingo. Skye tried not to appear too eager. "Sure, if it would help you out. I'm supposed to see her very soon"—not a complete lie—"and I'd be happy to pass it along."

Skye waited patiently while the woman gathered Nicki's mail. The bundle was large and stacked on top were several bulky packages. One in particular caught her eye. She couldn't wait to get back to the motel room and rummage through her find.

❖

Aimee kept glancing at the door. The coffee shop at Southside on Lamar was deserted, which made her furtive looks all the more noticeable. The owner finally strode over. "Do you need anything else?"

Aimee assumed a sheepish look. "No, I'm waiting on someone. I'm fine for now." She wasn't really. When she'd called Lieutenant Jane Dawson, she'd expected to get a simple rundown about Skye Keaton that would fill in some blanks to the information she'd gathered from the Internet. Instead, Jane suggested they talk in person. Aimee was a savvy enough businesswoman to know most bad news was delivered face-to-face. She nursed her now cold coffee and waited for Jane to arrive and the other shoe to drop.

Ten long minutes later, Jane slid into a chair across from her.

"Sorry I'm late. Something came up just as I tried to sneak away."

"No problem." Aimee took a deep breath and assessed Lieutenant Dawson. She hadn't seen her in a while. Jane used to be the department's liaison to the GLBT community, and when she was in that post, they had crossed paths on numerous occasions. Jane's calm, professional demeanor, as she handled difficult public relations issues got her noticed and promoted quickly to the position of official department spokesperson. Her easy good looks didn't hurt. The cameras loved her and she always made the department look good, even when doing so seemed an insurmountable task. Aimee hoped Jane's position in the department would make her the perfect person to fill in the blanks about Skye's background.

Jane leaned forward. "Disciplinary reports are public record. For the most part."

"You're saying I could just request Skye's record?"

"Yes."

"Through regular channels, that could take weeks, am I right?" Jane nodded.

"I'd like them sooner."

"I understand. Mind if I ask why?"

Aimee hesitated. Bottom line, Jane was a cop. Aimee might refer to her as a friend, but in truth, they were really only acquaintances. She didn't know how Jane would react to her story about her on-the-lam niece and her attempts to find her before the feds did. If she knew Skye was looking for Nicki, would Jane feel compelled to tell her law enforcement brethren to tail Skye in hopes she would lead them to Nicki? In books and on TV, local authorities usually hated the feds. Maybe she was blowing the situation out of proportion, but she wasn't prepared to take that chance. She lied. "I'm thinking of hiring her to work security for some property I own. I need her to start right away." She spoke the words rapidly and avoided Jane's look, certain that a trained professional would know she was lying.

"Oh, okay." Jane reached under the table and pulled a thick folder from her briefcase. She set the folder on the table, her hand rested on top. "Since it's public record, I don't think there's an issue with me giving you this copy."

Aimee tried not to stare at the document in the center of the table. She wanted to grab it and run to her car where she could pore over the contents in private.

"A few portions are missing."

Aimee forced herself to look from the folder to Jane's face. "Missing?"

"I guess missing isn't the right word. Sealed is more appropriate. In other words, some of the information you mentioned on the phone may not be in these files."

Aimee nodded. She got it. If she requested the file through regular channels, she would have received this same stack without an explanation. She would have realized some chunks were missing, but her questions would go unanswered. Jane was here in person to fill in the blanks. Aimee wondered how cooperative Jane was prepared to be.

"I don't have any personal information about the Burke case," Jane said, as if she could hear Aimee's thoughts. Aimee heard the big, silent, "but." She waited. "But I have heard things."

"Anything you could share would be helpful."

"Skye was a dedicated cop."

Not the thunderbolt of information Aimee had been expecting. She stared at Jane. Her pained expression told her she was just warming up. "Skye tended to believe more in the order part of law and order. She would do just about anything to get a conviction. Most of the time, her actions were justified."

And sometimes they weren't. Aimee heard the unspoken cut, but she detected not a hint of disdain. Whatever Skye had done, Jane didn't think it had warranted her separation from the department.

"She had a habit of cutting corners. Constitutional corners. Her actions sometimes tied a prosecutor's hands, placed them in a difficult position. Legally."

"But she was a victim in the Burke case."

"Yes. Some people think she brought that on herself."

But you don't. Interesting. Aimee's curiosity ran rampant, but Jane's locked up expression told her she wasn't likely to get much more. She chose her next question carefully.

"Would you trust her to guard something very important to you?"

Jane glanced around. No one else was in the tiny café. Aimee guessed the action was symbolic. Jane was about to tell her something she truly meant, but wouldn't admit to in her official capacity.

"I would trust her with my life."

Back at her office, Aimee reflected on her meeting with Jane. Frankly, she wasn't sure what to make of it. She knew now that Skye had been asked to leave the department for infractions that violated department policy, but she had earned the secret respect of more than a few higher-ups. Aimee flashed back to the swarm of federal agents who'd invaded her home and swept through it like a well-oiled machine. She shuddered. She didn't want to take any chances when it came to finding Nicki and getting her to Morgan and Parker. She wondered what tricks Skye might have up her sleeve. Tricks were the last thing she needed. Aimee picked up the phone. "Natalie, do I have any messages?"

"Yes, ma'am."

Aimee cringed. "Any from a Skye Keaton?"

"No, ma'am."

"Okay, thanks. Shoot me an e-mail with the messages." *Like I've told you to do a thousand times.* Aimee kept the phone in her hand and considered her options. First, never again hire temporary help as a favor. Second, get hold of Skye Keaton. She couldn't believe Skye hadn't called her. If she didn't return client calls, she'd be out of business. Apparently, Skye didn't possess a lot of business savvy. *Well, I can teach her a thing or two.* She punched in the numbers and waited for the mechanical outgoing message.

"Keaton here."

Aimee jumped at the sound of Skye's husky voice, her bravado fading now that Skye had actually answered the phone.

"Skye, it's Aimee Howard."

"Oh." Skye sounded decidedly disappointed.

Oh? No, "I'm sorry I haven't returned your message." No, "I realize I work for you and I should probably check in every once in a while." Aimee chided herself. Had she really expected Skye to check in? She took a deep breath and plunged in. "I thought of some information that might be helpful."

"Okay."

"Wow, you really don't like to waste words, do you?" Silence. Well, that answers that, Aimee thought. "Forget I said that. I wanted to let you know I had a discussion with my dad the other day and he said he was in contact with Nicki in the last week. I think he's been sending her money, and knowing him, we're not talking about small sums."

"How not small?"

"Probably in the thousand dollar range. Maybe more."

"Your father is Gordon Howard, the developer?"

Even though her parentage was easy information to locate, the fact that Skye had checked her out was at once flattering and disturbing. "The one and only."

"I'm guessing a thousand bucks is nothing to him."

"Technically, no. He's got plenty, but Dad guards every dime like it's his last. The money he's been sending her is from her trust account, not his personal fortune."

"How would he have gotten her the money?"

"I'm betting a wire transfer. Apparently, he took down her banking information when he talked to her last."

"Interesting."

"What?"

"Nothing. I was just thinking that if we had her bank information, it might be easier to find her. See where she's spending her dough." Skye paused. "I went by her apartment. Someone paid Nicki's rent through the end of the semester."

"That was probably my brother. He's out of the country, so he probably has all her expenses paid up for a while to make things easier on him."

"If your brother pays for everything, I wonder why Nicki would need to dip into her trust account."

"Good question."

"It doesn't look like she's been here in a while. The apartment manager gave me a bunch of mail that's been piling up."

"Why did she give it to you? Isn't that a federal offense?" She heard Skye chuckle into the line.

"Oh, that's rich. I'm pretty sure the feds are worried more about little Nicki than any federal offense her apartment manager may have committed by giving me her mail."

Aimee felt stupid. Of course, Skye was right. All she wanted to do now was end the call. "Anyway, I thought you should know about her contact with my dad. And the money. In case it helps." She was feeling pleased with herself for providing what Skye obviously considered pertinent information, but Skye's next remark doused her self-congratulations.

"Why didn't you tell me this before?"

"I just realized it might be important."

"Any other important information you've forgotten to share?"

Aimee bristled. "What's with the tone? I thought you worked for me." She instantly regretted the statement and softened her tone. "I'm sorry I didn't tell you sooner, but looking for missing college students isn't really my forte."

"I work for Morgan and Parker."

Aimee was confused by the seeming non sequitur. "Excuse me?"

"I don't work for you. If you have information that could help me find Nicki, call me, but if you have a problem with the way I do my job, call your lawyers."

Where did Skye get off talking to her like that? Aimee thought of a thousand retorts, but only one made it past her lips.

"Apparently, I'm not the only one who has a problem with how you do your job. But rest assured, I won't put up with as much as your last employer did."

As she clicked off the line, the sour taste of regret overshadowed the triumph of her zinging last remark.

Skye stared at the phone in her hand. What the hell? The not so thinly veiled reference to her former cop status was crystal clear. Her only question was who had filled Aimee in on the details of her forced resignation. Parker? Morgan? Skye started punching in the numbers to their law office, anger her driving force, but she clicked off the line before the call rang through. Surely neither of them would have told Aimee things that would cast doubt on their decision to hire her. No, that would only reflect poorly on them.

Aimee had to have found out the background behind Skye's separation from the department another way. It was probably easy for her to learn whatever she wanted. As Gordon Howard's daughter, she had not only limitless funds, but also unfettered access to the upper echelon of city government. Clearly, Aimee was used to having whatever she wanted, which made Skye resistant to give her anything. If Aimee wanted to convey or receive any more information about this case, she'd have to consult Parker and Morgan, and if those terms weren't acceptable, she was done with this job.

She tossed the phone down and resumed reviewing Nicki's mail. She'd received several large brown envelopes from an address in Wyoming. No name on the return address, only initials: C.O.P.S. She picked the phone back up and scrolled through the features to see if it had a camera function. *Guess this smart phone will come in handy after all.* Skye snapped a picture of the return address. She was sorely tempted to open one of the envelopes. From the outside, it looked like junk mail, maybe a catalog or newsletter. Did the drafters of the legislation really mean for it to be a federal offense for someone to open junk mail? She could always say she found it in the trash.

She tossed one of the envelopes in the round, tin wastebasket and reflected for a moment on why the trash can wasn't bolted down like everything else in the room. After a respectable three minutes, she snatched the envelope back and ripped it open.

CHAPTER NINE

Skye scanned the contents of the envelope.

Federal taxes are a foreign conspiracy. The IRS, along with most other federal agencies, has become an arm of the infidel, reaching into the pockets of Hardworking Americans, STEALING the fruits of their labor in order to fund the works of despots in corrupt foreign lands. Citizens, you must exercise your rights under the CONSTITUTION to blunt the dilution of our Great nation. Every time a dollar goes overseas, it turns into a piece of filthy LUCRE, not fit to be called AMERICAN. Stop the flow of support for the unbelievers, the unpatriotic, the un-American. You know what to do. Recall the teachings of our forefathers, Thomas Jefferson, Benjamin Franklin, and the Reverend Bill Gale, and follow their example.

Skye stared at the paper in her hand. It was a newsletter of sorts, though not professionally produced. It consisted of three sheets of plain white typing paper with a banner headline: THE CONSTITUTIONAL HERALD, a publication of C.O.P.S., the Coalition of Patriot Sectarians, an unorganized militia of the sovereign republic of Texas.

C.O.P.S., seriously? She rechecked the return address on the envelope. Why was an organization in Texas using a Wyoming address? *The Herald* contained several stories, one paragraph after another, complete with blaring headlines and sloppy clip art. The story she'd just read was positioned under the headline: *Render unto God what is God's. Caesar can get money from liberal Jews, Wops, and Spics*, and was accompanied by a picture of the tax code in flames. Skye glanced through the rest of the newsletter and found advertisements from various gun dealers, shooting ranges, and army surplus stores as well as articles dealing with a number of controversial subjects including the military, racism, abortion, and guns. She read another one with interest.

ARM YOURSELF

Every Coalition member has not only a RIGHT, but a DUTY to bear arms. How else will we protect our families against the plots and violence of the infidel who lives among us? Especially in these times when we cannot KNOW for sure who it is who will rise up to take away our rights. The DANGER slithers among us, and many times the most dangerous are dressed like we are, living in our neighborhoods, their children going to our schools. At neighborhood parties, they talk about sports and the weather and you relax, thinking you are of the same mind, but later, they go into their homes and pledge their allegiance to the PSEUDO government. They send their money to causes that would deny you and your children a truly AMERICAN way of life. They send money to feed the poor in countries whose name you can't pronounce. They send money to protect nonbelievers from their own path toward SIN. They send money to teach outrageous ideas to schoolchildren who will grow up to build bombs and other weapons designed to defeat you in wars waged against freedom. You have no way of knowing from where and when the enemy will come—you must be VIGILANT. Protect your FREEDOM. Use it. Exercise your rights. PROTECT yourself. You have a right to own and use the weaponry GOD gave you.

Why was a rich sorority girl getting this kind of whack-job mail? Skye turned the envelope over and confirmed it was addressed to Nicole. *Bizarre.* What was even more bizarre was the presence of at least three other envelopes with the same return address. And the package. Skye pulled out a pocketknife and sliced through the tape on the medium sized box, no longer giving a shit about federal law.

To the untrained eye, the contents of the box would look like junk, but a weapons expert would know exactly what she was looking at. PVC pipe, rubber disks, washers, short aluminum pipe. Skye had been shooting guns since she was six. She'd developed an intense fascination with firearms and, as she grew older, learned everything she could on the subject. She was an accomplished markswoman, proficient with a wide array of guns. She had no doubt the seemingly harmless random assortment of parts was exactly what someone needed in order to make a silencer. A homemade, illegal silencer. *Jeez.*

Skye dropped the box and rocked back on her heels. She had to be wrong. No way was spoiled Nicki Howard spending her time making accessories designed to kill. If Skye hadn't seen the kind of crazy mail Nicki had been getting, she might have a better chance at shrugging off her concern. She pulled the receipt from the Freedom Army-Navy Surplus store from her pocket. Extreme right-wing propaganda, weapons, purchases from a store selling survivalist equipment. She glanced back at the C.O.P.S. newsletter. The front page featured a quarter page ad for the store. Pieces started to click into place, and the picture was frightening. She'd worked on a task force investigating extremist militia groups before she entered homicide. Their constitutionally protected hate speech hid a string of illegal activities—guns, bombs, and tax evasion. Before her thoughts could run off on a tangent, she reeled them back in. She packed the box and shoved it in the back of the closet. A trip to the surplus store was in order. It was time to find out how Nicki was spending the money she'd wheedled out of her trust account.

Aimee decided an in-person visit was the best way to alleviate her concerns, but when the receptionist told her Morgan was in court, she instantly regretted not calling first.

"Can Ms. Casey help you?"

She felt the beats of silence as she considered the option being offered. She'd gotten to know Parker since she met Morgan last year, but their acquaintance was at arm's length. Parker was a former cop and so was Skye. Did she really want to do her venting with someone who might very well be a good friend of the source of her consternation? Aimee quickly adjusted her perspective. If she really wanted to know more about Skye Keaton, Parker might be the best source of accurate information. She faced the receptionist who waited patiently through her long, twisted thought process. "If Ms. Casey is available, I'd be happy to talk to her instead."

Moments later, she sat in Parker's office and contemplated her approach. Parker's first words opened the door.

"I think it's too soon for us to have heard anything, but I passed on your message to Skye. Did she call you?"

"Well, not exactly. I mean I e-mailed her and asked her to call, but I didn't hear from her so I called her." Aimee told herself to stop babbling and get to the point. "She's fairly gruff, don't you think?"

Parker smiled. "Skye's not known for her bedside manner."

Aimee felt the red-hot blush rise up her neck. As much as she was certain Parker's choice of words was unintentional, she couldn't help the slow creep of embarrassment at the images it provoked. She cast about for a way to change the subject, but since Skye was the reason for her visit, there was no escape.

"I guess I'm used to a more professional approach." As she delivered the words, she noticed an almost imperceptible tightening of Parker's demeanor, but she couldn't read the source. She considered ignoring Parker's reaction, but decided she might get more information with a direct approach. "Did I say something to offend you?"

Parker's smile was still in place, but the change in her bearing was evident. "Not really." She paused and her smile turned sheepish. "Well, maybe. We cops do our best to be professional, but we generally like to be left to our own devices when it comes to how we conduct an investigation."

Aimee knew Parker had been a police officer before law school, but the smooth, polished professional seated behind the desk bore no resemblance to the rough-around-the-edges Skye Keaton. She decided to say as much. "I don't think you're anything like Skye."

"I'm not." Parker's words were staccato.

Hmmm, must be a story there. Aimee waited to see if Parker had anything to add before she resumed her questions. Silence. She plunged in. "How do you know Skye?"

Parker stared at a spot on her desk for a very long time before finally facing Aimee. "Skye and I were partners. We were both homicide detectives."

Partners? Parker's information raised more questions, but Aimee wasn't sure of the line between personal and professional anymore. She ventured one more. "I assume you know about the circumstances behind her separation from the department?" She didn't wait for an answer before plunging ahead. "And you still feel confident she's qualified to do detective work for your firm?"

Aimee braced herself for Parker's reaction. It was stoic. "Rest assured, I would not have hired Skye if I didn't feel like she was supremely qualified. She will find Nicki and she will do it quickly. We'll contact you as soon as we have word."

Aimee left feeling dismissed. She didn't wear the feeling well. Federal agents had torn a path through her home and office, but she was supposed to sit quietly and wait while a has-been cop wandered around Austin looking for Nicki. Granted, she hadn't been close to Nicki in a while, but she trusted her own instincts more than she trusted those of a stranger. She was tired of feeling like she didn't have options. She fished her iPhone from her purse.

"Tom? Hi. Look, I'm going to take a few days off. With everything that's been going on, I think it would be a good idea if I took some time to regroup. I need you to handle the contracts on the Donaldson sale, but if she needs handling, I'll be available by phone. You okay with that?" She didn't need his permission to take off, but she wasn't in the habit of ditching the hard files on her employees. Tom assured her he would handle the sale with kid gloves and told her to take as much time as she needed. She glanced at her watch. Three o'clock. She had plenty of time to work out a plan.

❖

Skye felt the buzz in her pocket as soon as she turned off her bike. Another e-mail from Aimee.

I found info that should be helpful. Will have it delivered to you. What hotel?

Skye contemplated ignoring the message. Couldn't Aimee just tell her what the information was? Well, at least Aimee wasn't calling or ordering her to call. Skye dug a matchbook from her pocket and thumbed the address of the motel along with her room number into a reply. Maybe Aimee had managed to get hold of Nicki's bank records. Those could be helpful.

Skye shoved the phone back in her pocket and sized up the surplus store in front of her. The run-down building was not the type of place Skye expected someone like Nicki to frequent. Upon entering, she noticed dusty, ill-arranged military leftovers strewn throughout the narrow building that looked like an old shotgun style house now converted into a casual family business. With competition from lots of bright new shiny sporting good stores, Skye figured this place couldn't be more than someone's hobby or tax write-off. What in the world could Nicki have spent three hundred dollars on in here?

"Looking for something special?"

Skye turned to the hulking figure standing behind her and studied him. The man wore an odd assortment of his own inventory, from the dusty black combat boots, camo pants, and beret to the olive green utility belt armed with a hunting knife strapped tight around his beer gut. She thrust out a hand. "Not really. Just checking out your stuff."

He grunted. "Authentic."

I bet. "You a vet?"

"Staff Sergeant Davis. Desert Storm, Marines, First Division." He looked her up and down. "You?"

"Army. First Calvary. Didn't see any action. Unfortunately. "

His nod and grim smile signaled the lie bought her credibility. She'd actually thought about joining the service, but her father had talked her out of it. She followed the path of her siblings directly into police work. She'd taken a few courses at one of the local community colleges in a half-hearted effort at giving herself some options, but her heart was never in it. When her shift schedule started to conflict with her class schedule, she abandoned her courses without any consideration for the ragged transcript full of incompletes she left behind. Maybe if she'd actually joined the Army she would've gotten an education and had some other options now.

Skye shrugged the thought away. She probably would've fucked up no matter which career path she'd chosen. At least she had this chance to try to regain some professional cred. She considered the best way to approach Mr. Desert Storm about his ad in the C.O.P.S. newsletter.

"You own this place?"

"Yep."

She was going to have to work harder for an opening. "I've been looking for a place like this." She invited his question.

He hedged. "Lots of surplus stores around."

"Not all the same."

"True." He was making her work for it.

"I think it's important to support businesses that support the community, that have a conscience, so to speak. I pay attention to who advertises in the publications I read."

He rubbed his chin, but didn't say anything. Skye could tell he was sizing her up. She waited. She would wait as long as it took, but she was done talking. If he didn't respond to that remark, she would have to try another, more circuitous approach.

He reached around her. Skye held herself still though she was unnerved by his closeness. He pulled back and waved a dusty pair of combat boots in front of her face. "You like these?"

Skye nodded.

"Try them on."

She did. Surprisingly, they fit.

"They look good," He grunted. He jerked his head in the direction of the front of the store. "That your bike out front?"

"Yep."

"Nice ride. Softail?"

"Yep. Gets me where I need to go." Skye knew her expression more than her words spoke the pride she felt about her most expensive and prized possession. She'd purchased the 1995 Harley Softail when she was nineteen, over the angry protests of her mother. Her father had sided with her, though his support was more of a backhanded compliment. He assured her mother Skye's head was too hard to suffer any damage from a wreck on the two-wheeled instrument of death.

Skye watched the man admire her bike while she considered her strategy. She looked down at the boots on her feet and rubbed the tips against the back of her jeans. They were no longer dusty and she could see her reflection in the glossy black shine. She cracked a smile just to see a friendly face. When she lifted her head, Mr. Surplus was staring at her instead of the bike. She kept her smile. "I think I'll take these," she said. "And I'm probably going to need a bunch of other supplies." She turned her head in a sweeping gesture. "I see some of what I need, but I may need your help to locate the rest." She paused and fixed him with a pointed look. "Do you think you can help me?"

His stare lasted forever, but Skye didn't waver against his gaze. She had no idea what she would say if he called her on her request, but she'd played bluff enough to know that winning usually paid off big.

After what seemed like an hour, the man reached around her and grabbed a card from the counter. He scratched a single word and a phone number on the back and shoved it her way.

"Call the number. Eight p.m. tonight. Opportunities abound for those who seek the greater good."

A chill ran up Skye's spine, but she forced her half-smile to stay in place. So Mr. Surplus did possess the ability to string together an entire sentence, even it if was a scary, ominous one. She took the card, nodded, and walked to her bike with deliberate slowness.

CHAPTER TEN

Getting there was the easy part. Arrangements were only a phone call away. Aimee chose not to think beyond the destination.

She assumed her best syrupy voice. "Daddy, it's your daughter, Aimee. Remember how we were talking yesterday about all the good things you do for your children and grandchildren? Well, I need a favor." She listened patiently through the grunts that always accompanied her father's effort at bestowing favors. As cantankerous as the old man was, he usually came through. Today was no different.

She had two hours to get ready. After a quick run by the office, she drove home and parked her car in the garage. She left a detailed note for Elsa, called for a car, and packed a bag. The drive from her house to Love Field was fifteen minutes. Aimee glanced at her watch. She had time for a quick bite, but she was so keyed up, she wasn't sure she could keep anything down. Her cell phone lay on the counter, a guilty reminder that what she was about to do would not be well received. *Should I call her first?* Aimee may not know Skye very well, but she could predict her reaction, and she'd rather witness the surprise in person.

Precisely an hour and a half after her call to her father, Aimee rode through the airport security gates to the Signature Flight Support Terminal. As they approached the Jetway, she motioned for the driver to pull over. She handed him a generous tip and grabbed her own bag from the backseat. The uniformed man who greeted her at the foot of the stairs leading to the sleek Gulfstream G450 leaned for a hug.

"Ms. Howard, to what do we owe this pleasure? I can't remember the last time you flew with us."

"Captain Rick! It has been too long." She whispered the next words. "Don't tell anyone, but I've been flying commercial." She mocked a shudder. "I'm not as rich as the rest of my family, after all."

"Oh, please." Rick grabbed her bag and escorted her up the stairs into the Gulfstream. "If charm equals wealth, you're the richest one of the bunch."

Aimee smiled at the old family friend. Rick Gains was the lead pilot of Howard Enterprises' small air fleet, and he had worked for her father as long as she could remember. The fleet consisted of two identical Gulfstream jets, used for both personal and professional travel. She was grateful one of them had been available for her use today. With no long airport lines or traffic to deal with, the private jet would get her to Austin considerably faster than any other form of transportation.

The moment she slid into one of the roomy leather seats, another familiar face appeared at her shoulder. "Welcome aboard, Ms. Howard. Good to see you again."

"Ken!" Aimee rose to greet the tall, lanky young man. Ken Gains was Rick's son, and she and Ken had practically grown up together. Ken always said he was going to be a pilot like his father and, after a stint flying commercial, he'd joined his father as one of the team of pilots on the Howard payroll. She delivered a fierce hug. "Since when am I Ms. Howard?"

"Dad's a stickler for protocol."

"Our fathers definitely have that in common." She glanced around. "I don't see any dads in the immediate vicinity, so it's Aimee, okay?" She waited for his nod before asking, "Are you flying me to Austin?"

"I'm Dad's wingman for the flight." He cocked his head at her. "Haven't seen you in a while."

"Real estate business has been keeping me pretty busy. We've just hit the slow season." She felt a tinge of guilt. "Sorry I haven't kept in touch."

Ken laughed. "Like I would've had time to do anything if you'd called. Your dad's business keeps us hopping. I'm lead pilot on this plane now."

"Wow, that's amazing. You totally deserve it." She smiled. "I remember in fourth grade when you announced you were going to be a pilot. Do you still love it?"

"More than ever. By the way, for old time's sake, Dad's going to fly us down. I think your dad may have asked him to. I'll be his co-pilot, which leads me to my next question. Can I get you a drink?"

Aimee considered for a moment, before she resolved one drink would be perfect to fortify her for Skye's reaction when she showed up unannounced. "I'd love a glass of champagne."

Ken moved to the galley to take care of her request. She fought the instinct to serve herself. Her father's strict demand for a certain protocol meant that even his pilots were trained to serve. It was easier not to fight it. Instead, she continued to talk to Ken as he poured her drink as if she were merely a guest in his home.

"What's the flight time to Austin?"

"About thirty-five minutes. What's up with the last minute trip? Real estate emergency?"

"An emergency, but definitely not real estate related. I don't think thirty-five minutes is long enough to tell the whole tale. Nicki, Neil's daughter, is in some trouble and I'm flying down to help sort things out." She nodded at the glass of champagne he offered. "Let's get together soon over a bunch more of these and I'll tell you the whole story—what I know anyway."

"Sounds like a plan. Seriously, call me sometime. I'd love to catch up." He stopped at the sound of his father over the intercom. "Looks like we're all ready to go. Buckle up and I'll see you shortly." He squeezed her arm then made his way to the cockpit.

The flight was quick, but the thirty-five minutes of relative solitude gave Aimee the chance to question her decision to join

Skye in Austin about a thousand times. And that was just in the first ten minutes. Not only was she ignoring her attorney's advice, she was fairly certain Skye wouldn't welcome her sudden appearance. She leaned back in the comfortable seat and closed her eyes to ward off the constant second-guessing. The backs of her eyelids began to run vignettes of Skye Keaton. Skye on a motorcycle. Skye asking her to dance with only a look. Skye touring her house. Skye hot with anger. Skye hot with passion. She lingered on the last image, massaged it so she was now in the scene. This time she took what she wanted, what she sensed Skye wanted to give, without regard to the boundary Skye had erected between them.

"Aimee, we'll be landing in just a few minutes."

She kept her eyes shut, willing the pictures not to fade. But they did. Aimee looked up at Ken. His stare held concern and she waved it away. "I must've been daydreaming. Are you flying right back to Dallas?"

"Yes. Why? Do you need something?"

"No, not really. I just thought if you were hanging around, we could grab a bite to eat later. Silly really. I have a lot to do. I'm sure you do too."

Ken handed her a card. "Here's my cell. If you need any help with Nicki, give me a call. We've all had our youthful challenges. Remember that time we snuck up to Plano Senior High and dyed their duck pond blood red?"

Aimee laughed, but she didn't bother explaining that Nicki's troubles with the federal government made the criminal trespass tickets they'd received in high school seem like chump change. Besides, it only took a few phone calls from Daddy's attorneys to get them out of hot water. Nicki's situation was likely to be much harder to navigate.

A few minutes later, Aimee descended from the plane and stepped into the waiting Town Car. She gave the driver the address Skye had given her and pulled a notebook from her bag. She tamped down the twin feelings of enthusiasm and dread she felt at the prospect of seeing Skye in person, and jotted a few notes about people and places she should check out while in Austin. The notes were sparse. She couldn't believe how little she knew about the everyday life events of her favorite niece. They had grown apart quickly after she left for college. Aimee blamed herself, in part, for substituting expensive gifts for actually showing up in town and just hanging out. Hell, her parents were never around either. No wonder she'd gotten herself into trouble. Once she found Nicki, things would change.

Aimee was lost in thought and didn't notice that the driver had stopped the car until he cleared his throat to get her attention. "Ms. Howard, are you sure this is the right address?"

Aimee looked out the window and wondered if Skye was fucking with her. She considered calling her, but she didn't want to ruin the surprise. She told the driver. "Wait here. I'll be right back."

She walked by the glassed-in lobby and cast a glance inside. The front desk clerk had dinner spread out on the counter. She couldn't tell what it was, but it looked homemade and she could smell the garlic and other spices. She hurried past and found the room number Skye had provided. A few loud knocks later, she determined Skye wasn't in. Time for Plan B. Aimee took a deep breath and charged into the lobby.

"That darn sister of mine. I told her I would be here in time for dinner, but she can never wait on a meal." She hovered at the counter, ignoring the startled look on the desk clerk's face. "Is that garlic I smell? It sure smells wonderful. If I weren't a true lady, I might just reach over and snatch that nice looking meal away from you." She stopped her barrage of comments and stared into his eyes. With the most syrupy southern accent she could muster, she said, "If I promise not to steal your supper, will you help me?"

He cheeked the bite he'd just placed in his mouth and nodded.

"She has the only key and I left my money in the room."

He nodded again as if what she said made perfect sense. Aimee waved a hand toward the window. "If I don't pay that driver, I don't know what he'll do." Again, the clerk nodded. "I just need you to let me in the room real jiffy like so I can make good on my debts, of which your kindness will be one." She could tell she lost him with the last part, but fixed her face into a sad, pleading expression and waited.

He chewed, she waited. He chewed some more. Aimee didn't budge. Finally, he swallowed. He glanced out the window at the waiting Town Car, then back at Aimee who was dressed in a designer suit.

"What room?"

"One twenty-seven."

He handed her a key. "Five minutes."

She smiled broadly, grabbed the key, and practically skipped out the door. She had the door to Skye's room open in under sixty seconds. She wedged a piece of paper in the doorjamb and returned the key to the desk clerk with a broad smile and moments to spare.

She reached into the back of the car and grabbed her bag before the driver could protest.

"Ms. Howard, surely you don't intend to stay here?"

"I'll be fine." She glanced back at the dingy building behind her, and then repeated the words as if saying them again could make it so. "I'll be fine."

❖

Skye was cold, tired, and hungry. The kolaches from the morning had long ceased to fuel her body, but determination to get this job done quickly pushed her to work through meals. After leaving the surplus store, she started checking off her list of anyone who might know Nicki's whereabouts.

So far, she was discouraged at her results. She'd managed to wrangle a copy of Nicki's class schedule out of a naïve student working in the registrar's office, but the instructors she went looking for had already left for the day. She'd spoken with a couple of Nicki's friends, but all they could tell her was that Nicki had dropped out of sight some time ago. None of them knew much about Nicki's boyfriend, except for his name, Earl Baxter.

Skye resolved she would start running through the remaining list of Nicki's friends first thing in the morning, but her immediate goal was to make the call to the number Mr. Surplus had provided in the quiet of her room and then grab a bite to eat.

"Skye, I thought you'd never get here."

Skye heard only the voice; the words were a jumble. She shook her head as she tried to register the fact Aimee Howard, complete with suitcase, was sitting on the edge of her bed.

"What the hell are you doing here?"

"Last I checked, I was free to travel wherever I wanted."

Skye glared. "What are you doing in my room?"

"I'm delivering the information I mentioned in my e-mail."

Skye was furious. She'd barely been in Austin long enough to accomplish anything and suddenly her client appeared in her motel room. Was Aimee here to check up on her?

"How did you get in?"

"I have my ways."

"I bet you do. Did you show some skin to the desk clerk?" Skye regretted the statement as soon as the words left her mouth, but she had no intention of backing down.

"Where do you get off talking to me like that? What have I ever done to make you think that's the kind of woman I am?" Aimee's eyes burned bright with anger.

Skye bit back a sharp retort. Aimee was right. She had no right to talk to her the way she had. She didn't know her at all, and her suppositions weren't enough to merit passing judgment. Why did Aimee's oozing sex appeal rub her the wrong way? She didn't have the time or energy to process the thought. She filed it away for future inspection. She didn't have the time or energy to argue either. She needed to get rid of Aimee before eight so she could call the number on the back of the surplus store card.

"Look, you startled me. I didn't expect to find you or anyone else waiting in my room. Let's start over. Did you have some information for me?"

Aimee reached into her bag and pulled out a file. "I managed to get Nicki's bank records." She opened the file and pointed within. "Check them out. There are several rather large wire transfers initiated by my father followed by cash withdrawals for the exact same amounts."

Skye glanced at the records. Aside from the large deposits and subsequent withdrawals, there was no other activity. She sighed at the apparent dead end.

Aimee handed her another file. "And then almost identical deposits wired into another account."

Skye nodded for Aimee to continue. "The other account is a joint account, and the co-signer is listed as William P. Gale. Is this helpful?"

Skye examined the paperwork Aimee had handed her. *Gale.* The name sounded familiar. "It may be. How did you get this?"

"Cleavage. Works every time."

Skye refused the bait. "I said I was sorry."

"I'm trying to inject some levity here. You and I obviously got off on the wrong foot. I'm sorry for showing up unannounced, but I'm really worried about Nicki. I didn't do anything nefarious to get these records. I happen to have several large business accounts at the same bank and I merely expressed to my personal banker my need for assurances that my dear niece was being responsible with her funds. He probably shouldn't have given me her online access codes, but I may have made some comments that led him to believe he might lose my business if he didn't. I need to feel like I'm contributing something to the effort to find her. Can you understand that?"

Skye nodded. She did understand, but Aimee needed to learn to trust the professionals she hired to get the job done. If the feds showed up at the bank asking questions, they'd probably think Aimee's show of power was a poorly disguised attempt to cover her niece's tracks.

She'd think of a way to broach that subject after she'd had a chance to thoroughly review the bank information. Right now, she needed to get rid of Aimee because the clock was ticking toward eight. "I get what you're trying to do, but you being here is more distracting than helpful." Skye instantly regretted her choice of words. She rushed to clarify. "I have all the information you provided and I know how to use it. I'll find Nicki if you'll let me focus." Not much better, but Skye was done digging herself out of this hole. She glanced at her watch. Seven thirty. Aimee needed to go now.

"What did you learn today?"

"Huh?"

"Today? What did you find out?"

Skye resigned herself to giving a brief report. "Frankly, not a lot. After I searched Nicki's apartment, I talked to a few of the names on the list you gave me. The friends I've spoken to say she hasn't been in class, but I got her schedule and plan to check with her professors tomorrow. I have her boyfriend's name, Earl Baxter, and I'll work on finding him tomorrow as well. I have a few more of her friends to talk to."

She purposely omitted her trip to the surplus store and strange mail Nicki had received. She wasn't sure why. Her gut told her the strange encounter at the store would offer more of a lead into Nicki's whereabouts than talking to all her friends and teachers, but she wasn't prepared to tell Aimee since she didn't know herself. Better to keep this information to herself until she had something concrete to offer. She tried to ignore the disappointed look at Aimee's face. "I'll find her. I promise."

The room was quiet. Skye watched as Aimee's disappointment morphed into enthusiasm. She waited with dreaded anticipation.

"I'll help you."

"Help me?"

"I'm here. I've taken a few days off from work. We can split the list of people to talk to and knock it out faster." Aimee looked around the room. "We're going to have to move you out of this place, though. You're bound to come down with some dreadful disease if you spend the night here. Besides, we'll need Internet access. I think they barely provide electricity here. Didn't Morgan give you an advance?"

Aimee paused for breath and Skye jumped in, certain it might be her only opportunity to get a word in. She needed to set things straight before they got completely out of hand.

"You are the client and I am the investigator. We're not working together on this case. If you want to find Nicki yourself, more power to you, but if you want me to find her, then we'll do it my way. Got it?"

Aimee bristled. "You would seriously turn down my help? That seems pretty shortsighted. I could offer a new perspective."

"I work cases my way. Period."

"I've heard about your special ways of working cases."

Skye stood and walked to the door. She had enough of Aimee's innuendos about her past. She contemplated quitting on the spot. She could probably still beg back her job from Ernie. Hell, with the hours she'd expended on this case already, she was temporarily flush with cash.

The memory of Morgan's hand on her arm when she threatened to walk out yesterday stilled her haste. She wasn't going to like every client she had. As a cop, she hadn't always liked the victims whose wrongs she sought to vindicate. Still, she always did her damnedest to get the job done. Was she going to let the tension between her and Aimee get in the way of her success?

She took a deep breath. "I don't know what you've heard about me, but here's the truth. I work hard. I always have and I always will. And I'm good at what I do. Whether you trust me or not, I will find Nicki before the feds do. Now, I paid for this motel room, and I'd like the courtesy of some time alone." Skye opened the door. She'd said all she was going to say.

❖

Aimee stood outside Skye's room and counted to ten. Five times. She was still angry, but was no longer gripped by a strong desire to topple Skye's Harley. Finally, she convinced herself to leave and regroup. A short cab ride later, she arrived at the Four Seasons in downtown Austin and, once in her room, she tried to convince herself this junket to Austin wasn't a big mistake.

She wasn't used to leaving important things to chance. Writing a fat check to Morgan and Parker was one thing—they were lawyers, trained in their field. But as for finding Nicki, she still wasn't convinced a private investigator could do a better job than she could. Skye's tactless approach would probably send Nicki running in the opposite direction if she ever got close. Aimee had to admit she was a little intimidated when she first saw Skye as well. She was generally attracted to lace over leather, but she couldn't remember ever seeing leather look so fine. On the other hand, straight Nicki wouldn't be swayed by the strong feminine power. All she would see was a thug on a motorcycle headed her way.

Aimee pulled a photo from her purse, a candid shot of Nicki taken at a party the previous summer. Her smile was bright, her bearing relaxed. She looked as if she didn't have a care in the world. *Nicki, what happened to you? Where are you?*

Aimee placed the photo on her nightstand and vowed she would get the answers to those questions. Soon.

❖

At seven fifty-nine, Skye dialed the number on the back of the business card. When the clock struck eight, she pressed the talk button on her phone.

"Good evening, thank you for calling the Institute. How may I direct your call?"

Skye stared at her phone. The greeting was not at all what she had expected. Maybe she dialed the wrong number. Nope, there it was on the display, same one the man at the store had written down.

"May I help you?"

Skye looked at the back of the card again and prayed for an inspiration. The one word he'd included with the number was White. When he was writing on the card, she'd assumed he was writing his own name and number, but he'd said his name was Davis. She cleared her throat and prayed for a good guess.

"Yes, thanks. May I speak with Mr. White?"

"Mr. White isn't in right now, but you can meet with him tomorrow at seven p.m. Please call this number at that time for the address." The friendly voice clicked off the line. Skye fumbled for a pen and paper and scrawled down the information before it faded from her memory. She held the paper in one hand and her phone in the other, staring at both as if some revelation would occur if only she kept watching. No revelations, only resolve. Tomorrow at seven, she would have answers.

CHAPTER ELEVEN

Aimee yawned. Seven a.m. was too early for anything. After hitting the snooze button three times, she'd finally convinced herself to get out of bed. Skye was probably already out talking to people. *Well, let her be the early bird.*

The first thing Aimee did was order up a big breakfast to fortify herself for the day's events. When the omelet, toast, bacon, fruit, and coffee arrived, she groaned. What she'd ordered up for energy seemed more likely to send her into a food coma. She nibbled on a point of toast and drank heavily from the coffee pot. She'd tackle the rest after a quick shower.

Freshly showered, Aimee slid back under the covers with the room service tray on one side and her iPad on her lap. A Google search for Earl Baxter turned up a ton of hits. Who knew Earl was such a common name? Who named their kid Earl, anyway? She tapped the screen and brought up the Central Appraisal District for Travis County. A few taps later, she learned that Earl Baxters weren't all that common in the property ownership database. Her search returned only two hits. Earl and Donna Baxter owned a ranch style home on the western edge of town, and Earl Baxter, Sr. owned a nineteen fifties bungalow in South Austin. She saved both listings into a file on her tablet and recorded the addresses into the maps program. She dialed the concierge and was assured a car would be ready for her use within the hour. Refreshed and ready to start the day, she dug into her now cold breakfast with gusto.

❖

Skye lamented the absence of her laptop. When she'd started as a cop, the Internet was a sketchy proposition and search engines were nonexistent. Back then, cops relied on their instincts to gather information, not what some preprogrammed machine spit back as the top ten search results. She had finally learned to accept the assistance a computer could provide, but when it came to running down clues, she still preferred to eyeball her sources.

It was cool outside and would be colder on her bike, so she wore layers in anticipation of the afternoon sun. Austin morning traffic was always heavy, but Skye deftly wove between the cars as she made her way toward the university campus. She had a strong hunch and was determined to catch one of Nicki's professors before class started so she could follow up on it.

The campus was huge, nothing like the rinky-dink community college she'd pretended to attend. After driving around in circles, she finally gave in and asked for directions to the building listed on Nicki's transcript. When she finally reached the auditorium she was looking for, the room was filling quickly. Hundreds of students took their seats while a tall, striking woman glanced through note cards at the podium. Skye surmised she was Nicki's political science professor.

Skye was discouraged by the size of the crowd in the auditorium. No way would Professor Latamore remember one of her students out of a group this large. Oh well, nothing ventured, nothing gained. She approached the stage.

"Professor Latamore?"

"If I tell you there's going to be a pop quiz, it won't be a pop quiz," the woman answered without looking up.

Skye chuckled. "Well, I guess I should've studied just in case."

Skye's response elicited eye contact and a grin. "You're not one of my students, which is a good thing since there's a high likelihood of a pop quiz."

Skye gestured at the crowded auditorium. "You know everyone in your class?"

"Not at the beginning of the semester, but by this time of year, yes. I think these huge class sizes are crazy, but I make it a point to get to know something distinctive about everyone in my class." She cocked her head. "Is this a pop quiz about my teaching skills?"

Skye shook her head and returned her easy smile. "No, ma'am. I have a few questions about one of your students and I was hoping you could help me out."

"Oh, this *is* a pop quiz of sorts. Which student?"

"Nicole Howard."

Professor Latamore froze. Skye held her breath.

"Who are you?"

"A friend."

Her stare was long and piercing. "I'll talk to you, but not here." She scribbled a note and handed it to Skye. "I'll meet you there after class, a little over ninety minutes from now." Professor Latamore turned back to the podium. Skye was dismissed.

Skye resisted the urge to drag the professor away and grill her. She sensed she was on to something—something important. The last thing she wanted to do was wait through a ninety-minute class. She checked her watch, then pulled up the address the professor had given her on her phone. She had about an hour to kill. She consulted a much folded piece of paper in her wallet and made a call to one of Nicki's friends who lived a few blocks from campus. Within ten minutes, she was seated in an apartment at least three times nicer than her own, sipping jet-black espresso from a tiny cup.

"Would you like another?"

Skye looked at her cup. It had contained one swallow, maybe two, but she was already starting to feel the effect of the tarlike substance. Why not have another? She had a long day ahead. "Sure."

While her hostess, Diane Burch, worked the levers on a fancy black and chrome contraption, Skye pulled out a notebook and opened to a fresh page. "When's the last time you saw Nicki?"

"Gosh, it's been a while. We used to hang out together all the time until she started seeing Earl. I mean, I did see her a few weeks ago, but just in passing. She was with Earl and they were at the grocery store. We didn't really talk. They were in a hurry. They had a cart full of stuff."

"Like what kind of stuff?"

"Actually, they had two huge carts and they were full of cases of bottled water, canned food, and batteries. Weird."

"What can you tell me about Earl?"

"Not much. The guy barely spoke two words whenever I saw him, but I didn't see him much. Nicki was weird around him, not herself. She used to be fun. Now she's all serious. She talks about politics all the time."

"And that was unusual for her?"

"Nicki's smart and all, but we used to have fun. She got good grades, but she didn't let study time spill over into fun time."

"What's your major?" Skye felt silly asking the clichéd question.

"Fashion design, minor in business. I'm going to open a boutique, sell my own designs."

"Little risky in this economy, don't you think?"

Diane looked at her like she'd grown an extra head. "Hello, Highland Park? No worries about wealth there. I think rich people make better financial decisions. That's why they're better equipped to deal with a downturn in the economy at large."

You're fucking kidding me. Skye choked the words back, but she wanted to choke rich little know it all, Diane Burch. Choking wasn't going to get her any information, and that's what she was here for even if she didn't think whatever Diane had to tell her was worth her time. She snuck a look at the time, anxious for her meeting with the professor. Her gut told her the professor and the mysterious Mr. White were way more likely to be good sources of information about the trouble Nicki was in than the piece of fluff sitting across from her. She struggled to focus and changed the subject back to Nicki.

"What's Nicki's major?"

"You know, I'm not sure. She was all hot on journalism when she started. She was going to be the next Diane Wallace, but she had some run-in with the faculty advisor of the school paper so she quit.

Then she started taking a bunch of classes about government and political science. Not that it really matters. I hear she hasn't attended a class since mid-terms."

"Too busy with her boyfriend?"

"Probably. I heard he was a student here, but dropped out."

"Any idea where he lives?"

"No." Diane dropped her voice. "He's kinda creepy."

"How do you mean?"

"Doesn't talk much. Dorky clothes. You know, Unabomber."

Skye scrunched her face to match Diane's serious look and nodded. "I know exactly what you mean. Do you think he was dangerous?"

"Maybe."

Good enough. Skye would find Earl Baxter right after her meeting with the professor. Earl, Professor Latamore, and Mr. White were the keys to this case. She was sure of it.

Austin was a completely different place now than the town Aimee had lived in as a student. Big box stores lined I-35 and its offshoots and new residential developments were evidence of the city's wavering acquiescence to the pull of commercial progress. Fortunately, her career in real estate meant she possessed great navigational skills.

The Baxter house in west Austin was home to a lovely couple, Earl and Donna, neither of whom had ever heard of Nicki Howard, nor did they recognize the photo Aimee showed them. Aimee had only seen Nicki's Earl from a distance, but she was quite sure the sixty-year-old Earl at this house was not stepping out on his wife. At least not with Nicki.

She'd purposely chosen the west Austin residence first so she could swing by Skye's motel and apologize for her ambush the night before. She pulled into the lot and glanced around, but Skye's bike was gone. She knocked anyway, just in case, but no one answered. Aimee scrawled a short note, wedged it in the door, and drove away.

The South Congress area was the last vestige of the funky culture that made Austin unique. Colorful shops and Airstream trailers featuring gourmet to-go food lined South Congress Avenue. The houses were generally small, but all unique, unlike the cookie-cutter developments on the northern edge of town. Even the humble, unkempt Baxter home was prime real estate.

Aimee knocked on the door. She heard shuffling feet, and eventually, the door swung open to reveal a wizened old man wearing a tattered bathrobe and slippers.

"What the hell do you want?"

Aimee hoped a big, bright smile would squelch his foul mood. "Mr. Baxter?"

"Who wants to know?"

"My name is Aimee, Aimee Howard." She assessed his age and decided to take a risk. "I know your grandson, Earl."

He grunted and a strong odor of alcohol wafted forth. "Then you know what a pain in the ass he is."

"He can be a bit much, but I think that's what attracted my daughter to him in the first place. You know my daughter, Nicole Howard?"

He squinted at her through Coke bottle lenses. "Blonde? Little bitty thing?" Aimee shoved Nicki's picture under his nose. He jabbed at the photo. "Yeah, that's the one. She's a hot little thing."

Letch. Aimee assumed an appropriately shocked expression. She really didn't care what the old coot had to say if he could lead her to Nicki.

"Does Earl still live with you?"

"His stuff does. I don't know where he's taken off to. Good for nothing. I let him live here so he wouldn't have to pay for one of those fancy dorms. He's supposed to contribute to the household, but I've yet to see a dime. If you see him, you tell him I'm going to sell off that pile of shit he left in my den. At least then I can afford to buy some of the things I need."

The idea crept up her spine, slowly forming into a half-baked plan. "When's the last time you saw Earl?"

"I don't know. Maybe a few weeks. Long enough for his mail to start piling up."

"You know, Nicki's been gone around that long. Think they ran away together?"

He cackled. "Now that would be a hoot. Two unemployed college wannabes run off to find their fortunes."

Aimee joined his laughter. "You're right about that. I need to find them though. I have some very important papers for Nicki to sign." She rubbed her fingers together. "We have a mutual investment, if you know what I mean."

He nodded, and she offered up more of her tale. "It's worth a lot to me to be able to find her. I suspect she's with your Earl." She switched to a wistful tone. "I was hoping to find her here." Aimee paused then pretended a light bulb blew up in her head. "I have an idea!"

"Yeah, what's that?"

"You want to get rid of Earl's stuff? Well, I'm sure to find him when I find Nicki. What if I take his stuff? Maybe I'll find something that will lead me to Nicki. I can keep it safe and give it to him when he turns up." Aimee reached into her bag and pulled out a bank envelope. "Of course, I would want to compensate you for helping me out." She fanned out several hundred-dollar bills while she waited for his response. She didn't have to wait long.

❖

Skye found a parking space directly in front of Jo's Coffee. The shop, located in the center of the action on the South Congress strip, bustled with business even though it was chilly outside and there was no indoor seating. It was eleven a.m., and Skye idly wondered if anyone in this part of the city actually worked for a living. She was a few minutes early and took the time to contemplate the drink menu. Soy lattes, chai, natural cigarettes. Really?

A light squeeze on her shoulder sent her spinning around, with her hand shoved in her jacket. She grabbed the hand that had touched her and scowled into the startled face of Professor Latamore.

"Shit. You scared me." She unclenched her grip. "I'm sorry."

The professor grimaced and shook out her hand. "Quite strong, aren't you?" Skye started to respond, but she interrupted. "Cop?"

For a brief second Skye considered lying. She couldn't say why, but she chose not to. "Used to be."

"I dated one of you once. Challenging."

"Is that so?"

"Absolutely. Worth it in the short run. Coffee?"

Skye's head spun at the abrupt change in topic. She resisted the urge to ask more about the challenges of dating a cop, and responded only to the coffee question. "Do they actually serve coffee here?"

"It's what they're known for. Drip? Black?"

"Perfect."

"Grab a seat and I'll order."

Skye obeyed. She selected a small table at the edge of the covered patio, farthest from the window where Professor Latamore placed their order. The professor was an imposing woman. Skye guessed her height at six feet. Long, dark hair was locked into a tight French braid. She wore her classic suit carelessly, sleeves rolled up and jacket unbuttoned, as if defying its sharp, tailored lines to define her. Her glasses framed piercing blue eyes and perched on a distinctive nose. Her strong bearing likely intimidated her students into hard work. Skye wasn't intimidated, only curious.

"Your coffee, Detective."

"Thanks." Skye accepted the blazing hot brew, choosing to ignore the moniker. Her mission was to get information, not give it. She could easily slip into casual conversation. Something about Latamore invited confidence, but she had a job to do. "Professor—"

"Call me Dixie."

"Well, Dixie, as I said, I need to get some information about Nicole Howard. Can you help me?"

"Is she in trouble?"

"Yes."

"I might've known. I'll help you as much as I can."

"Frankly, the reason for my visit this morning was to see if Nicki has been showing up to class. When you said you'd talk to me, you got my hopes up that you might have information that could help me find her. I have to say you seemed pretty shocked when I said her name this morning. Care to clue me in?"

"You're not the first person to ask me about Nicole in the past week."

"You don't say." Skye knew when to play it low-key. Dixie would tell her whatever she was going to tell her in her own way.

"Two FBI agents came by my house last Friday."

"Did they say what they wanted?"

"Not specifically. They were very cagey. Asked a lot of questions about my class, Nicki's attendance. They wanted to know who she hung out with."

"And if I were to ask the same questions?"

Dixie spread her fingers and ticked off her answers. "I teach an advanced political science curriculum. We explore the subject of government structure in more depth than introductory classes. Nicki showed up for every class until three weeks ago. The only person I ever saw her hang out with was Earl Baxter, another student in my class."

"I was under the impression Nicki had a lot of friends."

"Maybe she did, maybe they weren't in my class. Besides, Earl was pretty possessive."

"Was Earl as faithful about attendance as Nicki?"

"Yes. They were quite a pair. They shared interest in a particular part of my curriculum."

Latamore must be a great teacher. She certainly knew how to keep her listener intrigued. "And what part of the curriculum was that?"

"I teach a section on the history and development of the militia movement."

Alarm bells clanged in Skye's head. "I assume we're not talking about the guys with muskets defending against Redcoats from overseas."

Latamore laughed. "No, more like guys with money they printed themselves and cars full of fertilizer parked outside government buildings."

Skye masked her excitement. Finally, she was on to something. "And Nicki and Earl were especially interested in this topic?"

"Especially Earl. Nicki asked a lot of questions too, but there was something different about her interest. To her, the pursuit was academic. To Earl, it was more prurient, if you know what I mean."

Skye did. "I'd like to talk to him. He might have some ideas about where to find Nicki."

"Funny, the agents thought so too. Except I think they were certain wherever Nicki was, Earl would be too."

"I don't suppose you had any ideas on that front?"

"None I shared with two uptight suits."

Skye leaned back in her chair. The strange professor gave off no vibes, sexual or otherwise, but Skye knew her own charm could melt ice when she chose to turn it on. She started with a low dose, served with a wink and a smile. "I guess your time with the cop was well spent."

"Sure was, if you call a constant stream of broken dates and sleepless nights waiting to hear she made it through each raid unscathed, well spent." Dixie drank deeply from her coffee as if to let her words sink in. "Actually, I prefer quiet, studious types." She waved her hand in the air. "No offense."

Skye laughed. She didn't need a hammer to the head to tell she had just been blown off, nicely. "None taken. Back to Nicki—any idea where she might be?"

Dixie cast subtle glances around the coffee shop. She eased out of her chair. "Walk with me."

Skye stood. Her own spot check of the patio revealed nothing alarming, but for some unidentifiable reason, she trusted Latamore's instincts. They strolled along Congress Avenue. Dixie tucked her arm in Skye's and leaned in close.

"There was a raid near here a little over a week ago. A compound full of right-wing extremists holed up with enough weaponry to blow us all to kingdom come. Unlike other such operations, the feds were able to take the so-called patriots down with little public fanfare, though I doubt any bullets were spared. Word is the leader of the misguided bunch got away and the feds are falling all over themselves trying to find him."

"How do you know all this?"

"I may have given up cops, but lawyers, especially those who work for the Justice Department, have a certain special appeal."

"I see. What does this have to do with Nicki?"

Dixie shrugged. "Look, I really don't know anything about Nicki's whereabouts. Remember I told you that I make it a habit to learn something about each of my students to distinguish them from the masses? Well, in Nicki's case I learned about her affinity for challenging the establishment and her alliance with a young man who was committed to do more than challenge.

"Maybe the raid had nothing to do with Nicki, but I do think it's interesting that a particularly precocious student, who argued with me ad nauseam about the constitutionality of most federal laws, and who was dating the son of one of the men killed in a recent federal raid, has fallen off the face of the earth."

Skye jerked to a stop and pivoted directly into Dixie's path. "Whoa, there. Earl Baxter's father is a member of an extreme right-wing militia?"

"Was."

"Do you know where this compound is?"

"Former compound. Just outside of Wimberley, I think." She shot a glance at the slight bulge in Skye's jacket. "How many guns do you have with you?"

"Excuse me?" She silently dubbed Latamore the queen of the non sequitur.

"There won't be anything left at the compound. The feds will have grabbed what the escapees didn't take, but if you're intent on finding the ones who got away, be prepared for a fierce and well-armed resistance. These people weren't playing around. They have designs on overthrowing the government, as crazy as that may sound. Word is they developed ties to illegal dealers who provided them with state-of-the-art weaponry. Those ties are likely dried up now, but I understand the authorities are concerned that they kept a cache hidden off-site in the event of a raid and they'll develop another source soon."

Skye opened her mouth to ask one of the many other questions she had, but stopped when she heard a voice call her name.

"Skye?"

She instantly recognized the voice. Aimee Howard. Still in Austin. Right on her tail. Skye squelched her first response. Latamore didn't need to see her tangle with her client. She forced a bright smile to mask her frustration.

"Aimee. I didn't expect to run into you here."

"Nor I, you." Aimee delivered a pointed look at Dixie Latamore. "Hard at work?"

"Matter of fact, I am. Aimee Howard, meet Dixie Latamore, one of Nicki's professors."

Aimee thrust out her hand. "Pleasure to meet you. I'm Nicki's aunt, Aimee Howard."

Dixie clasped Aimee's hand between her own. "You're an alumnae—I recognize your name. You fund a scholarship for GLBT students."

Aimee felt her skin warm. Her grant wasn't anonymous, but the scholarship didn't list her name. "And you know that because?"

"I'm the faculty liaison for the GLBT student group. I head the committee that reviews the scholarship applications." Dixie squeezed Aimee's hand and gushed, "You're a generous woman. Thank you for supporting our future. "

Aimee was in full-on blush now. She moved to withdraw her hand from Dixie's grasp, but Dixie wasn't yielding other than to lightly stroke the hand she held captive.

Was Nicki's professor flirting with her? Sure felt like it. The advance, however subtle, screamed improper for several reasons. Topping the list was the fact that they were there to get information about Nicki, and the "they" included Skye, who was surely observing this interaction with a keen detective's eye.

Propriety be damned. Aimee took advantage of the proximity to size up her admirer. Handsome yet bookish summed up her impressions. Definitely not her type. *As if you have a type. All the vapid young women who've lived on your dime haven't brought you an ounce of fulfillment.* Maybe a tenured professor, steady, learned, and stable would fill the void.

She snuck a glance at Skye. She was the antithesis to Professor Latamore. Rough, edgy, stability in question. Windblown, sexy, grouchy, gorgeous. Her look lingered. Aimee couldn't help herself. Skye was damned adorable in her heavy black boots, sleek leather jacket, and jeans. Her layered hair spun around her head in wayward waves, untamed. Appropriate. And damned attractive.

Skye cleared her throat. "I'm sure you ladies can talk about scholarships later. Right now, I need to find Nicki." She shot Dixie a pointed look. "Is there anything else you can think of that might be helpful?"

Dixie shook her head. "I can't think of anything right now."

Skye handed Dixie a card with her number on it, effectively forcing her to let go of Aimee's hand. "If you think of anything else, please call me." She walked toward her bike, determined not to witness the budding relationship between the two women she left behind. Two steps later, she felt a tug on her arm. She knew without looking who was trying to catch her attention.

"Skye, wait. I've done some checking around. I may have a few leads. Let me buy you lunch and we can talk."

Skye shot a look at Dixie, who, even from a distance, was fixated on Aimee's every move. She couldn't blame her. Aimee's suit hugged her curves in ways decidedly distracting to accomplishing any business. In a low voice she said, "Wouldn't you rather have lunch with the esteemed lesbian professor?" Aimee and Professor Latamore were perfect for each other. Well educated, worldly. Maybe they could discuss the scholarship fund over tea. Dixie could come to Dallas and peruse Aimee's art collection.

Aimee tossed a smile at the professor. "Jealous?"

Skye flinched. The single word pierced. Lord knew she'd rather have her eyes poked out than look at art, and hot tea was swill, but she didn't begrudge Aimee's right to engage in those activities. Alone.

Did that mean she was jealous? Of what? She'd been having a great conversation with Dixie until Aimee showed up. The connection severed as soon as Aimee appeared, and Dixie focused all her attention on Aimee. Skye knew the score. Dixie might not be rich like Aimee, but she was educated, cultured, connected. Skye could count her connections on one hand. Her culture was limited to rock 'n roll artists and biker magazines, and her education consisted of on-the-job training for a career neither of these women would ever consider pursuing. A career that was over. Jealous? No, she wasn't jealous at all.

Aimee grabbed her arm. "Come on, I'm craving queso and I hate ordering a whole bowl by myself, even if I can eat it all. We can walk to Guero's."

Skye looked at Aimee's hand on her arm, and then glanced across the patio at Dixie. She shrugged at the professor, allowed Aimee to tug her along as she walked down Congress Avenue and concentrated hard on ignoring the implications.

CHAPTER TWELVE

The moment they ordered, Skye launched in. "What're the leads you're so anxious to share? You know, the leads you got while ignoring my request that you let me do my job?"

Aimee ignored her in favor of the large bowl of steaming queso the waiter delivered to their table. Skye would be pissed off when she heard about Aimee's trip to the Baxter house, and she wasn't going to let her crankiness ruin this meal. Aimee doctored the cheesy goodness with heaps of salsa and pico de gallo, then wrapped the concoction in a warm corn tortilla and shoved it at Skye. "Eat. It will soothe your soul."

Skye wrinkled her nose at the dripping mess. "My soul's fine."

"Eat." Aimee dangled the mess closer. Skye took a bite before a large glop of queso fell onto her jacket. She groaned. Aimee smiled. "See, I told you."

"Fine. You're a queso connoisseur."

"Don't forget the corn tortillas." She pointed toward the back of the restaurant. "They make them fresh here." She sighed. "I could live here."

"Here in Austin, or here in this restaurant?"

"Both. Seriously, couldn't you eat this goodness every day?"

"Why don't you? Live in Austin, I mean."

Good question. "I don't know. I guess because my friends and family are in Dallas. I'm not sure geographic distance would make any difference with my family. We're distant enough as it is, but my friends? Well, I don't think I could make it without them. We went to college down here, but we're all from Dallas and moved back when we graduated. We hang out together all the time." *Like that night at the bar when I first saw you.* "They're my real family." *Lame answer.* Aimee dove back into her food to avoid extending her pitiful sounding response.

"You're lucky to have a group of friends you can count on."

Aimee didn't miss the wistful tone in Skye's voice. "I suppose most of your friends were cops?" Skye pushed her chair back and crossed her arms, her demeanor shifting from wistful to defensive. Aimee immediately wished she could yank the words back. "Sorry. None of my business."

"Yeah, well, speaking of business. You hired me to do a job. Any reason why you are running around doing it behind my back?"

"As you're fond of pointing out, I didn't hire you. Morgan and Parker did. I'm not doing anything behind your back. I told you last night I would help. Not my fault you can't accept help." At the rate this conversation was going, Aimee didn't think there was ever going to be an appropriate moment to share the news about her find.

"I don't need your help. I'm making progress. Before you interrupted, I learned some valuable information from Professor Latamore."

Ah, an opening. "About?"

"Nicki's boyfriend, Earl Baxter."

"Interesting." Aimee's steady composure burst into a smug grin.

Skye pounced. "What the hell is so funny?"

"Nothing's funny. I'm merely waiting to hear what you found out about Earl so we can compare notes." She plunged back into the queso as Skye contemplated her statement.

Big sigh. "Okay, junior detective, tell me what you found."

"I found out where Earl lives, or at least where he lived until a few weeks ago." Aimee filled in the details of her search, ending with the story of her visit with Earl's grandfather.

"So he's long gone. I bet Nicki's with him, wherever he is." Skye's words were rote. Aimee could tell by her glazed expression, her mind was processing this new information, refocusing on new ideas of how to find Nicki. Ideas she wouldn't share. She contemplated not telling Skye the rest of the information she'd managed to wrangle. Skye hadn't acted the least bit impressed at her handy bit of detective work. Why should she show hers if Skye wasn't going to return the favor? *Because you both have the same goal.*

Fine. I'll be the bigger person. She waved a hand to get Skye's attention. "There's something else."

Skye rolled her hand, urging her to spit it out.

"My trunk is full of Earl's stuff from his grandfather's house. All of it, even his laptop and"—she paused on purpose to convey the importance of the information she was about to share—"his diary."

Skye sped along I-35. She'd practically jumped out of her chair at the restaurant when Aimee announced her find. Aimee insisted they eat the lunch they'd ordered, but Skye downed a few measly bites then tapped her foot impatiently until Aimee finally gave in and agreed to meet at her motel.

Aimee pulled in seconds after she reached her door. Skye was impressed since she'd broken at least half a dozen traffic laws on the drive across town.

Aimee spoke first. "My hotel would've been closer. I'm staying at the Four Seasons."

"You really want to haul Earl Baxter's possessions through the lobby of a four-star hotel?"

"Fair enough." Aimee inclined her head at the door. "Are you going to invite me in?"

Skye's plan was half-baked. She wanted to look at the stuff Aimee had, but she wanted to do it alone. She hadn't had time to process the strange feelings she'd experienced while she watched the interplay between Aimee and Professor Latamore. The pangs of jealousy still rankled, and close proximity wasn't the right environment to sort them out. There was also the matter of the stack of Nicki's mail and the box of silencer parts she'd left spread on her bed—more information she'd prefer to keep to herself. Aimee's persistent personality killed her plans to work alone, at least for now.

"Sure, come on in."

Skye inserted the key in the lock and turned. Something was off. A tug on the door confirmed her suspicion. She'd just locked her door, which meant someone had been in her room. Someone who hadn't bothered to lock up when they left.

"What's wrong?"

Skye masked the concern churning a hole in her gut and turned to Aimee. "Nothing. Looks like my key isn't working. Why don't you wait in the car while I check with the front desk."

"But that's a regular key, not one of those electronic cards. Did it work when you left this morning?"

"Aimee, please, will you just wait in the car? Trust me." She watched Aimee's internal struggle play out on her face, first a shake of her head, then a tight grimace of consent before she finally stalked to her car and slipped behind the wheel.

Skye stood in place for a few seconds to make sure Aimee wasn't inclined to follow, then she made her way to the motel office. The same man who checked her in was back behind the desk. Skye forced a smile.

"Hi, I'm in room one twenty-seven. What's your name?"

"I remember you." He smiled brightly. "My name is Farhad. Can I help you?"

"Maybe. I was supposed to have some visitors, but I've been out all day. I'm worried they stopped by when I was out and I missed them. Did anyone stop by to see me?"

Farhad morphed from confident to anxious. "I haven't been here all day. Perhaps your friends came before my shift started. If they show up again, I'll be sure to let you know."

"I didn't say they were my friends."

"My apologies. I assumed. Anyway, thanks for stopping by."

Skye placed both hands on the counter and leaned in. "So they did come by, but they said they would be back?"

Skye knew Farhad was lying, but she wasn't sure about what. What she did know was that someone had been in her room. The Do

Not Disturb sign still hanging from the doorknob made it unlikely her visitor had been the housekeeping staff. She'd worked enough cases in hotels to know what a relief the DND sign was to underpaid maids. At first she was willing to consider her overly cautious instincts were on hyperdrive, but Farhad's cageyness signaled her concern was well placed. His nervous, rambling answer confirmed her suspicions.

"I don't know if they'll be back. I mean, I don't know if they were here. Were they two middle-aged men in dark suits?"

Now she knew for sure who'd been in her room. Chances were good they'd threatened Farhad not to warn her they'd been here, probably even flashed some guns to make their point. Leave it to the subtle feds to show up at a dive motel wearing suits. She needn't have worried about sharing Nicki's mail with Aimee. No doubt her visitors had carted it away. Thanks, gentlemen, happy to help with your investigation.

Skye stalked back to Aimee's car and spoke to her through the open window. "Change of plans. We're going to your hotel. I'll meet you in the lobby and we'll unload your car together."

"But I thought you said—"

"Changed my mind. I'll be there in a few." She tapped the roof of Aimee's car. "Go on." She immediately turned away to brook any argument. The feds were probably long gone, but no way would she expose Aimee to the flashback of her own house being tossed by government agents. When she heard Aimee's car pull away, she counted to ten before unlocking the door to her room.

Skye would've known she'd had visitors even if Nicki's mail wasn't conspicuously absent. Her zipped tight duffle bag had been wide open when she left that morning and she knew she'd left her towel on the floor, not neatly hung over the shower curtain. Skye shoved her scattered belongings into her duffle while she sorted out her strategy. If the feds were following her, then they were probably following Aimee as well. They may have followed her all morning and were waiting at the Four Seasons, ready to take the contents of Aimee's trunk off her hands.

Skye scrolled through the e-mails on her phone until she found the one from Aimee that had irritated her the day before. She dialed Aimee's cell and waited impatiently through the rings.

"Aimee, Skye here. Another change of plans. Don't go back to your hotel." In a calm voice, she explained her belief the feds were following one or both of them.

"Are you sure? Could they be following me now? Should I take evasive action?"

Skye coughed to shield a laugh as she imagined Aimee sneaking furtive glances over her shoulder and making erratic lane changes. "No, no. Don't do anything out of the ordinary in case they're watching. We need a different plan, though. They could be waiting at your hotel." She paused and considered what she was about to ask before deciding she didn't have much choice. If she wanted Aimee to trust her, she had to show a little trust herself. "I need a place where I can go through what you found in private. You know this city better than I do. Any suggestions?"

Aimee's response was quick and sure. "Absolutely. Meet me at the 7-Eleven on the corner and I'll take you there."

❖

Aimee drove along back streets at Skye's suggestion. She fought to remain calm, but pumping adrenaline and Skye's urgently spoken traffic directions through her cell had her feeling like she was about to burst through her skin.

"You're doing great. Keep changing lanes every hundred feet or so, but remember to signal. Make all the left turns you can. Don't worry if it takes us a little longer to get there. I'll be right behind you, even if you don't see me."

Aimee bit back an "I know how to drive" retort. "Okay."

"I'm going to hang up so we can both concentrate. Call me back if you see anything unusual. As soon as we get there, let's call Parker and update her on what we've learned so far."

The "we" was a nice touch. Skye probably didn't even realize she'd used the word. Right now Aimee cared more about the "we" arriving safely at their destination than teasing Skye about their teamwork. For a brief moment, she allowed her mind to wander past their professional pursuits, into a more personal "we." Until the encounter with Dixie Latamore, she'd begun to wonder if the desire Skye had telegraphed at the bar weeks ago had been a figment of her imagination. Had Skye forgotten the surge of attraction or had she only shelved it? The other possibility, that she might have imagined the chemistry between them, was too much for Aimee to process. Twenty nerve-wracking minutes later, Aimee pulled up in front of a three-story brick home on the edge of campus. She waited in the car until Skye pulled alongside.

Skye shut off the engine and removed her helmet, but remained astride her bike. "What's this place?"

"A house where men in suits aren't allowed entry." Aimee pointed at the Greek letters over the front door. Alpha Alpha Beta. "I'm a legacy. Welcome anytime."

Skye's furrowed brow told Aimee she had no idea what a legacy was. "I was a member of this sorority, as was my mother and her mother and so on. You get the idea. Anyway, this girls-only house is the safest place I know, for now anyway."

"Okay, fine. If this is the best you can do. I'd prefer we weren't parked right out front."

Just can't please this woman. But I'd like to try. Aimee shrugged away the distracting thoughts and pointed to the side of the house. "There's a drive there and a parking lot in the back. I'll meet you there."

"Fine." Skye replaced her helmet and sped around back, apparently satisfied Aimee knew how to drive on her own now. As Aimee parked her car, she watched Skye standing near her bike, engaged in an impromptu grooming session. She adjusted the collar of her shirt, then she used a piece of cloth to wipe road dust from her heavy black boots. Skye's last task was her hair, and her frustration was palpable. She stared at the tiny mirror on the handlebars of her bike and raked both hands through her static filled mane. Aimee almost called out to her, to say it would be criminal to try and tame those wild and sexy layers of golden beauty, but she knew the compliment would be overshadowed by Skye's embarrassment at having been caught primping. Instead, Aimee cast her gaze in the opposite direction and made a noisy show of emerging from her car. By the time she turned around, Skye was at her door.

"You look great." *Dammit.* Aimee bit her tongue before she could say anything else. The words had just tumbled out.

Skye looked down. "Yeah, well, I didn't know where we were going or I would've changed."

"Honey, it's a college sorority house. Any girls in the house this time of day are likely to be wearing pajamas and watching soap operas." Aimee pointed to the trunk. "If you help me, we should be able to carry this stuff in one trip, but let's tell them we're here first." She grabbed Skye's arm. "Come on."

Skye couldn't verbalize the source of her nerves, but she couldn't ignore them either. She stalled. "A sorority house, really?"

"Sure, it's the perfect place."

"Are you sure it's a good idea to haul this stuff inside in front of a bunch of college students?"

"Like I said, anyone on the premises this time of day isn't going to be paying attention to anything except the television or getting their nap on." Aimee looked around. "Not to be the cautious one or anything, but shouldn't we get inside in case we didn't completely lose our tail?"

"Tail?" Skye laughed at Aimee's attempt at cop speak. "We weren't followed. Now that I'm looking for them, they don't have a chance."

"Spoken like a true badass." Aimee's tone was affectionate, and Skye's confidence shot up a few notches. So what if she hadn't gone to college, and hadn't—God forbid—pledged a sorority. She possessed more useful skills than these pampered rich girls would ever learn in their cushy classrooms. She let Aimee lead her into the house.

Aimee was a popular presence. Several of the seniors knew her on sight and volunteered to help bring in the stuff from her trunk. Skye bit back a protest. As much as she might resent these young women, she didn't want to involve them in something illegal. Aimee had assured her she had come by Earl's belongings honestly, or at least with honestly earned cash, but Skye couldn't help but think what they were doing could be construed as obstruction of justice by some eager prosecutor.

Since when did you become concerned about breaking the rules? It was one thing to skirt the line of legality when her fate was the only one at stake, but she felt oddly protective of the innocent strangers in this house. And Aimee too.

While she stood around contemplating, Aimee and the girls carried several loads from Aimee's car into the house.

"Here you go, Ms. Howard. No one's using this room. You should have plenty of privacy."

Aimee thanked the girl and cautioned her to keep the fact that they were in the house private as well.

"They seem to like you," Skye observed after the girl left them alone.

"I'm one of the more active alumni. As stifling as sorority life can be with its rules and rituals, I had an instant family once I pledged. This is a huge campus and it can be pretty overwhelming, but this house and the people in it helped me navigate my way through my first two years of school."

"And then what happened?"

Aimee smiled. "And then I finally came across the great group of lesbian friends I was looking for. We're still friends. They were at the bar with me that night..." Her voice trailed off and silence wedged into the space between them.

Skye waited for a respectful few seconds, then asked, "But you didn't break ties with the sorority?"

Aimee looked surprised. "Once an Alpha, always an Alpha. True, I got a mixed bag of reactions from my sisters when they found out they'd been living in the midst of a woman-lover, but I suspect I wasn't the only one. I stayed active, but I moved out of the house. Besides, I needed a private place to bring home all my dates."

Her last comment was delivered with a smile, but Skye recognized the hurt behind the jest. Skye had always been part of a tight-knit group too, relying on the security of the police fraternity to provide security, friendship, and acceptance. But she'd been careful not to let her personal and professional life merge. Most of the time, anyway. "They didn't try to kick you out of the sorority when they found out you were a lesbian?"

"Honey, when you have as much money as the Howards do, you don't get kicked out of anywhere." Aimee's response was delivered with a piercing bite that deterred Skye from further questions on the subject, but she did bask in the warm sensation of being called honey for the second time in the last hour. She didn't pretend to understand the feeling, but she nuzzled against it like a warm blanket. Across the room, Aimee's eager digging through the detritus of Earl Baxter's existence signaled she was past indulging in personal revelations.

Skye shook off warm and fuzzy, strode over to the bed, and placed her hand in the middle of the pile. "Hold it, there, junior P.I."

"What?"

"I think we should check in with Parker and Morgan before we go through this stuff."

"You're not serious."

"I am."

Aimee crossed her arms and scrunched her brow. "I don't get it. I bought this stuff from Earl's grandfather, fair and square. Besides, you're not..." She paused as if struggling for words. "It's not like you...Never mind. Do whatever you think is best."

Go ahead, say it. You're not a cop anymore and, even if you were, you never cared about the rules. Aimee's unspoken words punched Skye in the gut. Why would Aimee believe any differently? She'd broken into Nicki's apartment, lied to get her mail. Skye didn't regret what she'd done and she'd happily lie to cover, but Earl's possessions, well, that was Aimee's deed, and while it may have been stupid, Skye wasn't about to let her face charges for a brilliant, though careless, move. Skye dialed Parker's number.

"It's Skye. I have Aimee here and we're on speaker. Are you in the office?"

"Are you still in Austin? Aimee what're you doing there?"

Aimee piped in, "Just a little impromptu trip. I thought I might be able to help Skye make contact with some of Nicki's friends."

Skye cut in. "We need to talk."

"Should I get Morgan on the line too?"

"Probably not a bad idea."

"Hang on."

Skye used the moments spent waiting to caution Aimee. "Let me do the talking. Okay?"

Aimee opened her mouth, but shut it without a word and merely nodded her head.

"Skye, Morgan's here," Parker said. "We have you on speaker too."

Skye launched in. "Here's the deal. We found out where Nicki's boyfriend lives. He's been missing for several weeks, same as Nicki. His grandfather isn't real fond of his namesake grandson, and told us he planned to toss all of Earl Junior's things in the garbage. We saved him the trouble and paid him to let us do the tossing instead. We haven't gone through anything yet, but we have it in a safe place." Skye looked around the girly bedroom, her gaze falling to the pile of Earl's crap resting on the lacey bedspread. Safe place— definitely a relative term.

Morgan chimed in. "I get where you're going. Certainly, Earl Junior could come back and say no one had the right to sell you the stuff, but his beef's with his grandfather, not with you. Parker, what do you think?"

"A prosecutor could always make the argument you're obstructing, but since we don't know what the investigation's about, it's kind of hard to obstruct it."

Skye debated whether now was the time to share what she'd learned from Professor Latamore. The raid on the militia compound was certainly public knowledge by now. If Morgan and Parker knew about it, they might be able to use that knowledge to get the prosecutor to give up some other details about the charges against Nicki. But the sight of Aimee, hovering over her shoulder, sealed her lips. Skye could see it now—Aimee rolling up on the bullet-riddled compound to poke around for clues. No, she'd call Parker back later when she could speak freely. There was one thing she did need to let them know, and she hoped by divulging it, she could enlist Morgan and Parker's aid in her immediate goal—to work alone. She cleared her throat. "There's another thing."

Silence, then expectant dread in Morgan's tone. "What?"

"We're being followed. Pretty sure it's the feds." She sketched out the details of her motel room being tossed. Because Aimee was listening in, she left out the specifics about what had been taken from her room. She wasn't sure if she would have told even if Aimee weren't present. She wasn't in the habit of sharing leads before she fleshed them out. "I think they've been following Aimee for a while. They may have had her house staked out in Dallas."

"Was Aimee with you at Earl's place?"

Aimee opened her mouth to answer, and Skye placed a finger over her lips. "Yes. They also searched my motel room, but I'm certain we lost them after that."

"What's the plan now?" Parker asked.

"I have a few ideas." Skye willed Parker not to ask for specifics. Tonight's meeting with Mr. White was a solid bet, especially after Latamore's revelation, but she sensed Parker and Morgan would nix a true undercover operation, not that that's what she had in mind. She just needed to get in the door tonight. If she could, she was certain she would find the key to why Nicki had disappeared and where she could be found. Losing Aimee would make it easier, and she took advantage of Morgan and Parker's presence to make it happen.

"It'll be easier for me to stay under the feds' radar if I'm working alone." She ignored the hard glare from across the room.

Morgan spoke first. "Aimee, why don't you come back to Dallas? I can try again to get a meeting with the prosecutor and we can discuss our next steps."

Aimee sensed a rat. Skye paced the room, obviously anxious to finish this conversation and move forward with her plans. Secret plans. Plans that didn't involve her. Bullshit. If it weren't for her, Skye wouldn't have a bed covered in potential leads. She offered Skye a sweet smile and answered Morgan in her best syrupy southern voice. "Oh, I'm sure you're doing everything you can up there. If the prosecutor will meet with you, that's great, but you don't need me, do you? Since I'm down here, I think I'll visit with some old friends and catch up on college memories. Don't worry about me. Y'all do what you think is best to find Nicki and just give me a ring when you've located her. All right?"

"Uh, sure. Will do," Morgan responded. "Skye, you need anything else from us right now?"

"No. I'm good. I'll be in touch as soon as I have a good lead."

Skye clicked off the line and strode over to Aimee. "What's with the helpless female routine? You've done nothing but try to control how I do my work from day one."

"Is there some reason you feel the need to take all the credit?"

"All the credit or all the blame? Do you even understand the difference?"

"I don't get it."

"You will if a herd of federal agents show up at your door again, this time with a warrant to arrest you. I was trying to protect you."

"I don't need your protection."

"That's what you think," Skye muttered.

Aimee ignored the whispered editorial and changed the subject. "It's pretty clear you're holding something back. Care to share?"

"Actually, I think we're done sharing. Time for you to stop playing detective and go home to your sheltered Highland Park life. You might get your hands dirty."

Skye's bravado tipped her off. Aimee spent her life negotiating and she knew a bluff when she saw one. "You do know something." She scrutinized Skye's face for a clue. Nothing. Where had Skye spent her day before they ran into each other at Jo's? Suddenly, she knew, not what, but who. "Wait a minute—what did Professor Latamore tell you about Nicki? By the time I saw you, you and she made your way through coffee and the conversation to go with it. I don't imagine you're big on small talk. What did she tell you?"

"How about this, we go through this stuff together"—Skye gestured toward the bed—"and then you go home, and I'll report in. Daily even."

"Oh, aren't you generous? I bought this stuff. If you want to go through it, we'll do so on my terms."

"And what are those?"

"Tell me what Latamore told you."

Skye contemplated her options, which didn't take long. If she weren't working for her, Aimee's stubbornness would be attractive. Skye had to admit Aimee had more layers than she suspected. The moment of their initial connection in the bar, she hadn't cared beyond the bolt of magnetic physical attraction that hovered on the surface. Now, after a few interactions, she knew the layers beneath—intelligence and resourcefulness—were powerfully attractive in their own right, even if they had the potential to get under her skin. She could use Aimee's insights, as long as she could guard against the pull of attraction that threatened to distract her from her mission. Find Nicki. The goal was simple, but the process had turned out to be more complicated than any of them had thought. Another head might bring some good ideas to the mix. Besides, she wouldn't put it past Aimee to pay a visit to Professor Latamore herself. The idea of Dixie Latamore fawning over Aimee left Skye restless. She settled her emotions by resolving to share a few choice pieces of the information she'd learned. She chose her words carefully.

"Latamore believes Nicki's disappearance might be associated with a federal raid on a compound near Wimberley." She braced herself for the onslaught of questions, and she wasn't disappointed.

"Federal raid? Was Nicki on the compound? What kind of compound? Was it one of those wacky cults, like Waco? Or FLDS, like on *Big Love*? How does Latamore know about this?"

Skye held up a hand. "Stop." She cast about for a censored version of her theory, then listened with dismay as all the details she knew tumbled from her mouth.

"Nicki's boyfriend Earl? He's the son of a member of the Coalition of Patriot Sectarians, the Texas branch anyway. Apparently, Earl and Nicki took a special interest in the rights and culture of extreme right-wing militia groups." She took a deep breath. Aimee leaned forward, waiting expectantly while Skye considered whether she should continue. "Latamore said Nicki stopped coming to her class several weeks ago. Prior to that, she'd never missed."

"Earl's grandfather said he hasn't seen him in about three weeks."

"Chances are good they're together."

"Do you think they were involved with this group, what are they called?"

"Coalition of Patriot Sectarians. They call it C.O.P.S. And, yes, it sounds like they are involved."

"What do we do now?"

Skye ignored the "we." There was no "we." She had plenty of ideas about what to do on her own: finish searching through Earl's belongings, meet Mr. White, take a trip to Wimberley, and research everything she could find on the Coalition. While she thumbed through her mental to-do list, Aimee waited with an eager expression on her face. Nicki was her family and she wanted her to be safe. Would Skye trust someone else to do the job if one of her brothers was in trouble?

Not the same. She was qualified to find lost souls. Aimee was not. She'd done pretty well so far. Skye weighed the pros and cons, but she couldn't rule out a basic fact. Aimee was motivated, and she wasn't likely to stop looking for Nicki, no matter what Skye said. The last thing Skye needed was a half-cocked amateur scaring off witnesses. The only way she could avoid that was to manage the amateur herself.

"Where are you staying?"

"Four Seasons."

"Not anymore. Get a couple of the girls you trust to drive your car back to the hotel, while we go through this stuff. What's in your room?"

"I packed light. I have a few things with me, like my iPad. The only thing in my room is a small suitcase, some clothes, and toiletries."

Skye surveyed Aimee's suit and heels. "Are the clothes in your room like the ones you have on?" Aimee nodded. "Leave them. We have to go shopping later for a few things anyway. You're going to need a helmet." She tried to ignore Aimee's wide grin. "Now help me go through Earl's things."

CHAPTER THIRTEEN

Aimee surveyed the items Earl Junior had left behind. It was a strange mixture of stuff. In addition to the laptop and the diary, they found a collection of empty Skoal cans, several books about guns, and a heap of dirty laundry. Aimee tossed the latter items on the floor and leafed through his diary while Skye fired up his laptop.

"You think he would have taken his computer," Aimee said.

Skye shook her head. "Not if he planned to come back. Same thing at Nicki's place. The feds got her laptop, which means she left it behind along with a full set of luggage and a closet full of clothes. I get the impression these kids left town in a hurry. Anything interesting in that diary?"

"Hard to tell. Lots of blathering about the injustices of the federal government. There's a string of numbers on every other page, but I can't find a connection. You may be able to make sense of it." She set the book aside. "Any ideas about where they went?"

"A few."

Aimee watched Skye's face, her expression displayed her struggle about whether to say more. She knew it had to be hard for Skye to include her in the investigation, and she had no idea what sparked Skye's sudden reversal on the subject. She resolved not to push, at least not too much. For now.

Her patience paid off. Skye waved her over. "Did you say you have an iPad?"

"Yes."

"So you know your way around a Mac?" Aimee nodded and Skye rotated the laptop toward her. "Can you check the Internet search history? Let's see what Earl Junior's been looking into on his laptop."

"Police department still stuck on PCs?"

"It's kind of amazing we even have computers, considering our budget is always the first to be cut. I mean…" Skye's voice trailed off and Aimee immediately recognized she'd referred to the job as if she was still employed there. Was this the right time to venture a question about why she no longer did? Skye's stone face was a clear answer. Aimee changed the subject.

"Why do you think the feds didn't search Earl's house?"

"Maybe they don't know about him. Well, no, that's not right. I got the impression from Latamore, the feds were asking about both Nicki and Earl when they came to visit her." She shot up in her chair. "Wait, I remember seeing some men's toiletries when I was at Nicki's. Maybe he was living with her, or at least the feds assumed he was."

Aimee nodded, more focused on her search of the laptop than Skye's theories. "Lots of searches here for 'patriot' sites, most of them featuring guys in camouflage toting automatic weapons. Look, here's a site that tells you how to make a silencer."

"Hey, let me see that." Skye reached around her and leaned in. As Skye scanned the page, Aimee focused on controlling the arousal she felt. Skye obviously felt nothing, her attention entirely focused on the computer screen.

"Can you really make a silencer out of all that stuff? Why would you want to? Can't you just buy one?"

Skye rolled her eyes. "Yes, you can make a silencer out of all this stuff. No, you can't just buy one unless you have a connection to the black market. To make a legal purchase, you have to get a permit, which requires a pretty rigorous federal background check."

Aimee resisted the urge to whip her concealed handgun license out of her handbag to show Skye she knew a thing or two about background checks. She didn't appreciate Skye's condescending tone, but they were finally getting along and she didn't want to ruin it. "Why do you think he was interested in this stuff?"

"I don't know, but Nicki got a package in the mail with all the ingredients to cook up a silencer."

"What? Why didn't you tell me? Where is it?"

Skye shot her an annoyed look, opened her mouth to answer, and then closed it. A slow smile crept across her face. "Do you always ask questions in threes?"

Not the response Aimee expected. "What?"

"Never mind. There was a package in Nicki's mail, no return address, postmark Wyoming. It contained all these parts." She pointed at the screen. "The feds must have taken it along with the rest of her mail when they searched my motel room. I didn't tell you before because I was hired to work this case on my own."

"Why are you telling me now?"

"Because I've learned if I don't include you, you're going to include yourself. Seems like it will be a lot easier to keep you out of trouble if we work together."

Skye turned back to the computer and scrolled through the Internet history Aimee had located. Aimee resisted the urge to punch her for her impudence. For now, she would be content just to be included, but she silently vowed to gain Skye's respect, among other things.

❖

Skye clicked through the saved websites, most of them extremist craziness. Lots of chatter about the overreach of the federal government and musings about why the Internal Revenue Service was an illegal government enterprise. The scariest sites discussed the need to stockpile provisions and arms in preparation for the ultimate war—the uprising of the people against the treachery of the socialist government of the United States of America. Skye envisioned a bunch of slack-jawed, tobacco-chewing hillbillies dressed out in still creased camo, toting automatic weapons, extra ammo spilling from their pockets.

"Why would Nicki be hanging out with these people? Was she really that messed up?"

Aimee shrugged. "Haven't a clue. She had everything she could ever want. She didn't work, so she didn't pay taxes, and I can't imagine she was subjected to any of the other so-called treacheries these whack-jobs are spouting off about."

Skye started to pose another question, but was interrupted by her ringing phone.

"Keaton."

"Skye? Is that you?"

She instantly recognized the low tones of Professor Dixie Latamore. "Yes, it's me. Professor Latamore?"

"Please call me Dixie."

"Okay, Dixie. What can I do for you?" Skye shot a look at Aimee who had given up pretending not to eavesdrop on the conversation. "Actually, do you mind if I put you on speaker? Nicki's aunt Aimee is here with me."

"Oh no, not at all. Hello, Aimee, how nice to be able to speak to you again."

Skye wished she hadn't shared the call. Aimee and the professor could gush all they wanted. Later. Right now, Skye needed them to focus. "Professor, did you think of something else that might be helpful?"

"It's Dixie, and I did think of something, though I'm not sure how helpful it is. One of the journalism professors is a good friend of mine, and he was in my office when the feds stopped by. Later, he mentioned he and Nicki had a nasty fight at the beginning of the semester, which resulted in her quitting the university paper."

"Any idea what the fight was about?"

"You can get the full story from him, but the gist of it was Nicki didn't think her assignments were meaty enough. Not sure it will amount to anything, but I took the liberty of calling him to let him know you may want to talk. His name is Mike Drees." Dixie rattled off a number. Skye thanked her for the call and hung up.

Aimee protested. "Hey, I wanted to ask her something else."

Like what she prefers for dinner? Skye started punching numbers in her phone. "I need to make this call."

Aimee reached out and placed her hand over the keypad. Skye stopped dialing, but she shot Aimee an angry look to let her know she wasn't happy about it.

"Why don't you like her?"

"Huh?" Skye was genuinely puzzled.

"Dixie. Professor Latamore. You get all snarfy around her."

"She and I got along just fine." *Until you came along.* Skye's silent thought wasn't lost on Aimee.

"I heard a 'but.' Care to share?"

"Oh please. She practically slobbered all over you. If you're interested in picking up women, then go on and do it. I've got work to do."

"You're ridiculous." Aimee shut the laptop and glanced at her watch. "Come on. We've got work to do. Call Drees and tell him we need to meet with him. Now, what were you saying earlier about a helmet?"

❖

Aimee clutched Skye's waist and thanked the universe she was wearing pants. Skye had insisted she wear her helmet for now. It felt strange on her head and she spent most of the ride trying to figure out how to see out of it. As much as she wanted to concentrate on the feel of Skye against her, the fear of falling off, coupled with the dread of what she'd look like when they reached her destination, robbed her of the pleasure.

Skye, on the other hand, was fearless and dashing. Her blond waves were tightly confined under a red do-rag, and her sleek body hugged the bike like a second skin. When they arrived at their destination, Skye would simply shake out her tousled hair and be ready to go about her business. Aimee would have helmet hair and a crumpled suit. Maybe that look would suffice for a meeting with a journalism professor, but their next stop would be a mall, no question about it.

Drees's office was in the newspaper office. Students moved quickly through the room as if to simulate the real life hustle of a big city newsroom. The university paper was actually the next best thing. With a circulation of over fifty thousand, and the locale of the capital city in the second largest state in the country, there was no shortage of big headline breaking news to share with an active readership. Aimee recalled Nicki's descriptions of the newsroom, the paper, and her aspirations of becoming a big name journalist. When had those dreams died and why hadn't Nicki shared any of that with her? She hoped Drees would have some answers.

Skye paused outside his door.

"What?"

"Let's talk about how to play this."

"What? Oh, wait, I get it. Bad cop, good cop? You can be whichever one you want."

Skye's scowl caused her to regret the cop reference and promise to behave. "Sorry. Tell me what to do and I'll do it."

"I have a healthy distrust of the press. Follow my lead and don't bring up anything I don't specifically mention. Deal?"

"Deal." Aimee meant it. Besides, she wasn't interested in drawing attention to herself since she was certain she looked like she'd been dragged behind a car for a few blocks. A quick stop in the restroom to fluff out her hair and smooth her clothes hadn't done much for her self-confidence. She nodded at the door and Skye gave it a few solid knocks.

"Come in."

Mike Drees looked more like a harried city desk editor than a college professor. The tufts of hair that lined his bald scalp jutted out at odd angles, and his sweater vest was marked with a couple of sizeable coffee stains. His desk was covered with messy stacks of paper, and Post-it Notes waved from every page. He was apparently immersed in the particular stack in front of him because he didn't look up until Skye cleared her throat.

"Yes?" The word and his glance were directed at Aimee, but she kept her promise and didn't speak. He was probably only focused on her because of her own bedraggled appearance, which she itched to explain. Skye stepped in quickly and saved her from herself.

"Professor Drees?" At his nod, she continued. "I'm Skye Keaton."

"Oh, yes. You're here about Nicole Howard. Dixie Latamore mentioned you might be in touch."

Skye introduced Aimee and eased in to the reason they were there. "Professor Latamore mentioned Nicki used to be in your class and on the newspaper staff. It seems she kind of fell off the face of the earth a few weeks ago. We're talking to everyone who knew her as part of our search. Any ideas on where she might be?"

"I guess Dixie didn't tell you Nicole quit the paper and dropped my class at the beginning of the semester."

Aimee opened her mouth to correct him, but shut it abruptly when Skye subtly reached over and gripped her arm in a death vise. Aimee bit back a yelp, but delivered a menacing scowl in Skye's direction, which she shrugged away.

"Wow, Nicki quit?" Skye asked. "I thought she loved journalism."

"Oh, she loved it all right, but she wasn't willing to work her way up. I was surprised since she took my intro class last semester. I'm sure I made myself clear about what was expected."

"What do you mean?"

"She wanted to jump right into bylines and undercover exposés." He chuckled. "I know this may surprise you, but a lot of the material we print is not Pulitzer worthy. Most of our staffers work their way up by writing a combination of fluff pieces and straight reporting on daily news. I hate to admit it, but even what we might consider cutting edge journalism wouldn't merit more than a few column inches in the *Austin Statesman* or any other big city paper. Nicki and I had a bit of a row about her position on the paper and she quit. I was sad to see her go, but I have a few hundred students. If I'm not consistent with them, then I'll have chaos."

"Understood." Skye paused while she calculated a timeline in her head. "Was this fallout right at the beginning of the semester or a few weeks in?"

Professor Drees reached for his keyboard and began typing. "I can look up her exact drop date. Here it is. September ninth, right after Labor Day. Semester was still pretty young. I can't imagine what got her in such a lather just days into the class."

Skye couldn't either. At least not now, but she felt the familiar itch of a clue begin to fester. She wanted to get back to Earl's laptop. She had one last question. "Do you know if Nicki had any specific story ideas in mind?"

"She did pitch some ideas my way. I don't recall what most of them were, but I remember they weren't school paper material for the most part." He started clicking keys again. "I actually have them here if you'd like a copy."

Golden. Skye smiled. "We'd love a copy."

As they walked back to the parking lot, Skye leafed through the papers Drees had printed off. Each one consisted of a paragraph summary of a story idea. While they were inside, the sunny day had turned cold and a rising wind whipped the edges of her papers.

"We need to find a place to go through these, and I want to look at Earl's laptop again." Earl's laptop and diary were in a duffle on the back of her bike. Skye looked up from the paper and studied Aimee's appearance. She looked like hell, her expensive suit crumpled from her ride on the bike. Her perfectly coiffed hair was a tattered bird's nest. She had to be miserable, but she hadn't complained. She was probably freezing too, even with Skye's jacket on. Skye suppressed an impulse to wrap an arm around Aimee, squeeze some warmth her way. The urge threatened to distract her, which was precisely why she didn't give in to it. She could help Aimee in less personal ways, ways that wouldn't compromise her own resolve to remain professional. "But, before we do that, we need to get you some clothes. Let's hold it down to two stops, and I get to pick one of them—it's in Roundrock. You pick the other. No malls."

Aimee acted surprised to even have a say. "What is it about malls?"

"I don't want to be trapped inside a building if someone comes looking for us."

"Gotcha. There's an outlet mall in Roundrock, open air. Stop there and I'll grab some casual clothes."

Skye groaned, but gave in. Aimee desperately needed a different wardrobe. "Fine, but no more than thirty minutes. I hope you know your way around."

Aimee's eyes sparkled with a "who me?" expression.

❖

Forty-five minutes into the shopping trip, Aimee sensed Skye was beginning to come unhinged. She'd been to three stores, but the selection was hit-and-miss. Her choices consisted of struggling into skinny jeans or floating around in pants that made her look like the backside of a barn. Skye, meanwhile, stalked the pavement outside each store, impatient to get to the next stop. As if her impatience wasn't stressful enough, at store number four, Skye followed her in.

"How hard can it be to buy a couple pairs of jeans, shirts, and a sweater?" She swiped through the clothes on the rack, yanked a green button-down shirt, and held it up to Aimee's chest. "This looks great. Get a couple of these."

"This does not look great. I look like hell in that shade of green, that's not my size, and I'm too well-endowed to ask those buttons to strain across my chest."

Skye blushed. "You're not entering a beauty contest."

"Mind telling me what we are doing? It might speed the process if I knew what activities I'm dressing for." *Especially since the activities on my mind don't require being dressed at all.*

Skye pondered the relative disadvantages of sharing her plan with Aimee in advance. She didn't really have a plan other than a couple of tasks ahead: clothes, helmet, hotel. The rest was a hazy mess she hadn't completely sorted out. A trip to Wimberley to check out the raided compound was on the list, but she hadn't decided if she was taking Aimee with her to her meeting with Mr. White. Aimee didn't need clothes at all if all she was going to do was hang out at the hotel. Skye's heart skipped as she pictured Aimee lounging on pillows, dressed only in a bra and panties. Her thighs clenched as she fought to stave off the flood of desire the image provoked, and she spoke to break the spell. "The paper says the weather's going to get cooler. We may be spending some time outdoors. Jeans, not designer, boot-cut, and stuff you can layer. T-shirts, sweaters, that kind of thing."

"Okay. I'm going to need a jacket and some shoes, too."

Skye nodded. *Perfect, more clothes, less chance for distraction.* "We'll pick up both of those at the next stop."

Mercifully, Aimee didn't argue. "Okay." Aimee pointed to a row of benches in the walkway outside the store. "Go sit over there. Wait for thirty minutes. If I haven't come back by then, and only then, you can stalk me. Deal?"

Skye sighed. "Deal." She spent the next thirty minutes studying the other people wandering around the outdoor mall. No sign of federal agents lurking, but she couldn't believe the volume of shoppers in the afternoon on a weekday. Had the economy recovered when she wasn't paying attention? *Better do a good job on this case if you care about your own personal economy.*

She fished a pen and a small notebook from her jacket pocket and jotted a list of tasks: helmet, hotel, meeting with White, trip to Wimberley. She tapped the pen against the paper, but nothing else came. She had no doubt Nicki was wrapped up in the investigation of the compound in Wimberley. If she'd been present during the raid, she'd obviously escaped and was on the run. Was she with Earl? Where would two kids hide out in the Texas hill country? Nicki's upbringing suggested she would check into the nearest five-star hotel, but maybe she'd acquired survivalist skills courtesy of the Coalition. If so, she'd be harder to find. Skye looked forward to the challenge.

"Are you ready?"

Skye looked up. She had no idea how much time had passed, but it was enough for a complete transformation. Aimee was campfire ready, dressed in plain denim jeans and a sky blue sweater layered over a plain white T-shirt. If not for her full figure, she would've looked like she had stepped from the pages of an Eddie

Bauer magazine. Skye preferred Aimee's lush curves to the rail thin women that usually modeled these clothes. She was gorgeous.

Aimee pointed at her feet. She was wearing Nikes. "My heels didn't exactly match. I had to grab something to wear for now." She hefted a big sack. "I put my unsuitable suit and shoes in here. There's a Salvation Army up the road. Mind if we swing by and I'll drop this off. I don't think we have room on the bike."

Skye hadn't given any thought to what they'd do with all Aimee's stuff, including the articles from her hotel. Now that they had Earl's stuff too, storage space was tight. As if she could hear Skye's thoughts, Aimee said, "I'll get the hotel to ship the stuff in my room back to Dallas."

"Perfect."

CHAPTER FOURTEEN

A n hour later, they pulled up to the San Jose Motel, steps away from Jo's Coffee. The layout was similar to Skye's previous accommodations, but the atmosphere was a total three sixty. Instead of concrete walkways and large metal trash cans bolted to the ground, the landscape was lined with graveled paths and desert fauna.

Aimee didn't immediately slide off the bike. Skye removed her helmet and looked over her shoulder.

"You okay?"

Aimee pulled off her brand-new helmet. "Yep. I'm great." Their last stop had been the Harley dealership in Roundrock, where Skye personally supervised the purchase of a leather jacket, boots, and a perfectly sized helmet. Now that she had the appropriate attire, biker chick was a role she could get used to, especially when it meant she got to press her entire body, against Skye's tight, lean self. The short ride to Austin had been tame and uneventful, but Aimee imagined a different ride, where she and Skye rode like rockets, locked limb in limb. Daring fate, they would ride without helmets, their hair whipping wildly in the wind. The steady vibration of the bike, the heady abandon of the crisp night air would drive them to the brink of orgasm. Finally unable to take anymore, they pulled to the side of the road and Skye would take her—

"You mind if we get checked in?"

Aimee looked up to see Skye wearing a knowing grin. Shit. She shook away the fantasy, and slid off the bike, which freed Skye to do the same. Skye cast a long, lingering look of appraisal her way. After a slight nod, she motioned for Aimee to follow.

"You think I look hot in leather, don't you?" Skye stopped in her tracks, but didn't turn. Aimee almost regretted the slight tease, but she genuinely wanted the reassurance. It wouldn't kill Skye to say she was attractive.

Skye turned slowly, her eyes focused on Aimee's leather jacket. She slowly lifted her gaze and studied Aimee's face. "You look hot in everything I've seen you wear." Her eyes flicked away. "Don't tell me you don't know that."

As Skye stalked away, Aimee whispered to herself, "I won't."

Skye strode into the lobby of the San Jose motel. Aimee had suggested it and touted the advantages: motel layout, walking distance to conveniences, less visibility from the street. This place had all that, but it was nothing like the dive she'd chosen. With desert landscaping and earth tone colors, the motel was simple, yet rich. Skye was glad she'd taken Aimee's advice.

"Samantha King. I have a reservation." Skye leaned casually against the counter. Aimee was anxious enough for both of them.

"Yes, Ms. King, I see it right here. Two rooms, two nights? May I see your ID?"

Skye slid a driver's license across the desk. It was an impeccable replica of an authentic Texas driver's license. The photo was genuine, albeit old, but the rest of the information was a total fabrication, a souvenir from her days in Vice. Rules required her to turn in the ID when she was transferred to homicide, but she'd conveniently forgotten. Like her set of lock picks, it was a valuable tool she always carried with her.

"And who will be occupying the other room? I'll need to see their ID as well."

Skye kicked herself. She should've known they'd ask, though what she would have done to prevent it, she wasn't sure. It wasn't like you could buy decent fake IDs at every corner. She reversed her early opinion about their accommodations. A cash only roadside motel was sounding better and better.

Aimee strode up to the counter. "Hi, I'm Ann Hartley. I'm with her." She pointed at Skye. "I lost my wallet, with my ID, credit cards, and everything." She pulled a huge wad of cash from her handbag. "Luckily, I kept my emergency stash all separate. I think we'll really only need one room and we'll just pay up front and leave you a sizeable deposit." She slid a tall stack of hundred dollar bills across the desk and fixed the desk clerk with a big, bright smile. He stared at the stack of bills, shrugged, and processed a receipt. Moments later, key in hand, Skye led the way to their room.

Once they were safely inside, she whirled on Aimee. "Ann Hartley?"

"I was following your lead. You know, keep the initials the same. Samantha King, Ann Hartley. I kind of like my new identity. Where'd you get that fake ID? Can I get one?"

Skye shook her head. "This is not a game. I'm trying to protect you by keeping us under the radar. Tossing a few thousand dollars at the desk clerk was like drawing a bull's-eye on your forehead. He's telling everyone he knows right now about a hot blonde in a motorcycle jacket who checked in flashing enough cash to buy the place outright."

Hot blonde? Aimee forced herself to ignore the description. Skye was too angry for it to be anything other than an objective observation. Maybe sharing a room was a big mistake. Her first instinct was to argue. If Skye wanted to play clandestine games, she could at least include her in the plan so she didn't have to carve out her role as they went. Working with Skye was like stepping through a minefield. Hell, she'd only been following in her footsteps, but instead of safety, she'd set off another explosion. No sense making it worse by arguing the point. "Okay, okay. I'm sorry. What's next on the agenda?"

Skye pointed at the duffle bag she'd placed on the bed. "Let's finish looking through this stuff."

Aimee surfed through the contents of the laptop while Skye tried to make sense of the diary entries. Other than a partial manuscript for a futuristic novel based on the premise China had started a war that lead to global destruction, the computer's contents were pretty boring. Mostly class notes and random video downloads. She clicked on the Internet browser again, and poked around. No Facebook page or Twitter account for Earl Baxter, Jr. She typed in Nicki's name and learned she had both a Facebook page and a Twitter account, but with no activity since the beginning of September.

"Look at this," Skye shouted from across the room, waving a folded paper. "It's one of the Coalition newsletters. Like the one I found in Nicki's mail." She handed it over. After skimming a few pages, Aimee tossed it on the bed.

"No way is Nicki into all that craziness. There's something else going on."

"Maybe Earl Junior charmed her into a life with the wackos."

"Maybe he coerced her."

"Maybe."

Skye's voice trailed away as she stared at the paper in Aimee's hand. Aimee waved a hand in front of her face. "What's our next step?"

Skye looked at her watch. Six p.m. She had an hour to figure out how to ditch Aimee before her meeting with White. Judging by her lack of success so far, it wouldn't be an easy task. She didn't have a car, so she couldn't just send her off on an errand. She'd already resigned herself to the notion she was going to take Aimee along to Wimberley, but hiking through the remains of a federal raid was decidedly different than walking into a possible ambush of militant crazies. Distraction wasn't the only reason she wanted to go it alone. She was genuinely concerned for Aimee's safety. Her antics at the desk aside, maybe she could convince Aimee it would be more practical for her to stay behind and wait this one out.

"Have a seat."

"This sounds serious."

"It is. Look, I appreciate your help." She gestured to Earl's belongings. "You getting this stuff? That was really helpful."

"I hear a 'but.'"

"I have a meeting scheduled for tonight and I need to go alone."

"Need to or want to?"

"It could be dangerous."

"And riding around town on a motorcycle isn't?"

"Not that kind of dangerous. The dangerous where you don't know what could happen so you don't know how to plan for it kind of dangerous."

"I'm up for that."

Skye pulled her Sig and her .22 Smith and Wesson revolver from her bag and placed them on the bed. "I'll be carrying both of these, loaded. No safety. If I have to use them, I will."

Aimee reached over and slid her manicured fingers around the grip of the Sig. She ejected the cartridge, pulled the slide back, and checked the chamber. Aimee hefted the weapon a few times, apparently testing the feel, and then she sighted down the barrel. "I prefer my Taurus Judge Public Defender, but this will do."

"Oh, it will, will it?" Skye reached over, scooped up the cartridge, and pulled the gun from Aimee's grasp. She was disconcerted by the sight of Aimee's decidedly feminine hand wrapped around her hefty black weapon. Dangerously attractive. Even more disconcerting was Aimee's casual reference to the Judge, a revolver capable of firing shotgun shells. Her fluster came across as anger. "This is my gun. *Mine.* Get it?"

Aimee shrugged. "I would've brought my own, but the feds took all my guns." She assumed a pout. "Surely, you don't plan to run off to your meeting and leave me here unprotected?"

Skye shook her head as she tried to process the mixed bag of conversation. *All my guns? Leave me unprotected?* Aimee sure looked like she knew how to handle a gun, a look totally at odds with the rest of her appearance. Skye almost didn't want to know, but she couldn't stop the flow of questions. The first one that made it out of her mouth sounded inane even to her own ears. "How many guns do you have?"

"A few. Well, at least I used to. They're all in the custody of the federal government. Morgan said she'd try to get them back once we find Nicki and get this mess straightened out." She placed a hand on Skye's arm and kept talking. "You're pretty butch, but I'd feel safer with the Judge in my purse. No offense. My permit's good for either a semi-automatic or a revolver, but—"

Her rambling blocked out any chance Skye had of processing her thoughts. She placed a finger over Aimee's lips. "Stop talking." Another layer peeled away. Aimee Howard was a modern day Annie Oakley. Well, at least she knew her way around a firearm, whether she was a decent shot was another matter altogether. Seventy percent accuracy was all it took to qualify for a handgun permit. Her thought process was interrupted by a rush of warmth between her legs. She knew the source, but looked anyway. Yep, Aimee's tongue was wrapped around her finger, possessive and passionate. She watched as if the seduction was happening to someone else, then—slam— Aimee's eyes met hers. The force of her gaze out-blazed the heat of her touch. This feeling was decidedly different from the regular responses she felt with her casual encounters. Her arousal was laced with more than the desire for climax; it was consumed with the desire for more. More touch, more warmth, more intimacy, and that last desire she hadn't experienced in so long she didn't know what to do with it, but it burned. She reacted the only way she knew how. She jerked her hand out of the fire.

Aimee hadn't meant to do it, but once she started, she couldn't stop. Skye tasted like candy, and she didn't want the sweet sensation to end. Skye responded, arched against her, urged her closer for a moment, but then she broke away, reacting as if the very idea of touching her was distasteful. As Skye abruptly withdrew, Aimee savored the seconds before. She could hardly blame Skye for her reaction. The two of them were completely unsuited for each other, and even a quick tryst was likely to have disastrous implications to their ability to focus on the task at hand. But the attraction was fierce and powerful. Surely, Skye was aware of the surging magnetism she generated. Aimee shook her head. She wouldn't act on her physical impulses again. She didn't need to suffer rejection from a surly woman with a sketchy reputation.

Her emotional impulses were another matter. Whatever Skye was up to this evening was pivotal in the search for Nicki, and Aimee refused to be left behind. Skye could either accept her company or not. She'd find a way to get what she wanted. Aimee acted as if the physical encounter had never happened and announced her plan.

"I'm going with you tonight. You can take me or I can follow you. And don't think I'm not capable, because I am. One way or the other, you're including me in your little adventure."

Three, maybe five, seconds passed before Skye answered. "Okay."

Aimee wasn't sure she'd heard correctly, braced as she was for a fight. "Okay?"

"Yes." Skye glanced at her watch. "I have to make a call to find out where we're going." She pulled her phone out of her pocket. "Be very quiet, okay?"

Aimee made a show of zipping her lips. She watched while Skye dialed a number, announced her name. Skye didn't say anything else and hung up after a few seconds. When she finally disconnected the call, Aimee thought she might burst, but she waited for Skye to speak first.

"Where's Kyle, Texas?"

"About twenty miles south of here. Just off I-35."

"Any chance you know where the Thunderhill Raceway is?"

"Sure, it's a short track raceway. NASCAR recently announced it's going to be one of their sanctioned tracks starting in 2011—" She stopped and tried to assess the strange look on Skye's face. "What?"

"You're just a fountain of information, aren't you?"

"What's that supposed to mean?"

"Are you really a NASCAR fan?"

"Not a big one, but I think the sport's intriguing. Besides, who doesn't like Danica Patrick?" she asked, referring to the female racecar driver sensation.

"Ah, I see. It's all about the hot women."

Did Skye really think she only cared about surface beauty? Aimee purposely looked Skye over, from head to toe, allowing the presumption to stick. Skye was a fine woman, for sure, but Aimee was attracted to her cocky self-confidence more than her edgy good looks. She cared about much more than surface beauty, but she had no plans to let Skye know that. "It'll take about a half hour to get there. What time's the meeting?"

"We should leave now. Give me your driver's license." Skye pulled out her wallet, fished out her own license, and held out her hand for Aimee's.

Aimee didn't move. "Mind telling me why?"

"Two reasons. I don't want this guy to know any personal information about us—at least not more than necessary. These people aren't real big on government-issued documents anyway. It's a show of good faith."

"I bet they don't feel the same way about dollar bills." Aimee dug her license out of her Birken and reluctantly handed it over. "I guess I can be identified by my dental records."

"If you're scared, you don't have to go."

"I'm not scared, just appropriately cautious. Anything else I should know?"

"Yes. Leave that monster purse of yours behind. Judging by the size, it's bound to house at least a dozen personal items." Aimee frowned, but Skye was not dissuaded from her litany. "For tonight, you're my sister. We hate the federal government, and we're interested in learning ways we can take care of ourselves and the coming revolution. Listen, don't talk, and follow my lead. This guy may be off-balance, but I'm willing to bet he knows his way around guns. Understood?"

Aimee nodded. "I can handle whatever happens." She hoped it was true.

CHAPTER FIFTEEN

Skye cast about for anything she could focus on besides the tight grasp of Aimee's arms around her waist. She didn't have a clue why she'd allowed Aimee to accompany her, especially after their heated encounter. They should've discussed what happened, but Skye had shied away from broaching the subject because she didn't have a clue what to say. *Your touch sets me on fire, but I can't handle the burn.* Nope, better to just let the subject drop and avoid it altogether. At least they'd overcome their initial antagonism. Maybe if she included Aimee in the investigation they would have something to discuss other than the flare of arousal that ignited every time they touched. Skye sighed. So far, it wasn't working.

She'd glanced at a map before they left. Kyle was a short drive from Wimberley. It wasn't her preference to check out the scene of the raid in the dark of night, but if the meeting ended at a decent time, she tucked away the thought they might do a drive by.

As she drove into the parking lot of the racetrack, Skye focused on the meeting ahead. She doubted they would be meeting with just one guy at a venue this large, and the several dozen pickups and SUVs in the otherwise empty parking lot, confirmed her suspicion. She pulled her bike to a stop several feet away from the row of parked vehicles, shut it off, and waited for Aimee to dismount. Despite her bravado earlier, Skye could tell she was nervous now. She was too, but no way would she show it. She considered passing one of her guns to Aimee as sort of a good luck charm, but decided she didn't want to display firepower here in the well-lit parking lot.

She gestured for Aimee to follow and walked toward the stands. A rail thin woman, with scraggly brown hair hefted a shotgun as they approached the gate. She didn't aim her weapon at them, but the message was clear. This was an invitation only event.

Skye silently willed Aimee to follow her lead. "I'm Samantha, and this is my sister, Ann. Mr. White invited us. He asked me to tell you 'let freedom ring.'" She breathed a sigh of relief when the woman nodded at the phrase.

"Where did you meet Mr. White?" Apparently, the code phrase wasn't sufficient to gain entry; now she needed references.

Skye settled on honesty. "We haven't met him in person, but we were introduced through a mutual friend. Mr. Davis. He referred us to Mr. White for what we needed to accomplish our special purposes." The woman's fierce cynicism softened slightly, and Skye thanked her good memory for spitting up the name of the Army-Navy surplus store owner.

"You armed?"

"I am." Honesty had gotten her this far.

"You can keep your weapons with you. Unloaded." She pointed to a table just inside the gate. Leave your ammo in one of those bags. You can pick it up when you leave."

Skye didn't like the idea. By way of a compromise, she decided the loaded .22 in her boot didn't constitute a real weapon. She pulled her Sig out of its holster, ejected the clip, and put it in a bag. She scrawled her name on the bag with one of the markers on the table, while the shotgun-toting gatekeeper watched her every move. Then she flicked her eyes to Aimee. Aimee noticed she was the subject of scrutiny and opened her jacket wide to demonstrate she was unarmed. Apparently satisfied, the woman waved them on.

Skye chanced a whisper as they walked to the stands. "Any idea who owns this place?"

"Not a clue. I know they rent it out for special events, but I hardly think this counts."

Skye agreed. Although there was a random assortment of people in attendance—men, women, and children—they were all white, and they were all dressed like they were about to either join the military or strike out on a wilderness trek. In comparison, Aimee's Eddie Bauer outfit looked like high fashion. Skye hoped they didn't stick out too much. She couldn't help a last minute reminder. "Don't do or say anything that could draw attention. Follow my lead."

She led them to the top of the bleachers. They sat with the rest of the crowd, staring at the empty podium positioned down by the track. Within moments, Skye felt a surge of energy leap through the crowd. People around them came out of their seats, pointing and waving. She motioned for Aimee to stand with her as she craned her neck to get a better view. A tall man in a black suit strode toward the podium, flanked on either side by a pair of guys dressed in fatigues with automatic weapons at the ready. Even with the distance between them, Skye could tell one of the bodyguards was Mr. Davis from the army surplus store, apparently decked out in his own merchandise. She was relieved to see a familiar face, albeit a crazy one.

Her relief was short-lived. The crowd burst into spontaneous song. "My country 'tis of thee."

Oh boy. Beside her, Aimee dutifully belted out the lyrics to "America." She joined in, simultaneously offering a silent prayer to help her remember the words. Thankfully, the man at the podium waved the crowd to silence after the first verse. He spoke softly and deliberately into the microphone.

"Sweet land of liberty."

"Sweet land of liberty!" The crowd shouted back.

"Land where my fathers died."

"Land where my fathers died!"

"Let freedom ring!"

"Let freedom ring!"

The repetition of the simple lyrics whipped them into an absolute frenzy. Once, when she was young, Skye had accompanied a friend to church after a Saturday night sleepover. If her sedate Catholic parents had known where she was going, they would have been mortified. The evangelical congregation sang, swayed, and roared back the pithy phrases of their pastor until they were exhausted and sweaty with belief. Young Skye had been both fascinated at the power of their conviction and terrified to discover her Catholicism rendered her a heathen bound for hell. She didn't believe in heaven or hell anymore, but the fervor of this crowd brought her youthful fears raging back, and she joined the litany to keep from being different.

"Brothers and sisters, we meet tonight to mourn a tragedy, but more importantly, we meet to plan an appropriate response. Mere miles from this place, the unauthorized forces of the pretender government have invaded one of our strongholds." He held up a sheet of paper. "I have here a list, a roll call of those who have made sacrifice. Members of our family have been killed, wounded, and captured. Those held by the unauthorized forces of the pretender government face trumped up charges of treason." He waved the paper in the air. "Yet I say to you, the brothers and sisters listed here are heroes, and their captors are the true traitors!"

Shouts from the crowd accented his speech and spurred him on. "What can you do? For those fallen, you can pray. For those wounded, you can offer solace. For those captured, you can fight, ever mindful that your efforts will ring in the hearts of those who remain falsely accused and held by the unlawful forces of a puppet government."

He waited for the cheers of the crowd to subside before offering his next litany. "But there is more. I have it on good authority that our Supreme Leader remains free. I have no doubt he will reappear to us and lead us once again. What can you do for him, for our cause? You can be ready—ready to fight for our great nation, ready to wrest control back from the usurpers that have transformed our sweet land of liberty into a communist regime. Meet with your ready leaders to discuss how you can fortify your homes, arm your families, and prepare for liberty. When our Supreme Leader returns, it will be a sign. The end of times is upon us, and we will *let freedom ring!*"

The crowd went wild. They spilled from the stands onto the track, and surrounded the black-suited man. Skye motioned for Aimee to join her, and they moved along the edge of the crowd. She considered whether meeting the man face-to-face was a wise move, but her thoughts were interrupted by a tap on the shoulder.

"You came." Davis seemed pleased to see her.

"I did. Thank you for the introduction. I'm sure we can find everything we need here."

He nodded. "Happy to help another veteran."

Aimee cleared her throat and Davis looked her way. He raised a questioning eyebrow, and Skye introduced them. "Mr. Davis, this is my sister, Ann." Silently willing Aimee not to interrupt, she continued. "Our parents died recently. When we were going through their estate, we learned of their sympathies for your cause." She took a chance. "They were acquainted with the Baxters, and we mourn their loss as well. We are ready to fight back. "

"You'll find help here, along with everything you need to achieve your goals. I'll be happy to introduce you around."

She nodded in the direction of the black-suited man. The crowd around him had thinned slightly. "May we meet him?"

"Sure. Come with me."

Skye pulled Aimee with her and followed him through the crowd. Aimee leaned in close and whispered, "I bet he knows where Nicki is." Skye motioned for her to be quiet, but she silently agreed. In a few short strides, they were standing in front of the man. She had a split second to decide how to play the situation. How close were the members of this group to the group on the compound that had been raided? She thought about revealing a connection to Nicki, but she had no idea if the feds had already tried to question these folks. If they had, she might raise unnecessary suspicions. She resigned herself to sticking with the story about their parents.

They waited a short distance away while Davis talked to the black-suited guy. Skye started to think meeting the leader at this point was a bad idea, but just as she leaned toward Aimee to say they should leave, Davis waved them over.

"Samantha, Ann, please meet Mr. White."

White extended a hand to each of them and grasped hard, preacher style. "Davis has informed me of your recent trouble. I understand you were acquainted with Earl Baxter?"

Skye opened her mouth to reply, but the voice she heard wasn't hers.

"Junior only. He's close to our cousin, Nicki Howard." Aimee delivered the words with a bright smile while pretending to ignore the exchange of looks between the two men. "They are such a devoted couple." Her acting skills were put to the test as she now had the additional distraction of Skye's finger jabbing into her back. "We haven't heard from either Nicki or Earl Junior, since the raid, but we fear the worst. Our goal now is to contribute all our efforts to the cause."

"Indeed," White answered. "Perhaps we can direct your efforts to the greater good, and in the process help you obtain knowledge of your cousin."

"That would be fabulous." Aimee turned to Skye. "Wouldn't it, sister?"

"Oh yes. Fabulous." Skye's expression belied her spat out words, and Aimee could tell she only had a few minutes more to let this scenario play out before Skye wrested control back from her. She addressed White. "I'm afraid we lack many of the skills necessary to"—she sought the word he'd used—"*fortify* ourselves. We do have access to funds, though, and can contribute our fair share to any who would see fit to help us with the rest. Our parents would want us to be charitable with their cherished causes." She could tell she was on the right track by the way their eyes lit up.

"Brother Davis will make a list of the materials you should stock. Do you live nearby?"

"We've been staying in Austin, at our parents' home. We'd hoped to eventually join the compound at Wimberley, but..." Aimee let her voice trail off into a light sob.

White grasped her hand again and murmured, "You poor dear."

She could only imagine the smirk on Skye's face, as she hid her own behind her free hand. "Thank you, Brother White. I would like to offer whatever assistance I can to the cause. I'm not as skilled with weaponry as my dear sister, Samantha, but I do have something of my own to contribute. My poor deceased husband left me a trunk full of gold bars. I've been at a complete loss as to how to invest them. All the advisors I've spoken to suggest foreign currency, but I believe gold is the best investment there is. Wouldn't you agree?"

No matter how hard they tried to project nonchalance, Davis and White's excitement was palpable. White played his part perfectly. "Some of our greatest gifts come to us in ways we do not expect. If you see fit to honor our mission with a golden tribute to your late husband, we would use your gift to further our cause. We would, in turn, make it our first priority to assist you in locating your cousin."

"Do you have plans to build a compound like the one in Wimberley? I think it would be lovely to name such a structure after him."

"A physical structure seems to be a rallying point for our detractors." He paused, as if considering his next statement carefully. "We do have a rallying point of our own, though. Once we become better acquainted, perhaps I can show it to you."

Aimee heard the unspoken words loud and clear. If she and Skye showed up with a trunk full of gold, she could have anything she wanted. "Excellent. I look forward to a long and prosperous acquaintance."

"As do I. Did you ever attend meetings at the Wimberley compound?"

"I never had the good fortune. Point of fact, I don't even know where it is located. Dear Nicki said there were too many privacy issues to give me an exact location. I suppose privacy is no longer a concern. I would very much like to visit and honor the fallen with my prayers."

"It is true, our Supreme Leader was very secretive in his mission. I do know the location if you would like me to escort you there. We could go tomorrow."

"I appreciate the offer, but Samantha can escort me if you would be kind enough to tell us where to go. Then we can make arrangements to meet with Brother Davis tomorrow and gather what we need for our future mission among our people. I would of course, bring an offering of good will when we meet again."

Aimee held her breath while she waited for White's response. She knew better than to rely strictly on her feminine wiles, but she was sharp enough to recognize when someone took a fancy to her. Too bad it was the black-suited cult leader and not Skye she was sucking up to. The latter would have been much more pleasurable, and the payoff bigger than a map into the wilds.

"Brother Davis, please draw a map for our sisters so they can pay respects to the cause of their cousin and her betrothed." He lifted Aimee's hand to his lips and she silently paid the price for his favor. "You may contact me through the same number. Let us meet again tomorrow to discuss your future. Back here, say one o'clock? While we talk about my future plans for our people, and Brother Davis can take your sister through our standard drills."

"Oh, she would absolutely love that. Thank you for your kindness. I look forward to our next meeting."

This time Aimee led the way as they left the stadium. She studiously avoided Skye's glances as they stopped to retrieve the clip to Skye's gun. When they reached her bike, only a few vehicles remained in the parking lot. She didn't have to wait long for the fallout from her impromptu role-play as a militant wannabe.

"I think I'm going to hurl."

"Gee, Skye, tell me how you really feel." She jabbed her in the side and waved the map Davis had drawn like a truce flag. "Aren't you glad you don't have to drive aimlessly in the dark in search of the compound?"

"Oh, sure. Now one of these nut jobs can follow us in the dark."

"You seem to be pretty good at eluding followers. Present company excluded."

Skye cracked a reluctant smile. "Yeah, okay. You were pretty resourceful. Let's make this a quick trip and get back to the hotel. I could use a good meal, and I bet you could too."

Aimee considered the single room back at the San Jose. A meal was the last thing on her mind.

CHAPTER SIXTEEN

It was too loud for them to talk during the ride, and Skye welcomed the opportunity to reflect. Thoughts about how Aimee made her feel were distracting her from the search for Nicki. Was Nicki like Aimee? Vibrant, headstrong, daring? She must be daring, or why else would she have risked her comfortable lifestyle for a walk on the wild side with kooks like White's band of militants? On the other hand, vibrant and headstrong weren't personality traits likely to translate into a blind follower, which is what you'd have to be to believe the crap White and his gang were selling.

Skye thought back to her time on the task force years ago. The people they'd arrested fell into two groups: power-hungry fanatics and deluded salvation seekers. Nothing she'd learned about Nicki allowed her to place the girl into either category. No, she seemed more like her aunt. Skye laughed at the thought of Aimee's earlier charade for White and Davis. She played the part of the salvation seeking zealot like a pro. Was Aimee's attraction to her an act as well?

Why do I care? She knew the answer. She was attracted to Aimee, aroused by her, and fast becoming respectful of her. She barely recognized the subtle signs of attraction. She'd experienced them so infrequently. Her profession had always been the singular source of her personal fulfillment. The closest she'd ever come to blurring boundaries had been with Parker, but even then their relationship had never crossed the line. She'd shared her body, but had never been truly intimate with anyone, not even sharing the kind of closeness partners on the job commonly enjoyed. She'd always held something back. Her excuses varied, but they all centered around a single theme. Work. She had to keep her mind sharp, free from emotion, clear of distractions. The job provided a built-in wall, insulating her from outside assaults on her emotional well-being. Assault—an offensive threat or touching. Aimee's advances were anything but, and the wall she'd built had started to crumble.

Skye shook away the thoughts. *Focus.* Based on the map Davis had drawn, the clearing up ahead had to be the place. A large portable building surrounded by a circle of tents was probably the headquarters of the "Supreme Leader." She pulled to a stop and parked her bike under a large tree.

Aimee climbed off the back like a pro. Skye followed, and they both removed their helmets.

"This the place?" Aimee asked.

"Looks like it." Skye pointed to a remnant of yellow crime scene tape flapping from a nearby tree. The scene had probably been released soon after the raid, but the clean-up crew had been lax about removing all signs of their presence. She led the way to the abandoned building in the center of the clearing. Empty cases of ammo, randomly scattered MRE packages, and a sleeping bag here and there were the only signs anyone had ever been in residence.

"Doesn't look like there's much left here for us to see."

Skye heard Aimee's unspoken question, "Why are we here?" She didn't bother with a response. Visiting a crime scene, even months after an incident, was an event she never missed. No matter how much time had passed, actually being on site almost always gave her valuable insights into her investigation. She didn't expect Aimee to understand.

As she surveyed the scene, she felt a flicker of regret. She'd never again get a call, urging her away from sleep, food, another case, to a crime scene. She'd never again show up, flash her badge, and instantly gain the respect of the uniforms who'd first arrived at what was often a grisly mess. She'd never again take control in the heat of the investigation, order what should be bagged, tagged, photographed, and processed. She'd gotten so involved in this investigation, that she'd almost forgotten she wasn't a cop anymore, but the reality of what had gone down here brought her memory roaring back. The list of what she'd lost was long, so long she wanted to give in to the emptiness, get back on her bike, and ride far away. She glanced at Aimee who watched her with a look that reflected an intense loss of her own. Aimee had lost her niece and Skye was hired to find her. She may not be a cop anymore, but at least she had this job and she would apply her well-honed cop instincts to the task. She would find Nicki. She would do her job for Aimee, for herself.

"Eerie, isn't it? Any ideas about how the raid went down?"

Skye stared at Aimee long and hard. Aimee got it, the sense and feel of a place that carried memories of tragedy. Once again, she'd underestimated Aimee. How many times was she going to do that? She resolved to stop right now, and included Aimee by speaking her thoughts out loud.

"I always get something out of these visits. There's a feeling about a place, especially after the dust of the initial incident settles. Sometimes I find a piece of evidence overlooked in the action. Sometimes all I get is a sense of who or what we should be looking for." She flashed a light on the side of the building. "Look at all the bullet holes. There are hundreds of them. Whoever was in there was probably dead or seriously injured when the feds finished their attack." She pointed to the dense woods surrounding them. "The only decent approach to this place is from the road. I bet whoever got away was hiding out there when the raid went down."

"Do you miss it?"

"What?" Skye knew what Aimee was asking, but her protective instincts kicked in with avoidance.

"Police work, you know, 'the job.'"

With every ounce of my being. If I were a cop, I'd have only to flash my badge to gain entrance to anywhere I wanted to go. I'd have a team of crime scene techs at my disposal, and I wouldn't be standing in the middle of a crime scene in the middle of the night skulking around for clues. Aimee's ability to read her mind did a number on her preconceived notions. She viewed herself as stoic and Aimee as focused only on her own needs. Obviously, Aimee cared enough to empathize, and her own emotions weren't as closely held as she would like to believe. Still, self-preservation kept her from admitting the details of her longing, but the fact it existed seemed harmless enough. "I do."

"If you want to talk about it—"

Skye was quick to cut her off. "I don't."

Aimee nodded, but wisely didn't say anything else. Skye struggled not to let her frustration show. Why was her personal life up for grabs? Did Aimee feel like Skye's knowledge of her personal life demanded reciprocity? Well, it didn't. This wasn't a first date, it was a job. Time for Aimee to realize work was the only reason they were together. She started to bring up their encounter in the hotel room, make it clear there would be no more such interactions, but the sound of an approaching car interrupted her plan. She grabbed Aimee's hand and led her to a cluster of bushes yards away from the clearing.

She took the time to whisper in Aimee's ear. "Don't say a word. Nod to show me you understand."

Aimee nodded, fear in her eyes as she flicked a glance at the approaching car. Skye followed her gaze. It wasn't the same sedan, but it could have been. How in the hell had the feds tracked them here? She was certain no one had followed them through the winding Wimberley roads. Two men got out of the car. The headlights illuminated their suited selves as they walked through the clearing, looking around with purpose. *Looking for us.* They spotted her motorcycle right away. Skye silently offered a blessing that she'd relocked the saddlebags after extracting her flashlight. She hoped these jokers didn't have the necessary tools with them to break the lock or remove the bags from the bike entirely. They whispered, and she could only catch snippets of their conversation. *Around here... couldn't be far...too dark...leave this...track...later...*

She heard them test the locks, then watched as they lingered over her bike. Without the light of her powerful flashlight, she couldn't tell what they were doing. She felt protective of her ride, and had to restrain herself from running into the clearing and warding them off with a few shots from her gun.

They saved her the trouble. As if they'd lost interest, they returned to their car, and left as abruptly as they'd arrived. Skye motioned to Aimee to remain in place and silent. They stayed still and quiet for a full five minutes after they'd pulled away. Then and only then, she crouched low and ran over to her bike. A quick search with the powerful beam of her flashlight revealed the locks were still in place and had not been disturbed. She signaled to Aimee who quickly joined her. "Let's get out of here. We can always come back during the day."

"Who were those guys?"

"My best guess is the feds. Somehow they followed us."

"I thought you said no one followed us."

"Well, that's what I thought, but obviously I was wrong." Skye couldn't believe she'd overlooked a tail. "Unless one of those suits was posing as a survivalist at the revival we just attended, I don't know how the hell they caught up with us."

A coyote howled in the distance. Aimee jumped and grabbed Skye's arm. "It's spooky out here. Can we go?"

Skye looked down at Aimee's hand. Her tight grasp felt so good, she feared she'd grant her anything. It was indeed spooky. Her usual tendency to do the opposite of whatever Aimee wanted faded in the face of her desire to grant this small wish—a wish she shared.

"Yeah, let's go."

❖

Even in the dark, Aimee could tell they were lost. After three passes through the same desolate country path, Skye finally pulled over. They both got off the bike and removed their helmets. Aimee was pleased with herself at how much easier the task became each time she slid off the motorcycle.

"Maybe we should head back that way." Aimee pointed to the left as she ventured her opinion.

Skye shook her head. "That's the direction we came from. I'm worried the feds are still out there. I don't want them catching up with us." She waved her hand in the direction they'd been traveling. "I hoped that road would take us back to the highway, but no such luck."

"Well, no need to worry, I have my trusty iPhone." Aimee fished the device from her pocket and stared at the screen. "Oops, no signal." She walked around a few feet away, holding the phone in front of her like a divining rod. "I don't know what the problem is. I had a signal at the compound."

Skye cocked her head. "I don't remember seeing you talking to anyone while we were stopped there."

"I didn't, silly, but I did mark the spot on the map so we could find it again in case you want to go back." She stared at the unlit signal bars again. "Of course, that wasn't much use considering I can't get a signal at all now." She shook the phone in frustration. Seconds later, she cried out as Skye grabbed her hand and peeled the phone from her fingers. "Hey, what are you doing?"

"You have GPS on this thing?"

Aimee nodded. She considered the GPS app on her phone a blessing, but Skye's tone was accusatory. She watched as Skye took the battery out of her phone and put it in her pocket. "What the hell do you think you're doing?"

"Saving you from yourself."

"Give me back my phone."

"Here you go." Skye handed her the powerless device. "You're the reason the feds found us. It's nothing for them to pinpoint our location with your handy GPS function."

Aimee held the phone away from her like an unwelcome insect. "Seriously?" She shoved it back toward Skye. "You take it."

"It's disabled now. They can only trace it when it's on." Skye pulled out her own phone and took the battery out of it too. "I doubt they'd be able to get a subpoena for this phone, considering the fact it belongs to a law firm. The feds would have no idea I'm using it, but I'm not taking any chances."

Aimee shuddered. "I'm sorry. I had no idea. What's next?"

Skye looked around. "We'll have to find a way out of here on our own. I think I remember seeing a cabin not too far from here. Let's see if anyone's home, and we can do the old-fashioned thing— ask for directions."

Aimee waited for Skye to slide back onto the bike, and then she joined her and waited some more. Skye pushed the starter, but the only response was a dead click. She removed her helmet and leaned forward before trying again. Nothing.

"It's not going to start. Probably a short, but I can't find or fix it in the dark. These rough back roads may have jarred something loose.

Aimee could feel her frustration. She pulled off her own helmet. "What now?"

"I think we're going to need to find that cabin on foot, and hope real hard that they have a phone we can use."

❖

Thanks to barbed wire, hills, and tangled underbrush, it took them over an hour to reach the cabin they'd seen in one of their earlier passes through the area. By the time they reached the door, Skye was fuming. She was probably perfectly capable of fixing whatever was wrong with her bike if she were back at home with all her own tools. Out here, in the middle of nowhere, in the dark, with just a simple tool kit, she was helpless. She hated being helpless. She hated even more the thought of depending on the kindness of strangers, although, judging by the darkness surrounding the cabin, she doubted anyone was home at this place, strange or otherwise.

She looked in the front windows and grew more discouraged. The furniture was covered with white sheets. She knocked on the door, despite her belief the effort was futile. After a few silent beats, she turned to Aimee. "No one's home."

Aimee shivered in the cold night air, her arms wrapped tightly around her body. "Try again."

"It's no use," Skye pointed toward the window. "House is all sealed up for the winter."

"It's Texas; there are no real winters here. Maybe they just don't like getting dirt on the furniture. Try again."

"No one's home. Look around and see if there's a key. Maybe we can at least use the phone if they have service."

A thorough search of the wide porch and all its nooks and crannies yielded nothing. Skye inspected the keyhole. She had no doubt she could get in easily. She considered ways to distract Aimee from what she was about to do.

"Why don't you check around back? See if there's another entrance. I'll test the windows up here."

Aimee glanced at the thick forest to the rear of the cabin. "No, thanks. Why don't I test the windows while you go around back?"

Skye sighed. They only had one flashlight and it was pitch black outside. She decided to let Aimee in on her plan. "I'm going to pick this lock. You have a problem with that?"

"You know how to pick locks?" Aimee's tone carried a touch of awe.

Not the response she expected. Frankly, she wasn't sure what response she did expect, nor why she cared. She wasn't a cop anymore, so she wasn't bound by expectations about what a cop should and shouldn't do in the pursuit of justice. Still, she wanted Aimee's respect, inexplicable though the desire was.

"Yes." She bent and retrieved her set of picks from her boot. "Here, hold this." She handed the flashlight to Aimee. "Shine it here."

The lock was no challenge, and within moments they were inside. Aimee hugged herself and remarked about the chill. Skye quickly located the source of the frosty breeze flowing through the one room cabin. The broken rear window and shards of glass on the cabin floor indicated someone else had found a way in, a messier, but more efficient method than Skye's work with the lock. Skye placed a protective arm in front of Aimee and drew her gun. She peered around the room. The only closed door was across the room. She figured it probably led to the bathroom, and judging by the light scratching sounds coming from that direction, someone was in there.

"Wait here," she whispered to Aimee. As she crept softly across the room, she felt a presence close behind. Why should Aimee start following instructions now? When they reached the door, she leaned in close. Silence. Whoever was inside had likely heard their approach. Skye waved Aimee back, and grasped the handle with her left hand while she covered the door with the gun in her right. With a quick glance back to make sure Aimee was out of any potential line of fire, she threw the door open and trained her gun inside.

She'd intended to surprise the occupant, but it was she who was surprised by the furry raccoon calmly working his way through the contents of the trash. He seemed only mildly startled by Skye's presence before he returned his concentration to the wastebasket. Skye didn't even try to hold back laughter, a mix of humor and relief.

"What is it? Why are you laughing?" Aimee stepped closer. "Oh. I guess he's not armed."

"Nope. I bet he's hungry though. No telling how long he's been trapped in here."

"Judging by the state of the room, I'd say not too long. Besides, he looks pretty fat and happy, and he probably didn't get that way off the tissues in that trash can."

Skye appraised her. "I didn't make you for an outdoorsy type. You know a lot about woodland creatures?"

"I know enough. Much to my mother's chagrin, I spent hours of my youth traipsing through the woods with my brother and my dad on my dad's hunting lease. I'm not big on shooting at the furry beasts, but I enjoy target shooting and being outdoors. Besides, when I was a kid, I'd do anything to hang out with my dad, who I thought was the coolest person on earth."

Skye heard the wistful tone. "I take it your opinion has changed."

"A bit. Don't get me wrong—I love my parents. We just don't agree on much of anything, and I no longer care about doing things just to please them."

"I thought you were in business together. I suppose I just assumed you were because both you and your dad are in real estate."

"Sure, I got my start based on my dad's reputation as a shrewd real estate investor, but I've had my own firm, completely separate from his, for years. Now the clients I have come to me by virtue of my own solid reputation, not my father's." Aimee's tone had shifted from wistful to challenging. Skye recognized the shift for what it was. She was still stuck in the stage of caring what her father thought, worrying her worth depended on his respect. Aimee was past that, and Skye grudgingly admired her for it.

"Sorry. I misjudged you. I can tell you're proud of what you've accomplished."

Aimee shrugged. "Don't worry about it." She changed the subject. "Shouldn't we be looking for a phone?"

They completed their search of the cabin within a few minutes. No phone, which Skye didn't find surprising. In this day and age, cell phones were the norm, and if whoever owned the cabin didn't live here permanently, it didn't make sense to install a phone line for occasional use.

"Someone's been here recently, and I'm willing to bet it was whoever broke the window," Skye observed.

"How can you tell?"

"Remember all the rain they had down here last week? Flash flood all over the hill country? There'd be water damage if the window had been broken then. And look at the trash. Those frozen food trays are still moist. Whoever was here before us, was here very recently. You're right about our friend, the raccoon. He's in great shape. He may have only been locked in the bathroom for a day." Skye leaned out the open window. "What I don't get is why whoever broke in here, didn't just walk out the front door instead of crawling back out the window."

"How do you know they didn't?"

"Unless they had a key, they wouldn't have been able to relock the deadbolt. And if they had a key…"

"They wouldn't have broken the window. Gotcha." Aimee stared at her. "You seem worried."

Skye shook her head. "Not worried, really. Just have a weird feeling. We should probably head out, see if there's another house nearby, but before we do, I want to take a look out back. Why don't you wait here?"

"Not a chance. I'm coming with you."

The ground to the rear of the cabin consisted of a graveled stretch of about four feet that dropped off into a steep grade down to the wooded land beyond. As they made their way to the site of the broken window, Skye heard a whoosh of rocks slipping and felt Aimee falling behind her. She planted her feet firmly and braced herself to stop Aimee's fall. She caught her, but the force of the fall took them both down the hill.

Skye was the first to move. She sat up on her knees and brushed herself off. Extending a hand to Aimee, she asked, "Are you okay?"

"Just shaken up a bit. I landed on something nice and soft." She felt behind her. "I thought it was you, but apparently not." She sat up and let Skye pull her to her feet.

As Aimee brushed the dirt and leaves from her clothes, Skye pointed the beam of her flashlight into the spot where Aimee had fallen. Aimee had fallen on something soft, all right, but it wasn't nice. No, it wasn't nice at all.

CHAPTER SEVENTEEN

G o wait in front of the house."
Aimee had never seen a dead body before, but her shock didn't keep her from bristling at the command. No way was she leaving Skye's side. Skye had the gun and the flashlight, and she didn't care if her protection came with a dead person on the side. "I'm not moving."

Skye shrugged. "Suit yourself, but go stand over there." She shone the flashlight on a tree a few feet away. Aimee didn't move. "Seriously, Aimee, this could be a crime scene. Do you really want to leave traces of yourself next to a dead body?"

"Well, when you put it that way." Aimee moved to the tree, half relieved and half frustrated to be physically removed from the action. "Is it a man or a woman? How did he or she die? Do you think they fell out the window?"

"There you go with the questions in triplicate again." Skye took her time over the body before she answered. "It's a man. He may have fallen out the window, but that wasn't what killed him. Judging by the amount of blood and br—I mean other stuff, I'd say he was shot at close range, maybe in the back of the head. Rigor has set in and the body's cool, but with the cool weather, I can't really estimate how long he's been dead. The softness you felt was his big down jacket."

Despite the dark, Aimee could tell Skye was riffling through the dead guy's clothes. "What're you looking for? Should you be touching him?" In deference to Skye's alleged expertise, she left the last question unspoken, but her implication hung in the air. *You're disturbing a potential crime scene.*

"I worked homicide for years. I think I know what I'm doing. I'm just trying to find some ID." She sighed. "No wallet, nothing in his pockets. Wait a minute, here's something." Skye shined the flashlight at the man's chest and leaned in. Aimee couldn't help herself, she moved closer until she was right behind Skye's shoulder.

"What is it?"

"Dog tags. If these belong to this guy, then he is Private Baxter of the Coalition of Patriot Sectarians."

Realization dawned quickly. "Earl Junior!"

"That's my guess."

"Holy shit. I can't believe we finally find him and he's dead." Aimee cursed their bad luck. She was sure Earl was the link between Nicki and the band of wackos the feds were after. Where were they supposed to look now? As she considered the possibilities, another thought crept along the edges of her disappointment, adjusting its way into her focus. Dread kept the thought at bay until she noticed she was the subject of Skye's intense gaze. She met Skye's eyes with a steady stare of her own. Suddenly, reality dosed her full force. "Oh my God, if Earl's dead, then Nicki's probably dead too." She strangled a howl of despair and sobbed quietly instead.

Within seconds, Skye slipped an arm around her and held her close. Her murmured words of comfort were stilted, as if she wasn't used to the role of consoler, but the force behind them was genuine. "Don't cry. She could be fine. I'm not giving up. You shouldn't either. I'll never give up. We'll find her. I promise."

Skye's arms felt strong, warm, inviting. She wanted to lean into Skye's body and forget they were lost, forget they were standing next to a dead body, forget she might never see Nicki again. As much as she wanted to stay in the safety of Skye's arms, she knew Skye was right. She shouldn't give up. She stifled her sobs and straightened. "Sorry for the meltdown. Should we look around to see if her—I mean, to see if she's here?"

Skye seemed startled by her abrupt change in demeanor. "Uh, okay. Sure. But wouldn't you prefer I look around myself?"

Aimee knew Skye's protective instincts were kicking in, but she was determined to face the situation head on. "Whatever there is to see, I want to see it for myself."

"Okay, but please walk right behind me to reduce our footprint. I meant what I said about this being a crime scene."

"Wait a minute; shouldn't we just call nine one one?"

"Well, we could, but there are a few problems with that approach."

"And they are?"

Skye ticked off the list. "We don't know where we are. What will we tell the police about why we're here in the first place? Do you think they're going to believe that we just found this cabin with the window already broken out and a dead body in back? And, on top of all that—"

Aimee held up a hand. "Enough. I get it." She sighed. "I assume you have a plan?"

Skye smiled. "Half-baked, but yes. I figured we'd look around to see if we can tell if Nicki has been here, and then call for back-up."

"Morgan and Parker?"

"None other."

"I thought you didn't want to use the phone?"

"I don't, but we need to get out of here faster than we can on foot, and I'd like to tell someone about this body, someone who's not going to arrest me on the spot. They can handle the details of reporting, if they think that's what we need to do."

"Sounds like a plan." Aimee held out her hand. "Give me the flashlight. I'll lead. You bring up the rear with the big gun."

Skye hesitated only a moment before giving up the light. "Lead on."

Within fifteen minutes, they'd searched the open space from the rear of the house to a few feet into the thick woods behind. They quickly determined there was nothing more they could do in the dark without a machete and stronger light. Aimee leaned back against a tree. "I think it's time to make that call."

"Let's call from inside the cabin. While we're in there, see if you can find anything that can tell us where we are."

❖

Parker grabbed her cell phone off the nightstand and flipped it open without looking at the number. Years as a homicide detective meant she was trained to fully wake on an instant's notice. Morgan was asleep beside her so she whispered into the phone. "Casey here."

"Parker, it's Skye. We need some help."

"I'm listening." Parker carefully slid out of bed and padded out of the room.

"Long story, but here are the highlights. We're somewhere near Wimberley, and we found Nicki's boyfriend, Earl Baxter, Jr. Problem is he's dead. Not of natural causes. Feds are still following us and my bike broke down. We're at some cabin. Pretty sure the feds are tracking us through cell phone GPS, but there are no other phones around. I'll figure out how to get us out of here, but dead bodies are no longer my specialty, and I'd appreciate some legal advice."

If she wasn't awake before, Skye's "highlights" were like ice water in her sleepy eyes. *Dead body?* "Sounds like you've been pretty busy." Something else Skye said was off. "Did you say 'we'? Who's there with you?"

"Aimee. She stuck around. She's kind of hard to shake."

Parker paused before answering. Skye's tone was more resigned than frustrated, but she decided now wasn't the time to ask about the change of plans. "Okay, how did Earl die?"

"Gunshot wound."

"Anything to tie you to the scene?"

"His body was outside the cabin. We found him after we entered the cabin and left our fingerprints everywhere. Someone before us had already broken the window. Oh, and Aimee took a tumble headfirst into his body. No telling if she left any trace evidence behind. For the most part, we haven't disturbed the scene, and any evidence left by whoever killed Earl should be intact."

"Great. My first instinct is for you to get out of there. I can call in a tip to the cops once you're gone."

"Sounds like a plan. Hang on a minute. Aimee's looking around the cabin to see if she can find an address. I'm going to help her and be right back."

"Sure." Parker set the phone down, sank into a chair, and yawned big. As she finished, she felt a warm blanket, followed by loving arms encircle her shoulders. She turned into Morgan's embrace.

"Hey, babe, kind of cold to be wandering around the house in your boxers, don't you think?"

Parker grinned. "Guess I forgot to grab a robe."

"I guess." Morgan nodded at the phone. "Client?"

"Kind of. It's Skye. She and Aimee ran into a jam." She quickly explained the situation. "You okay with the plan?" Parker valued Morgan's advice. Morgan had worked the defense side far longer than she had. Whatever agency showed up to investigate Earl's death would want to talk to the people who'd found the body, but she and Morgan could make arrangements to bring Skye and Aimee in for an interview later. She had one question she wanted the answer to now. She didn't have to wait long before Skye was back on the line.

"Hey, Parker, we got an address."

"Cool. Morgan's here. I'm putting you on speaker."

"Hi, Morgan. Sorry to wake you guys."

"Nature of the biz. Not like I need to tell you that."

Parker cleared her throat. "Skye, can Aimee hear us?"

"She's right here, but no."

"I hate to ask this, but do you think Nicki killed Earl?"

Beats of silence preceded Skye's answer. "To tell the truth, it hadn't occurred to me. I was more worried she'd met the same fate. No sign of that though."

"Okay. We'll worry about that when she turns up. Morgan talked to the prosecutor again. Based on her reaction, we're pretty sure you're on the right track with the militia connection. She's standing firm on her decision not to discuss the case until Nicki's in custody. I think it's time for you to give up the search. You think the feds are in your way? Once we report Earl's death, you're going to start tripping over cops. Jake should be free soon. We'll get him on it."

Skye glanced at Aimee. She owed it to both of them to finish this job. "No can do. We're working a lead, and I want to follow it through." She paused. "Look, I don't want to talk about it on a cell phone. I can fill you in tomorrow."

"Still stubborn, I see. Fine, we'll talk about it tomorrow. Give me that address."

As Skye rattled off the information, Morgan took over the conversation. "I know where that is. Skye, I can give you directions out of there if you need them."

"My bike broke down. We'll be walking, but we'll take any directions you have to give."

Morgan smiled. "I have a much better idea. Wait there."

CHAPTER EIGHTEEN

W ho's coming to pick us up?" Aimee asked.

Skye answered without interrupting her steady gaze out the front window of the cabin. "She didn't say exactly who, just that she knows people who live in the area. She was confident she could get us a ride out of here." Skye looked out the window for the umpteenth time since she'd disconnected the call with Parker and Morgan. She hoped whoever it was knew their way around the country roads in the dark. She'd turned off her phone as soon as she hung up the call.

"How will we know whoever shows up is a friend of Morgan and not the feds?"

"They'll flash their headlights three times and say Morgan's name."

"What if the feds were listening in on the call and heard that part of the instruction?"

Skye forced herself to be patient with Aimee and her questions. This was all new to her, and understandably scary. *Precisely why you shouldn't have let her come with you.* "They don't have that capability. Well, they do, but it's expensive and troublesome to use. Besides, they would have to have a wiretap warrant, and contrary to what you may hear, those are hard to come by. They're interested in following us to find her, but they're not going to go to the trouble to get a warrant to listen to us."

"If you say so."

Skye observed Aimee's folded arms and closed off demeanor, and softened her own stance in response. "Hey, Nicki's okay and we're going to find her."

"You don't know that."

You're right, I don't. And I don't usually make promises, especially ones I have no idea if I can keep. Skye didn't bother questioning her instinct to do so now. "We're going to find her and bring her home."

"I hope you're right. I just—"

Skye held up a hand to cut her off. "Look down there. I believe our ride has arrived." She drew her gun, but kept it behind her back. She wanted to be cautious, but she didn't want to scare the Good Samaritan Morgan had managed to drag out of bed to rescue them. "You wait here and I'll wave if the coast is clear." She shoved her helmet into her duffle bag, threw the bag over her shoulder, and started for the door.

Aimee was right on her heels. "Don't you know by now that you're not leaving me behind?"

"I guess I should." She sighed. "Come on." She reached out and Aimee grabbed her hand.

"Does it offend you to know I feel safer with you than without you?" Aimee asked.

Skye chuckled at the frank admission as she led the way to the waiting SUV. "No, it only surprises me. After all, the last time you followed me, you careened down a steep hill and fell face-first into a dead body." She experienced her own surprise at how natural, how right Aimee's hand felt, grasped in her own.

As they approached the waiting vehicle, the driver lowered the window and poked his head out. "Skye, Aimee?"

Skye motioned for Aimee to be quiet. "Who sent you?"

"Morgan Bradley."

Skye heard the click of the locks disengaging, and she opened the rear door. She helped Aimee inside, then slid into the seat beside her. The overhead light was on, and finally Skye could get a good look at their rescuer. She started to say thanks, but surprise robbed her breath.

Luckily, he spoke first. "Detective Keaton, good to see you again."

Aimee glanced back and forth between Skye and the driver, clearly picking up on their familiarity. Skye finally found words. "Good to see you too, Judge Bradley, although I must say you're probably the last person on earth I expected to see this evening."

He laughed and his good humor was infectious. "Call me John. I suppose you wouldn't necessarily know where I've chosen to spend my golden years. Morgan's mom and I have owned property down here for years, but now that I'm retired we can enjoy it year round." He turned his attention to Aimee. "John Bradley, at your service. I don't think we've met, but I know your father, Gordon, even if we run in different political circles."

Aimee was clearly unaffected by the late night appearance of a judge to escort them away from a crime scene. "Glad to meet you, Mr. Bradley. No offense, but would you mind if we put some distance between us and this spooky place?"

He laughed again and quickly complied. Skye thought it strange to hear someone address him as anything other than "judge." She'd appeared in Judge Bradley's felony court dozens of times as a witness for the state. The unwritten rule of courthouse etiquette was once you knew someone as a judge, they always merited the formal address. Of course, Aimee would only ever call him mister, and Morgan called him "Dad."

As they drove away, Skye felt she owed a duty of candor toward the judge. "Did Morgan fill you in on the circumstances?"

"She told me there's a body behind that cabin, and that you think you know who it is."

"Well, that's about the sum of it, except just to be clear, that's a crime scene back there."

John caught her eye in the rearview mirror. "I understand. Morgan tells me you came upon that body after the fact. She'll take care of reporting it and you'll make yourself available to the authorities to discuss what you found, am I right?"

"Yes, sir."

"Then I don't have any worries about helping out a couple of folks who happen to be stranded in the country." He gave them both a once-over. "No offense, ladies, but you look like you could use a hot meal and some rest. We'll take care of both once we get you to our cabin."

"Thank you." Skye spent the rest of the ride looking out the window. Morgan was lucky to have a father who took her at her word, trusted her to do the right thing. Skye reflected on her own father's reaction to her decision to finally do the right thing and suffer the consequences. She knew he hadn't fought for her to remain on the force, and the fact he'd found her a crappy security job was a sure signal of his disapproval. Where Morgan could do no wrong in her father's eyes, Skye could do nothing right. The realization stung.

The drive seemed short, and Skye wondered if she should have tried to find her way out of the woods without involving anyone else. When they pulled up in front of the judge's home, she almost laughed out loud. Judge Bradley's cabin was a mansion compared to the one-room shack in the woods they'd just left. The front porch featured tall cedar beams with an expansive outdoor seating area. The property appeared to be at least a couple thousand square feet. The judge opened the front door and invited them in. A large gourmet kitchen opened into a spacious den. She spied one closed door off to the right and a staircase to the upper floor to the left.

A woman entered the room from the kitchen greeting them warmly. "Hi, I'm Marilyn Bradley."

The warmth stayed, but concern flickered in her eyes as she focused on their disheveled appearance. "Are you two okay? I'll show you to your room and you can get settled in while I heat up some leftovers." She pointed to the staircase. "Right this way."

She took the stairs without waiting for a response. Her bustling manner reminded Skye of Aimee and her plunge-right-in attitude. As if she could hear her thoughts, Aimee grabbed her hand and tugged her along. Skye enjoyed the feel of Aimee's touch until they reached the threshold of a bedroom with one beautiful four-poster bed, and Marilyn announced, "We have a sofa bed in the study downstairs, but I think this room's more private." She opened the closet door.

"There are towels, robes, and a random assortment of clothes in here. Help yourselves. Come on down whenever you're ready."

She was gone before Skye finished processing her words. Aimee sank into the fluffy down comforter and leaned back into the pillows. "This sure beats sleeping in the woods."

Reality dawned and Skye shook her head. After the night they'd had, she'd have a hard enough time sleeping. She didn't need the added distraction of sharing a cushy bed with a sexy bed partner.

❖

Aimee patted the pillow beside her. "Take a load off. This bed feels great." Skye had become edgy ever since Marilyn had left the room. If she could get Skye to relax, maybe she could find a way inside.

Skye stood in place. "I'm good. I'm going to go see if I can find the judge and talk to him about locating my bike."

"Uh, Skye?" Aimee held up her wrist, and made a show of checking the time. "It's almost midnight. Do you honestly think you're going to find your bike in the middle of the night?" Skye's expression told her she hadn't thought her getaway plan through. "Besides, we just got here. Don't you think it would be rude to leave so soon?"

Skye gave in. She sat, more like she half sat, on the edge of the bed, but it was progress. Aimee offered small talk as a way to relax them both. "This is a nice place."

"It is."

"Out in the middle of nowhere has its appeal."

"I suppose."

"Are you going to give two word responses to everything I say?"

"No."

Skye cracked a smile, and Aimee laughed. "That's more like it." She sniffed the air. "Whatever Marilyn's cooking down there smells pretty darn good."

"I'm so hungry I could eat shoe leather."

"Then I'm glad all my Jimmy Choos are safe at home." Aimee wiggled her feet and admired her black leather bike boots. "Although I must say, I'm liking my new look."

Skye's grin was wide. "You make the boots look good." She hesitated then said, "Those shoes you were wearing at the bar? They were hot." Her voice was quiet, almost shy.

She noticed what I was wearing? Aimee wasn't sure how to respond. Skye was like a cat that shows you affection when it wants, then shies away the minute you initiate contact. Her desire told her to pursue the contact, but her instincts told her to approach with caution. She settled on neutrality.

"I dressed up that night. It was my birthday."

Skye reached out and brushed a strand of hair from her face. Her palm remained cupped on Aimee's cheek and she whispered. "Happy late birthday."

"Thanks." What was the wistful look on Skye's face?

"Every time I've seen you, you've been dressed up."

Aimee's laugh was bitter. "You should tell that to my mother. She thinks I'm a vagabond compared to the daughters of her friends. If it's not couture, you may as well stay home."

"I wouldn't know couture if it bit me in the ass."

"I'll take you to meet my mother. She'll tell you all about it."

"Sounds like an experience I'd rather avoid." Skye cocked her head. "I detect a hint of animosity. You don't get along with your mother?"

"Both of my parents think I'm deluded. They believe that one day their lesbian daughter will abandon her little business venture and return to the fold, marry well, and do her part in building the Howard empire."

Skye nodded. "Sounds rough. I—" She stopped abruptly.

This was the longest personal conversation they'd had and Aimee didn't want it to end. "What?"

Skye shook her head, but Aimee hung on. "What're your parents like?"

"My mom is a devoted wife and mother. She believes her duty in life is to cook, clean, and care for every need of my father. When my brothers and I lived at home, she did everything for us. She's the perfect housewife."

The muscles in Skye's jaw tightened as she talked. Skye hadn't mentioned her father, and Aimee debated delving further. The articles she'd read had supplied a few details. Skye's father and her brothers were all cops. What was it like for Skye to be summarily dismissed from the family business? Back at the compound, it was obvious Skye's cop instincts were deeply ingrained. She'd admitted she missed her career, but Aimee could tell the loss was as much personal as it was professional. Skye said she didn't want to talk about it, but she sensed the issue was the primary barrier to her giving in to their mutual attraction. She was determined to break through.

"It's hard to break from the family tradition."

Skye's expression was confused at first, then settled into granite. "I didn't."

"I mean—"

Skye cut her off in a cold, biting tone. "I know exactly what you mean. Look, I didn't choose not to be a cop. It was all I ever had. All I ever wanted. I dedicated my life to the department, but I had to leave."

The implication was clear—Aimee chose the break with her family, Skye hadn't been given a choice. Aimee felt the sting of her pain. She didn't doubt the source was genuine, and all she wanted to do was make it go away. Skye probably expected her chilly demeanor to make Aimee retreat, but it had exactly the opposite effect. She leaned in close, her mouth slightly parted, and slipped her arms around Skye's waist. Skye took her offering without hesitation. Their lips met and melted the barriers between them. The Skye who'd shied from any intimacy disappeared. This Skye couldn't get close enough. Without breaking the kiss, she edged her hands under Aimee's sweater. Aimee gasped at the feel of Skye's hands on her bare skin. She arched her back and urged Skye in.

The sensations were all over the place. Sweet, wild, commanding. She'd always been the one in charge, in charge of money, in charge of the house. She didn't want to be, but the parade of women she'd allowed in her life all looked to her to take care of them, see to their needs before her own. She did. It was the price she paid for companionship, and a fair exchange for never having to worry about whether they loved her because of her money. She knew they did.

Skye couldn't care less about her fortune. She loathed the trappings of Aimee's success. Yet, she needed the tender care Aimee had to offer more than any of the takers Aimee had let enter her heart and her home. Skye's gruff exterior housed a tender soul, one broken by the betrayal of her professional family. She no longer cared about Skye's past except to want to be there for her as she healed from the wounds it had inflicted. Skye would never ask for what she needed, but Aimee desperately wanted to give—her love, her care, herself. She pulled Skye close and savored the moment, hoping it would last.

Skye floated through the air, and everything fell away. She and Aimee were the only two people in the world. Aimee's lips, her hands, her tongue, were soft, tender, inviting. She reveled in the luxury of weightlessness. Aimee's touch was the only reality, and it told her truths. She cared. Hers was not the rapid seeking of release that Skye knew well from her conquests at the bar. Those women sought climax, quick and sure, over and over. She'd given them what they wanted. She didn't blame them for the shallow need. She'd told herself her needs were shallow too.

But were they? Did she really enjoy the emptiness that always followed a night of drinking and fucking? Stumbling from strangers' beds, dragging the floor for the scattered pieces of her clothing— was that her desire?

No. She desired more, but didn't deserve it. She'd lowered the barriers a couple of times, but raised them quickly when she learned compromise between her personal and professional life was required. She didn't have a professional life anymore. She'd been kicked off the force, and her first gig as a private investigator was destined to be her last. She failed to find the girl, failed to keep anyone from getting hurt, failed to maintain the boundary between herself and her client.

The weightlessness was gone. Heavy sadness settled on her shoulders. The tenderness was still there, but she couldn't feel it. She wasn't supposed to have what Aimee was offering, and she wasn't going to take it.

She pulled away. Aimee's half-lidded eyes reflected dreams she'd never permit herself to have. She detached herself from Aimee's grasp and stood. "I have to go." The statement was lame. She wasn't sure why she said anything at all, but it seemed the only way to transition from what had happened to what wouldn't.

"Where?"

Anywhere, but here. "I need to talk to the judge."

"I'll come with you."

"No."

"No?" Aimee's expression slowly moved from dreamy to aware. Skye saw a flicker of hurt, and she hated her own harshness even as she cloaked herself in it.

"We can't do this." She waved her hand back and forth between them.

"This?" Aimee echoed, and then ignored the boundary she erected, and moved back into Skye's space. "Sure we can." She circled her arms around Skye's waist and rested her head on her shoulder. "*This* feels good. Doesn't it?"

It did. It felt great. But it could never be. Skye placed her hands on Aimee's arms and gently pushed her away. "You're my client."

"As I recall, you made it perfectly clear you work for Morgan and Parker."

"And I never will again if they find out I had sex with one of their clients."

"Sex, huh? Well, you seem pretty sure of yourself. I thought we were just kissing."

"What?" Skye practically shouted her indignation.

"Calm down, I'm kidding. Of course I want more. Don't tell me you don't."

"I don't," Skye lied.

"Bullshit." Aimee's smile was at odds with the harsh word.

"Seriously, Aimee. We can't do this. I have a job to do, and I'm far from finished."

"And, as your employer, I'm prescribing a break for you."

Skye stood and walked across the room. When she turned back to face Aimee, she shook with anger. "Here's what you don't get. You're my client, not my employer. Morgan and Parker hired me. They gave me a real job when no one else would. No one.

"I have to find Nicki. If we don't, you'll go back to your fancy Highland Park home and move on with your life. I, on the other hand, will be forced to dress up in a polyester cop wannabe uniform and go back to protecting cars during the graveyard shift." She swept her gaze over Aimee's body, the only caress she dared give. "Sex with you would be fantastic in the moment, but when you go back to your life and I go back to mine, it'll just be one more thing I can never have again."

Skye didn't wait for a response before she left the room.

CHAPTER NINETEEN

Aimee watched the door close behind Skye. Her emotions ranged from defensive to defeated. She hadn't meant to make Skye angry, but she didn't deserve to bear the brunt of it either. It wasn't her fault Skye had no options. Skye's future pitfalls were the result of her choices in the past, not any she'd make here, with her, in the present.

What kind of information was in Skye's sealed police personnel file? Was it the key to her distance? Or were the walls around her heart erected in response to a personal, rather than professional, disaster? She desperately wanted to know, but feared she'd never have answers. She'd tried. Lieutenant Dawson and Parker had offered tidbits, but stonewalled when it came to detail. Of course, at the time, she'd been more concerned about whether Skye was worthy of a job. The prospect of wanting more from Skye hadn't even crossed her mind.

Hadn't it? From the moment she'd seen her, she'd wanted to fold herself in her strong arms. Their attraction had been immediate, sure, and mutual. Skye couldn't hide the fact she felt it too. She'd stopped trying. What had she said? *Sex with you would be fantastic. In the moment.*

Aimee knew it would be fantastic for more than just the moment. She knew if Skye would open up to her, she wouldn't want the moment to end. Would Skye? Was that what Skye was afraid of, the possibility of wanting more? She realized her desire for Skye went far beyond a physical craving. She wanted to curl inside her, learn her truths, embrace her weakness, and soothe her soul. She wanted to feel her strength, share the load, and relinquish her control to Skye's command. She knew what these feelings were, even though she'd never had them before. Love was a word she bandied about whenever she'd selected her latest catch. What she felt for Skye was completely different from anything she'd ever felt before, and she knew only these feelings were worthy to be called love. She vowed she'd never be careless with the word again.

❖

Aimee, dressed in a pair of sweats she'd found hanging in the upstairs closet, found Marilyn alone in the spacious kitchen, standing over a huge stockpot on the stove. Neither Skye nor Mr. Bradley were anywhere in sight.

"Hi, Aimee, are you hungry?" Marilyn didn't wait for an answer. She ladled steaming stew into a large bowl and pushed it her way. "I hope you like beef stew. I made this yesterday, and it's had time to settle and absorb all the flavors. Pull up a chair."

"Sorry I took so long up there. I desperately needed a shower." She nodded her head toward the bowl of stew. "It looks great." She'd lost her appetite after the scene with Skye, but she didn't want to seem impolite. Aimee blew on a spoon of the hot stew before forcing herself to take a small bite. She groaned. "This is amazing. Thank you. I didn't realize how hungry I was."

"I'm glad you like it. Secret family recipe. I can write it down for you if you like." Marilyn's grin was infectious, and Aimee couldn't help but smile despite the turmoil she felt inside. Where was Skye? She could hear quiet voices coming from the closed study door. Was she in there?

She looked up to see Marilyn following her gaze. "John's in there with your friend. I think they're plotting."

My friend? Aimee held back a laugh. They'd gone straight from strangers to almost lovers, skipping the friend part entirely. Maybe if she was Skye's friend, she would have better insight into the source of her pain, could help her find a way through it. Friendship wasn't all she wanted, but it was a start. "I should join them since it's my niece they're plotting about." She stood and walked toward the closed door.

Marilyn placed a hand on her arm. "Actually, Skye asked to speak to John alone. I swore we wouldn't interrupt. Give them a few minutes. I'm sure she'll come get you."

Aimee returned to her chair. She wasn't so sure. She'd continually pushed the boundaries Skye had erected with no regard for Skye's feelings. The parade of women she'd moved in and out of her home over the years had never minded when she directed the show. As long as her money and position afforded them all the worldly trappings they wanted, they were happy to relinquish control.

Skye was different. Her ability to control was her armor. She would never barter her power away. Aimee regretted every one of her careless remarks about how she was Skye's boss, how her money was funding the investigation, how her decisions were final. Why should she be surprised that Skye wouldn't be vulnerable to her? She'd made it clear she was responsible for Skye's professional success.

It may be too late to keep Skye from shutting down, but she resolved to stop acting like an ass.

She set her spoon down. "Marilyn, your stew is delicious, but I'm exhausted. Would you mind if I went upstairs? I need to lie down."

"Of course not. No offense, but you look exhausted."

"I am."

"What should I tell Skye?"

"Tell her...tell her I'm sorry I missed her, that whatever plan she makes will be perfect." *I only hope it includes me.*

❖

Skye described what she and Aimee had found at the cabin and finished with, "Judge, I'd rather not involve you in any of this."

Judge Bradley motioned Skye to a chair. "You didn't call me. My daughter did." He smiled. "Looks like I'm already involved. Morgan filled me in on the details of your investigation and asked me to do whatever I can to help. What's up next?"

Skye considered. "My Harley's out in the woods somewhere and it won't start. Hopefully, it's just a loose wire or simple short in the ignition switch, either of which I can fix, but if not, I'll need to find a mechanic." She pulled a piece of paper from her pocket. "I have the directions to the compound. I don't think it's far away. We drove for a while after we left there, but it was mostly in circles. If I can get back there, I can probably find it. It's not new, but it's very valuable to me and would be to anyone who finds it."

"Not in the dark you won't. Get a good night's sleep, and I'll take you in the morning. We don't get much traffic around here at night. It'll be safe until morning. Once we find it, we'll get a tow service to bring it here so you can take a look at it and decide what needs to be done."

Skye shuddered at the thought of being without wheels for who knew how long. As if he could read her mind, the judge said, "I have an old pickup out back. You're welcome to it for as long as you need."

Skye started to decline, before she remembered the list of supplies Davis had handed her before they left the assembly the night before. No way could she carry all that stuff on her bike, and they better show with at least some of it when they arrived at their meeting the next day. A pickup truck was the perfect solution.

If the plan was still on. She wasn't sure Aimee would want to do anything with her ever again. She could hardly blame her. She'd acted like the burn of Aimee's touch was painful when it was anything but. The only pain she'd felt was the sting of knowing she could never have what Aimee offered. The sex would be mind-blowing, but it would end. And when it did, Aimee would return to her pampered and privileged life while Skye picked up the pieces of her shattered existence.

This time the loss would be total. She'd thought her success centered around her career, but for the first time in her life, she wanted more. She wasn't sure when it happened, but somewhere along the way, her attraction to Aimee had become more than sexual. She respected her, admired her, liked her even. In Aimee's arms, for the briefest of moments, she'd let herself dream she could have everything.

The dream died as quickly as it came. She'd be lucky to come out of this with one thing, a salvaged career. She would focus all her efforts on finding Nicki, and move on.

"Skye?"

She looked up into Judge Bradley's concerned eyes. She must've drifted off. "I'm sorry, sir. I guess I'm more tired than I realized."

"You've had a tough year."

Skye caught the reference. The retired Dallas judge no doubt still kept up with headline cases back in his old jurisdiction. She nodded. "I have."

"You were a good cop."

Skye had testified in his court numerous times before he retired. She didn't remember specific cases, but she knew he would probably remember her trademarks: self-confident, well-spoken, friendly toward the jury, and unflappable to the defense. He had seen her at her best. He had never seen her shortcuts, never had to toss evidence she'd gathered because she'd skated the rules.

"I wasn't always. Your daughter-in-law could tell you stories."

"I doubt Parker would ever reveal a confidence." He paused. "We knew the Burkes, and since Morgan and Parker were both involved in the case, I followed it closely. All Parker's ever said about you is that you were the reason Teddy Burke was finally off the streets."

"Respectfully, sir, there's a lot more to it than that."

"There usually is." He leaned back in his chair. "You know, Skye, I was on the bench for thirty years. As much as my job was to protect the process, I've come to realize that sometimes the process protects the wrong people. In those cases, the outcome is really all that matters." He lowered his voice to a whisper. "If you ever tell my zealous daughters I said that, I will deny it to the grave."

Skye returned his chuckle. "Thank you, sir." She stood and looked at her watch. One a.m. "I'm sorry to keep you up. I didn't realize it was so late."

"Don't worry about me. I'm a night owl. But I imagine you're going to want to check on your bike first thing. Why don't you head on to bed so we can get an early start?"

As Skye trudged up the stairs to the room where she'd left Aimee, she realized what she really needed was a *new* start.

Aimee woke to the sound of light groans. She'd fallen asleep in her clothes, on top of the covers while she waited for Skye to come to their room. Heavy shades blocked out all light, and she had no idea what time it was. She felt the space beside her, but no one else was in the bed. A few fumbles on the nightstand, and she located the switch for a small lamp. In the dim light, she saw Skye across the room, curled up in a hardback rocking chair, shaking and moaning. Her arms were wrapped tightly around her chest, and at first Aimee thought she was cold. She grabbed a blanket from the bed and tiptoed across the room. As she covered Skye's restless, sleeping form, she considered waking her, inviting her to bed. She looked uncomfortable, thrashing about, but Skye had chosen the chair over the bed, and Aimee respected her choice. She couldn't resist one selfish act before she returned to bed. She leaned forward and kissed Skye lightly on the forehead.

As she turned back toward the bed, her arm was jerked behind her.

"No!" Skye yelled, as she wrestled Aimee to the floor. "Get out!"

Aimee gasped, her face pressed into the rug by the side of the bed, and Skye's weight on her back. "Skye, it's me. Aimee. Let me go!"

Suddenly, Skye released her arm and stood. Aimee rolled over, but she remained on the floor, unsure about her next move. Skye's eyes were wild, and Aimee wasn't sure she was fully awake. Skye leaned against the bed and slid to the floor. Aimee scooted over next to her, more concerned about Skye's condition than she was about another attack. She tugged Skye's head onto her shoulder and stroked her hair. "Skye, baby, it's okay, baby. I've got you. You're safe. You're safe."

❖

Skye was bound tight, facedown on the floor. She was no longer a danger to him—his well-timed kicks to her kidneys were all for sport. Blood ran down her face from where he'd struck her with the pistol when she opened the door. The blood pooled on the wood floor beneath her face. She choked on the metallic smell. She passed out before he tired of kicking her. When she woke up, she was still bound, on her back now, metal springs an inch above her face. She was under her bed. She cried for help, but the tape on her mouth rendered her silent.

Finally, she stopped crying out. No one could hear her. She'd brought this on herself. She was going to die because she'd been so interested in an easy conviction, she'd let a psychopath go free. She struggled to move, but she only succeeded in moving a few inches. Her eyelids felt heavy. If she could pass out again, the pain might go away. She closed her eyes and willed herself unconscious. As her world turned gray, she heard a voice calling her name.

"Skye, Skye."

Hands reached out to her. Her eyes fluttered open. Aimee was stroking her head, murmuring comfort.

"What happened?"

"Bad dream?" Aimee said.

Dream, no. Nightmare, yes. She felt the cold sweat pool under her clothes. She was used to it, although it had been at least a week since she'd woken to her own cries. Skye shuddered. The haze was gone, and she remembered where she was. Ironic she should have the dream in Morgan's parents' home. If it weren't for their daughter-in-law, she would have died that day.

She struggled to sit up. "I'm okay."

Aimee gradually loosened her hold, but she didn't let go. "You have dreams like that often?"

Skye looked into Aimee's eyes, and she saw her own pain reflected there. Her instinct was to turn away, but instead she held her gaze and answered, "I do."

"Care to talk about it?"

She didn't. Beyond a few sessions with the department shrink, she never had. She was as surprised as Aimee when she started talking.

"About a year ago, I worked the Camille Burke case. Surely you heard about it?"

Aimee nodded.

"Then you must know how it turned out. I stacked the deck, but it turns out all my instincts were wrong. I've paid the price. Teddy Burke beat me unconscious. Almost killed me. The job covered up my transgressions, but they kicked me out as soon as I did my part and testified against him. The nightmares are my souvenir."

Aimee's expression hadn't changed; the compassion was still there. Skye had no other explanation for why she kept talking.

"He rang my doorbell. He was wearing a hat, carrying a clipboard. Oldest trick in the book. When I opened the door, he knocked me out with the butt of his pistol. While I was unconscious, he tied me up, and then he beat me. Parker saved my life. Of course, the nightmare doesn't end that way. He just keeps beating me, over and over." Her voice trailed off as she felt Aimee's arms slide around her waist. She didn't move away. Instead, she shared another secret.

"The Burke case wasn't the first time I crossed the line. I made a habit of it."

If Aimee was shocked, she didn't show it. "Seems like the department enjoyed the benefit of your transgressions. Why did they let you go?"

"I ratted myself out. The ultimate sin. I could break all the rules I wanted as long as I didn't get caught." She feigned nonchalance. "It was time to move on."

"You still have plenty of admirers in the department."

She sized Aimee up. "You checked me out?"

"I did." Aimee didn't even try to act embarrassed. "I'm sorry I pried."

"It's okay." Skye wasn't upset. Instead, she felt strangely relieved to have shared as much as she did.

"Why don't you get some sleep? We have a busy day tomorrow." Aimee stood and tugged her to her feet. "Get in the bed. I swear I'll keep my hands to myself."

"I'm sorry about earlier." She fumbled for words to describe her need and why she couldn't give in to it. "I didn't mean to hurt you."

"Shh. We're good." Aimee patted her on the shoulder. "Let's find Nicki, and then you can go back to your life and I'll go back to mine."

Skye didn't have the energy to argue. She hauled herself into bed and closed her eyes. As she faded into sleep, visions of Aimee, not Teddy Burke filled her dreams, and she wondered what life would be like without her.

CHAPTER TWENTY

Skye wasn't there when Aimee woke. Through sleepy eyes, she glanced at the clock on the nightstand. Ten a.m. She hadn't meant to sleep late, but she could use another few hours before she felt human again. Propped against the clock was a folded piece of paper with her name printed neatly on the outside.

> *Aimee,*
>
> *I've gone with the judge to take care of my bike.*
> *I'll meet you back here.*
> *Sleep in. You'll need the rest.*
>
> *Skye*

Had Skye ducked out early because she was embarrassed about her revelations from the night before? Or was the idea of waking up next to her distasteful?

She remembered her own words from the night before, "You can go back to your life and I'll go back to mine."

Why had she said that? She hadn't meant it. After only a week, she couldn't imagine her life without Skye in it, but she had just as much trouble when she tried to picture how Skye would fit into her life back in Dallas. Funny, all the women she'd brought into her home loved her wealth and the access her position afforded them, but she'd never stopped to consider whether they would before she'd invited them in. It wasn't that she hadn't cared about the other women, but she'd always known, at least subconsciously, they were interesting stops along her life's journey, but not the destination. The incredibly strong emotional attraction she felt for Skye signaled destiny. What Skye thought, what she felt, mattered to her. She could tell Skye hadn't cared for the expensive trappings of her home, and would hate her fast-paced event schedule. But she sensed Skye had come to respect her and their interactions were now laced with desire rather than resentment. She wanted to explore these new feelings, and she sensed that despite her resistance, Skye did as well. Would they be able to find a common ground?

She traced a finger over the writing on Skye's note and saved those concerns for another time. Now she had to focus on the search for Nicki, not dwell on unlikely possibilities.

She considered exploring downstairs for coffee, but decided on a shower instead to wake herself up. The hot steam from the shower brought her back to life. She stayed under the pounding stream until the water ran cold. When she stepped out, she reached for the robe she'd left hanging on the door hook and noticed its twin hanging on the hook beside it. Skye must have used it earlier. She drew it to her face and breathed deeply before placing it back on the hook.

Dressed in her own robe, she opened the door. Skye sat on the edge of the bed, dressed in a fresh outfit with a couple of shopping bags beside her.

"I went to the hotel and picked up our things."

"Thank God." She sashayed in her robe. "I don't think the patriots would approve of me showing up in a robe."

Skye shot her a look of approval. "I doubt they'd mind."

Aimee ignored the veiled compliment. "Beat it. I need to get dressed. We only have a couple hours before we have to meet with the motley crew. We should probably get those supplies so they think we're serious."

"Already done."

"Well, you've had a busy morning haven't you?"

"I couldn't sleep. Decided I may as well be productive."

Aimee flinched inside. She should have ignored her promise to leave Skye alone. If she'd held Skye through the night, she could have chased the demons away. She changed the subject. "Have you figured out how we find our way back to the racetrack? And what about your bike? Is it fixed? How are we going to haul all those supplies?"

Skye laughed. Aimee shot her a mock glare. "What's so funny?"

"You've graduated to quadruple questions." Skye raised a hand and ticked off the answers on her fingers. "My bike's being towed here, I need more time to check it out and either fix it myself or find a shop in the area. In the meantime, the Bradleys have offered us the use of a pickup, and I have a map that will get us back to the racetrack. Did I cover everything?"

"You did."

"Okay, now that we've checked off your list, I have a checklist of my own." Skye paused and cleared her throat. "Have a seat."

"Sounds serious." Aimee sat on the edge of the bed. She shoved her hands underneath her thighs to keep from tapping them nervously on the mattress. "What's up?"

"About today. I've worked out an alternate plan. I'll show up for the meeting and convince White you've given me control over your vast wealth. I'll get whatever information I can find out about Nicki, then report back."

"You're cutting me out."

"No."

"Yes, you are."

"These people are dangerous. Don't tell me you didn't feel a wave of anger at the meeting last night? This guy White has only just begun to get that crowd stirred up. I have a bad feeling about today."

Aimee's instinct was to push back. No way was she going to let Skye cut her out now, especially not if they were drawing closer to finding Nicki. She studied Skye's face, but saw no signs of a power grab. No, she saw only concern. She flashed back to the image of Earl Junior's body. "You're really worried, aren't you?"

Skye didn't hesitate. "Yes."

"Then let's call the whole thing off. Go back to Dallas. We'll talk to Morgan and Parker. Make a new plan."

"You aren't serious?"

Aimee studied Skye's incredulous expression, and knew she'd found her hook. "Oh, but I am. If you show up without me, White will get suspicious. You'd be better off not showing up at all."

Skye didn't say anything for what seemed like an eternity. Finally, she stood, strode across the room, and pulled something from one of the bags. As she turned, Aimee gasped when she recognized the gun in Skye's hand.

"Where did you get that?"

"The store." She handed it over, grip first.

Aimee hefted the Taurus Judge in her hand. It was a big gun, but the weight felt good. "Mine is blue."

"Of course it is."

"What is that supposed to mean?"

Skye smirked. "Nothing." She reached back into the bag and pulled out a couple boxes of ammo. "I wasn't sure if you preferred forty-five or four ten bore shot. I got both." She tossed the boxes on the bed. "Guess we're on for our meeting. Bring your big-ass handbag this time. I'll see you downstairs."

Skye left before she could respond.

Aimee entered the kitchen and found Skye and the Bradleys clustered around the large table. "What's up?"

Skye answered first. "I figured we could use an extra set of eyes on Earl Junior's stuff." She picked up Earl's diary. "Marilyn thinks those numbers you found may be wire transfer confirmations."

"Occupational hazard." Marilyn raised her hands in the air. "I'm a retired banker."

Aimee sat on the bench seat next to Skye. "Let me see." She thumbed through the book, noting the dates on the entries. "There's something familiar about these dates." She tapped her fingers on the table in an effort to jog her memory. "Hey, do you still have Nicki's bank records?"

Skye shook her head. "They went missing after the feds visited my motel room."

"No problem." She turned to the Bradleys. "Any chance you have a computer I can use?"

Judge Bradley returned within moments, laptop in hand. "We may be out in the boonies, but there's a wireless card attached."

Aimee launched the Internet site for Nicki's bank and selected the account Nicki shared with the mysterious William P. Gale. As Skye leaned close to watch over her shoulder, she tried to ignore their close proximity, an increasingly difficult proposition. She gave Skye a task to keep her busy. "Read out the dates with the odd notations in Earl's diary."

As Skye called out the dates, Aimee checked the online records. A pattern quickly developed. "Earl was tracking the deposits into this account. Every single one of the transfers is represented in his diary."

"Who's William Gale?" the judge asked.

Aimee thought she knew the answer. "Maybe Earl was posing as this Gale person, although I don't get why she would use her real name and he wouldn't use his."

Skye leaned in close again. "Google that name. William P. Gale."

Aimee typed in the words for the search. Dozens of results showed up on the screen. She read a few tidbits out loud. "'Racial and National Identity, a Sermon by the Rev. William P. Gale…' 'William P. Gale became an honorary member of the Ku Klux Klan…' 'William P. Gale, the self-styled minister who headed the white supremacist Posse Comitatus and other racist groups has died…' I don't get it. Do you think she opened an account with this guy? He's dead."

Judge Bradley answered before Skye could. "He's dead, but his spirit lives on. He was one of the original all-American terrorists. Under the guise of his church, he preached his anti-government, intolerant views. Unfortunately, lots of people listened to him."

"Still do," Skye added. "It's been a while, but I worked a task force with the Feds around the time of the Oklahoma bombing. Gales's writings influenced people like Timothy McVeigh and Terry Nichols, and unfortunately renewed their movement. You'd think an event like that would drive them underground, but headlines only cause more of them to come looking for limelight."

Aimee shuddered. "All I know is they seemed like a bunch of kooks."

"You're right and that's exactly what makes them dangerous. They think the government is conspiring to take away their basic rights, so they believe they're perfectly justified in defying the government in whatever way they deem necessary. They don't believe in regulations, taxes, or banks—anything that represents a restriction on their basic rights to fire guns, keep all their money, and say 'fuck you' to Uncle Sam." Skye's face turned red. "Sorry, Judge, Mrs. Bradley."

Marilyn smiled. "Don't tell anyone, but I've heard my husband utter similar words, although usually in reference to other lawyers."

"I still don't understand how Nicki got caught up with these people," Aimee said. "I understand youthful rebellion, believe me I do, but this goes way beyond thumbing your nose at authority. If the feds pick her up, she could go to prison. Right?"

"One step at a time. We don't even know what the charge is. There's no way to predict what will happen. Besides, you've hired the best lawyers in the business. Right, Judge?"

"That's right, Aimee." He held up a small stack of papers on the table in front of him. "What are these? Did you find them with Earl's things?"

"No, we got those from one of her professors, Mike Drees. They're story pitches Nicki turned in."

The judge handed one of them to Aimee. "Have you read this?"

Aimee skimmed the page. "Looks like she wanted to write a story about extremist militia groups. Maybe she lost her journalistic distance and bought into their rhetoric."

"Read it again. There's a tone there. When she wrote this pitch, I think she shared our beliefs that these people are dangerous."

Aimee read the paper again. "You know, I think you're right. I wonder what changed her mind."

Skye stood. She'd hoped the final review of the evidence they'd amassed so far would give them additional insights, but she wasn't sure what they'd found. If Nicki thought the group was dangerous, why would she have arranged for thousands of dollars to be wired to them?

"We need to get going." She shook Judge Bradley's hand. "Thanks for your help, sir. I'll get your truck back to you as soon as possible."

"Don't worry about it." He led her out of the room and lowered his voice. "I don't mean to question your judgment, but…"

She followed his gaze to Aimee who was saying good-bye to Marilyn back in the kitchen. She shook her head. "I know, but I can't convince her to stay behind. She's likely to follow me if I go by myself."

"Strong women are always a challenge." He chuckled. "I've been surrounded by them all my life. Absolutely worth it. But seriously, Skye, be careful."

She nodded. She had no intention of being anything but.

As they pulled out of the driveway, Aimee asked, "Are you sure you know your way out of here?"

Skye patted a folder on her lap. "I brought a good ole fashioned GPS with me." She kept one hand on the wheel and used the other to open the folder and draw out a piece of paper. "Look—a map. I asked the judge to write out some directions that would take us in the opposite direction of the cabin. Morgan called the Hays County sheriff in the wee hours. When we drove by this morning, the place was still crawling with cops."

"Do you think…I mean, how will we know if…?"

Skye reached over and squeezed her arm. She knew exactly what Aimee wanted to know. "If they find Nicki, they'll call Morgan. Lord knows they'll be even more interested in talking to whoever found the first body if they find another."

Aimee's wince signaled that her attempt at sensitivity had failed miserably. "Sorry. Look, I don't think they're going to find Nicki. We are. Alive."

"How will Morgan call us? You made me leave my phone."

"Check out the glove compartment." Aimee pulled out two cell phones. Skye had carefully managed the packing for this venture. She'd made Aimee leave her iPhone and all identification behind. Aimee's big handbag contained two bundles of cash, ammo, her new revolver, and nothing else. She'd left her own phone and wallet behind. She'd told Aimee the same story from the night before about not wanting the militia members to be able to identify them, but she also wanted to have some wiggle room if the feds happened to catch up with them. That last she kept to herself. Aimee didn't need anything else to worry about.

"Phones?"

"Prepaid cell phones. Can't be traced. I gave the number to the judge. He'll make sure Morgan and Parker can reach us if anything comes up. There's one for each of us. I programmed the number for mine into yours and vice versa."

Aimee shot her a look of admiration. "You sure had a busy morning."

"Like I said, I wasn't sleeping. Besides, you're paying me to get results. Right?"

"You've exceeded all my expectations."

Aimee's look was seductive. Skye almost bantered back. Totally out of character. She cleared her throat and changed the subject. "Let's talk about the plan."

"Fine."

Skye could tell Aimee's pout was all play. She forced herself to focus. "They're going to try and get you alone. You're the one with the money. Make up whatever excuse you need, but don't let them separate us. Understood?"

"But, Sister Samantha, what about your drills with Brother Davis?"

"Drills my ass. Ten bucks says their drills consist of firing high-powered rifles at beer cans lined up on a fence rail."

❖

When they finally pulled into the parking lot at the racetrack, Skye sensed something was off. Davis and White both leaned against a fully loaded Ford F350 Dually pickup, and there were no other cars in sight.

"I thought we were here for another meeting."

Skye kept her eyes on the men as she responded to Aimee. "Me too. Something's up. Remember what I said. Keep your handbag close. If they ask you if you're armed, say 'Hell yes, it's my second amendment right.' Don't let them take your gun, and stick close to me."

"I know, I know. Don't elaborate on our story. I'll watch you for cues." Aimee flashed a smile and its brightness almost caused Skye's concern to fade. She was used to troubleshooting undercover situations, but she was usually by herself or accompanied by other experienced detectives. Grudgingly, she acknowledged Aimee had done as well or better than some of the newly minted vice cops she'd worked with in the past. She'd been protective of them too, but her instincts toward Aimee carried an extra layer. Even if she couldn't have a life with her, she wouldn't be able to live her own if something happened to Aimee.

Davis waved. They'd been sitting in the car too long. Time to get out and take the next step. She reached across the seat and squeezed Aimee's hand. "Let's go."

CHAPTER TWENTY-ONE

S isters, thank you for joining us on this fine day," White's voice boomed. His eyes were dark and hard, his smile wide and insincere.

"Greetings, Brother White, Brother Davis." Skye pointed back to their vehicle. "We've purchased the supplies you suggested."

White rubbed his hands together. "Excellent."

"I thought there would be another gathering here today."

White responded to Skye with his eyes focused on Aimee. "Oh, there is. We plan to show you the new capital of the coalition. It's not far from here." He stalled as if uncomfortable about his next request. "Many of our people have made sacrifices on behalf of the cause. I understand your enlightenment is a recent one, but a show of good faith would allow the others to embrace you as one of our own."

Aimee shot a quick look at Skye who gave her a slight nod. She reached into her purse and pulled out one of the thick bundles of cash. White stared at the money, but she didn't hand it over right away. "Of course, Brother White. I had hoped to secure one of the gold bars to bring to you this morning as a token of our allegiance, but my late husband believed in the security of banks and I wasn't able to gain access this morning." She dangled the cash in his direction. "Please accept this as our pledge to the cause."

Judging by the way he snatched the stack of cash from her hand and lovingly thumbed the bills, the government-issued greenbacks weren't as offensive as his previous rhetoric indicated. He placed the bundle in his coat pocket. "Thank you, sister. Would you like to see where your pledge will be put to use?"

"We would love to." Aimee stepped closer to Skye in an effort to make it clear they both wanted in on the fun.

White ignored her efforts. He looped his arm through Aimee's. "Excellent. You and I have much to discuss. Davis will ride with Samantha."

Aimee placed a hand on White's arm and gave it a gentle squeeze. "I would love to ride with you, but I can't."

"Of course you can. I insist."

She'd started talking without a clue as to what she would ultimately say. Skye's furrowed brow told her she better think of something quick, but she couldn't. Skye obviously knew how to drive. They'd seen her pull up in the truck. A host of explanations ran through her head, but none of them were plausible. She and Skye were both armed. If they were all going to the same place, it wasn't like they would be separated for long. She avoided Skye's penetrating stare and announced, "Okay. I'd be honored to ride with you, Brother White."

Skye had no choice except to lead Davis to the Bradleys' pickup. She hoped the drive was short. She didn't want to have to make up small talk about her time in the service and their mutual hatred of big brother government. She especially did not want to discuss Nicki Howard since she and Aimee hadn't discussed how they'd keep their story straight on that front.

Once again, she'd made a mess of things. She never should have allowed Aimee to come with her today. Her only hope was to get Davis to talk about the "cause," and then get Aimee alone as soon as they arrived at their destination. She needn't have worried. Her initial volley triggered a steady stream of one-sided chatter. "Brother Davis, we saw the compound at Wimberley. Tell me what you have planned for the new venture."

"No offense to our captured brethren, but the Wimberley compound was nothing compared to our new location."

"Really?"

"Absolutely. The Wimberley compound was child's play. The only structure was a portable building. No furnishings. Not enough space to house the means of our defense, and certainly not an adequate base from which to launch a revolution."

He droned on for a while about the injustices they were rebelling against and Skye uttered occasional grunts of agreement to keep him going. After about thirty minutes, he finally lost interest in hearing himself talk. As he drummed his fingers on the steering wheel, Skye took advantage of the break in conversation to search for a road sign. She considered asking him where they were going, but she didn't want to invite a back and forth. It seemed they were headed back in the direction of Wimberley, but by a different route. Would the coalition risk placing a new compound near the one the feds had raided?

She decided it was a brilliant idea. The authorities wouldn't expect them to regroup in such close proximity to the old compound, and it would be convenient for the locals who'd already thrown in with the "cause."

Apparently, Davis had used the silence to come to a decision. He confided in Skye. "You know, the compound at Wimberley was merely a training ground." He paused as if for emphasis. "Our Supreme Leader didn't bother to keep the location a secret."

Skye tamped down the urge to barrage him with questions. He was revealing a crucial fact, and she didn't want to scare him off. "Is that so?"

"Yes. Clever, don't you think?"

Hell, yes. And crazy too. If Skye was reading these revelations correctly, the so-called Supreme Leader must have known the feds were on to them. He'd set up a makeshift compound and allowed some of his blind followers to be captured in order to throw off the scent of his real enterprise. Was he at the new compound now, waiting for them to arrive?

She reflected on the night before when they'd met White and his expression when Aimee had mentioned Nicki's name. He'd acted like he knew who they were talking about. Was Nicki with the leader at the new compound? If she was with him, then she wasn't one of the ones he'd chosen to sacrifice. She must be more deeply involved than they had originally suspected. If that was the case, convincing her to leave with them was going to be more challenging than they thought.

After all they'd gone through to find Nicki, Aimee would be heartbroken if they failed to save her. But Nicki was an adult and they couldn't force her to leave the coalition. Skye hoped she could get Nicki to listen to reason, not because it was her job, but because bringing her home safe and sound was what Aimee wanted. As upset as she was at Aimee for allowing them to be separated, she'd go to any lengths to give Aimee what she wanted.

Aimee stifled a yawn. White had sucked up to her the entire drive. He yammered on and on about the new compound and its superiority. He made it clear there was still work to be done and her contributions would make her a true patriot.

"It's very fortunate that you chose this particular weekend to seek out the coalition."

Aimee perked up. When they parted back at the racetrack, Skye had been concerned about her safety. She needn't have. All White had done was bore her to death. Maybe he was finally ready to reveal important information. She joined in the conversation to encourage him to keep talking. "I believe all things happen for a reason. Don't you?"

"I do. Today we gather to welcome those that were lost. The oppressors have not vanquished us. We shall regroup and regain our strength, and our cause shall be triumphant!"

Aimee was tempted to look around to make sure they were the only ones in the vehicle. This guy probably preached to himself in the shower, so she wasn't sure why she was surprised by his exuberant sermon for one. *Those that were lost?* Could Nicki be one of those?

The prospect was both exciting and scary. What would she say if she saw Nicki? "Hey, crazy girl, why'd you hook up with these wackos?" No, probably something more along the lines of, "Thanks for running on the wrong side of the law because if you hadn't, I never would have met Skye Keaton."

She snuck a look in the side mirror. Skye and Davis were only a few car lengths behind, but they may as well be miles away. With her big Taurus in the bag beside her, she felt safe enough, but she missed Skye. Badly. She missed the gruff manner Skye used to hide compassion. She missed the way she was on constant alert for possible danger. She missed the way Skye's hands felt on her body, offering strength, comfort, and passion. She missed her so much she risked a question.

"I'm excited. Are we almost there?"

His laugh carried a hint of insanity. He pointed ahead and, barely slowing the big truck, he turned onto a narrow dirt road. Aimee hoped Skye wasn't too far away to witness the sudden turn, but she didn't risk a look back. The woods around them were dense and Aimee flashed back to the woods behind the cabin from the night before. White seemed focused on his cause, but maybe he was on to her. The thick forest surrounding them would be the perfect place for him to dump a body, and now that he had a big stack of her money, maybe that body would be hers.

As they drove deeper into the forest, her hands shook, and she fought to control her rapid, panicked breaths. She was consumed with fear and regret. She never should have gotten involved with these people, never should have allowed them to separate her from Skye. If Skye were here, she had no doubt she would be safe. Skye's absence was the source of her regret, and not because Skye would protect her, but because she hadn't shared her feelings. She'd let Skye think they would go back to their respective lives as if the connection she felt was temporary.

What if she never saw Skye again? She hadn't wanted to take a chance that Skye might reject her. What kind of woman was she that she would carelessly risk her life, but not her heart?

CHAPTER TWENTY-TWO

Parker had spent the afternoon reading court briefs, a lousy way to spend a Saturday afternoon. At least she was at home. Morgan was at the office, meeting with a new client who'd insisted he couldn't wait until Monday to hire counsel. Parker would've joined her, but Morgan insisted at least one of them should be able to enjoy the comforts of home. Dressed in sweats and propped on pillows, Parker drowsed her way through the boring reading material. The ring of the phone startled her out of a particularly tedious passage. She recognized the number on the caller ID as the line at the Bradley residence, and she scrambled to answer. "Skye?"

"No, it's John Bradley. Parker?"

"Hi, Judge. Sorry, I thought it was Skye checking in." She'd spoken to Skye earlier about her plan to meet up with the coalition leaders and she'd been itching for a report ever since.

"Actually, there may be some trouble on that front. She and Aimee left a couple of hours ago, but I just received a visit from a team of federal agents. They had recent pictures of Skye and Aimee and knew they were staying at our place. They all but admitted they had a tracking device on Skye's motorcycle."

"Bet they conveniently forgot to get a warrant for that. Nothing I hate worse than cops that don't play by the rules." Parker's refusal to take shortcuts was the primary reason she was no longer a cop. "Any word from Skye?"

"Not a peep, and frankly, I'm concerned. My visitors made some ominous predictions about what would happen if Skye and Aimee don't head on back to Dallas. Something along the lines of 'they don't want to find themselves in the middle of what's about to go down.'"

"Think the feds are planning another raid?"

"I think it's a good possibility. You think I should try to reach her?"

Parker considered letting her father-in-law take charge, deal with whatever trouble might be headed their way. She hadn't been convinced Skye's plan to hook up with the coalition members was the smartest move; now it looked like she might be right. As she considered what to do, she paged back through years of memories. She and Skye had attended the academy together. Though initially assigned to different units, they'd remained friends, swapping stories after their shifts while they worked out, drank beer, talked about women. Skye had always been more circumspect about her sexuality while they were on the force, but with Parker she'd let her guard down. Eventually, they both worked their way up to the homicide unit and became partners. At the time, Parker thought their partnership was the strongest bond she would ever have with another person. She'd been wrong for a host of reasons, but she still valued the connection they'd shared. *A partner always has your back.* Parker believed in the creed and she'd never wavered from her conviction. She decided her duty transcended whatever their relationship had become.

"Thanks, Judge, but I'll call her myself. One former cop to another."

❖

As they pulled into the clearing, the first thing Skye noticed was that there weren't as many vehicles as there had been the night before, which seemed strange because the area was teeming with people. They must have caravanned in from wherever they lived before to take up residence here. Three large log cabins were positioned around the perimeter, and in the center, under a wide canopy, they'd erected what looked like a revival tent, complete with a dozen rows of benches and a podium at the head. She wondered if White would be preaching today or if the big guy, the Supreme Leader, would steal the show.

Davis placed a hand on her shoulder. "Help me unload?"

"Sure." She hefted one of the duffle bags full of MREs from the back of the pickup and followed him to the nearest cabin. She'd rather take off on her own and explore the entire compound, but for now, she needed to blend in. She spotted Aimee exiting White's truck a few yards away. Even across the distance, she could tell Aimee was shaken. She detoured in her direction.

"Hey, sis. You okay?"

"I'm fine."

It was a lie. Brash, confident Aimee was gone. Skye read fear in her darting eyes. "What happened? Talk to me."

"Maybe we shouldn't have come."

Tell me about it. Skye didn't speak the words since Aimee obviously regretted their decision. All they could do now was make the most of their access to the inner circle. Skye's well-honed instincts told her they were right on the edge of discovering Nicki's whereabouts.

"No regrets. You're doing great. I bet you have White in the palm of your hand by now." With her free hand she risked a quick squeeze to Aimee's shoulder. "Hang in there. We'll be out of here in no time. Stick with White, and I'll be right there. I won't let anything happen to you. I promise."

Aimee nodded and appeared to relax slightly. "Skye, I need to tell you something. Something important."

Skye whispered back, "Did White tell you something about Nicki?"

Aimee shook her head. "No, it's not about Nicki."

Skye felt someone staring at her. She looked over her shoulder and spotted Davis standing by her vehicle, watching her with inquiring eyes. She called out, "Be right there." She turned back to Aimee. "Let me get rid of him and I'll be right back. Okay?"

"Sure, okay. Go on."

Skye offered a broad smile of encouragement before she jogged to catch up with Davis. "I need to join Ann while she meets with Brother White to discuss the future of the compound. My sister would like us to share this experience together. Since her husband died, she relies upon my advice in matters of business."

Davis waved a hand in the direction of the makeshift tent. "Our cause is not a business. Our cause is revolution and restoration of true patriots to the seat of power."

Crazy fucking zealot. "Hey, pal, no offense. I only meant my presence might facilitate my sister's contribution, if you know what I mean. I'm sure Brother White would welcome my assistance." She hoped Davis was more concerned about the money they had to offer than their allegiance to the revolution.

His hard mask of resolve softened. "Of course. Help me finish unloading, then join your sister. I'm sure Brother White will be grateful."

Skye hurried through the task, quickly transporting the ammunition and MREs to the cabin that functioned as the supply post. When they finished, Davis directed her to drive to another clearing about a hundred yards away where about a dozen vehicles were parked. The walk back to the compound seemed like a hundred miles. Davis chatted the entire way, but Skye barely heard a word. She was fixated on returning to Aimee's side.

When they returned to the compound, Davis pointed out the largest cabin. "Brother White and your sister will be in there. He's preparing for a very special announcement."

Bingo. Skye forced herself to walk, not run. Within seconds, she was inside. She heard sounds coming from behind a closed door to her right and heard White's voice and a couple others she didn't recognize. She gave a perfunctory knock before she threw open the door.

"Samantha, welcome," White greeted her. "Your sister has been waiting for you to join her."

She didn't respond. Her entire focus was on the two strangers standing between White and Aimee. The girl was Nicki. Skye recognized her right away, although the confident smile and careful grooming contained in the photo she'd been carrying around were noticeably absent. As for the man standing next to her, Skye had no doubt he was the Supreme Leader. He was huge. He stood over six feet tall and his solid frame easily held three hundred pounds. He was dressed in solid black from his broad-brimmed hat to his western style boots. Unlike Nicki, he exuded confidence and power, backed by a mean glint in his eyes that a broad smile couldn't hide.

He placed an enormous meaty hand on Nicki's thin, slumped shoulder. Her flinch was slight, almost imperceptible. Skye could feel her fear, and she was curious about the source. If Nicki Howard was a willing member of the coalition, what did she have to be afraid of?

When Aimee entered the cabin with White, all she could think about was how close she'd come to telling Skye she loved her. Crazy really. They'd been standing in the middle of a compound full of armed militants preparing for a revolution, and all she could think about was Skye's strong arms, easy confidence, and sweet assurances. She made a silent vow, when Skye joined her, she wouldn't let her go.

"Sister Ann, I have a very important person I'd like you to meet." White led her into a room that appeared to function as an office. It was furnished with a large desk and several chairs, and the walls featured portraits of a bunch of white men, none of whom Aimee recognized. As he shut the door behind them, Aimee saw Nicki, and she gasped. She was pale and haggard, and the giant man standing next to her held on to her like she was his property.

White made the introduction. "Brother Gale, I'd like you to meet Sister Nicole's cousin, Ann Hartley."

Nicki barely reacted to the cousin reference, and Aimee was certain Nicki was in the clutches of the Supreme Leader. Even though she'd fully expected to find Nicki with these people, the shock of actually finding her here, looking worn and afraid, shook

Aimee to the core. She hid her surprise by lunging forward and pulling Nicki into a tight hug.

"Dearest cousin! I haven't seen you in so long. I was terrified when I thought you'd been captured. If I'd known you were in such strong company, I would have never doubted your safety."

Nicki responded to her tight embrace by hugging her fiercely, as if willing Aimee to wrap her in her arms and spirit her away. Her grasp told Aimee what she needed to know. Nicki wanted to get away from these people. If she'd ever been here of her own free will, she was done with the adventure.

Aimee risked a few simple whispered words in Nicki's ear. "Play along with me."

As she drew back from the embrace, Mr. Gale, re-staked his claim with a strong hand. He drew Nicki back to his side, and Aimee pretended deference.

"Brother Gale, please forgive me for my outburst. I'm very pleased to make your acquaintance. I appreciate the honor of this opportunity."

He extended his free hand and Aimee reciprocated, thankful he didn't kiss it. "A pleasure to meet you as well. If you are half the patriot your cousin is, then our acquaintance shall bring great strength to the cause. Isn't that right, Nicole?"

"Yes, sir. We are all patriots in search of justice."

Aimee barely had time to digest the contrast between Nicki's words and demeanor, when Skye burst through the door. White said something, but she didn't hear the words through her relief. Skye was with her. They would be safe. Now all they had to do was get Nicki away from these people. She decided to start the action by making sure Skye knew who the players were.

"Samantha, look—it's dear Nicole. And she's here with our Supreme Leader, Brother Gale. Aren't we honored to be in such esteemed company?"

"Completely." Skye extended a hand to Gale. His grip was solid and long. "Nicole, it's good to see you again."

Nicki nodded. Aimee breathed a slight sigh of relief that Nicki was following her instruction. She picked up the conversation thread.

"I believe we were just about to discuss how my late husband's estate can benefit our cause. Who can tell me more about the plans for the compound?"

White motioned them all to sit, and they gathered around the desk, seated in an assortment of metal folding chairs. "Brother Gale, would you like to tell our sisters about your plans for the next stage of the coalition?"

Gale opened his mouth to speak, but a high-pitched ring interrupted. They all looked around the room as the ring continued, and finally Skye assumed an embarrassed expression and pulled a cell phone from her jacket.

She glanced at the screen. "I'm sorry. I have to take this call. This particular arms dealer is a difficult patriot to reach."

"Go ahead. You can talk to your contact here. You're among friends."

Skye's expression was reluctant, but she answered the line. Aimee tried to catch her eye, but Skye was laser focused on the call. Aimee didn't get much information from Skye's short, clipped responses, but she read the edge in Skye's tone as trouble.

❖

The caller ID read "Fred," but Skye knew it was either Morgan or Parker. She'd programmed in a few choice numbers before they left the Bradleys' house and assigned code names in the event the phones were lost or confiscated.

"Skye, are you at the compound?" Parker asked, her voice low and urgent.

"Yes. We found some of the ones we were looking for."

"You can't talk."

"No, we still need to work that out."

"Nicki's there?"

"Oh, yes."

"Good. You need to get out. Now. The FBI visited Judge Bradley a little while ago. He thinks they have another raid planned. We think it's going to happen soon."

"I'm sure we can come to an arrangement. I'll speak with the others and I'll contact you again shortly."

"Be careful. Don't do anything crazy."

Too late for that. Skye clicked the phone shut, and faced the rest of the group. The men made no secret of the fact they'd been listening in.

"Weaponry is an important component of our revolution," White declared. "I'm certain our Supreme Leader would be most thankful if you have access to a superior arsenal."

I'm sure he would. The sound of gunfire punctuated her thought. She'd seen a makeshift shooting range when she and Davis had walked back from the parking area, but these pops and cracks were closer, and were accompanied by the sounds of running feet. Parker's warning echoed. It was time to get out.

She ran to the window, but could only see people scattering for cover in the face of an invisible enemy. When she turned back toward the group, they looked at her as if she'd lost her mind. She shouted, "It's a raid."

She grabbed Aimee's hand and headed for the door, but Aimee stood firmly in place. Skye followed the direction of her gaze. *Nicki.* Gale watched them both, and as if he knew exactly what they were thinking, he tightened his grip on Nicki's shoulder.

"Go if you must. You have not yet cast your lot with us, but we will stand and fight. The pretenders will not triumph this time."

All Skye cared about was keeping Aimee safe, but it was clear Aimee wasn't leaving without Nicki. Skye drew her gun and leveled it at Gale, hoping like hell White was too thrown by the sudden attack on the compound to react to her show of force. She barked out orders. "Let her go. Nicki, come with us. Now."

Nicki didn't hesitate. She shook off Gales's now loosened grip and ran toward the door. Skye brought up the rear and covered Aimee and Nicki's exit. She slammed the door shut behind her. "Follow me and stick close. Davis showed me a path through the woods. It leads to where our truck is parked." Aimee and Nicki didn't ask any questions, and they followed her through the cabin. She quickly found a rear door and waved them through.

They ran toward the woods, and within moments they were crouched in the dense area that Skye was certain contained the path Davis had shown her earlier. She fished in her pocket and pulled out the key to the pickup. Across the clearing, she spotted men in black combat gear creeping around the cabins. "Here. Take this." She handed the truck key to Aimee and then she pointed to her left. "The path should be right over there. Follow it for about a hundred yards and the pickup will be in a clearing. There's no guarantee they don't have it surrounded, but it's your best shot."

"What about you?"

"I'll stay here for a minute and cover you. Start the truck. I'll be behind you."

Aimee hesitated. Skye longed to give her some assurance, but she wouldn't lie. "I promised I would find Nicki. If she doesn't get out of here safely, then I've failed. Please don't fight me on this." *If anything happened to you, I would never forgive myself.*

"When you get to the truck, if the coast is clear, count to twenty. If I'm not there by then, get the hell out of here. When you get to the main road, drive the speed limit. Don't draw attention to yourself. Go to the Bradleys' house and call Morgan. She'll know what to do."

Aimee's response was to pull Skye into a fierce embrace. The crush of their bodies almost caused her to forget where they were, the trouble they were in. Almost. She craved this closeness, and the danger made it more precious. Aimee raised her head and met Skye's lips. The quick touch wasn't the passionate embrace she craved, but it was too dangerous to savor the connection. Skye pulled away. Aimee's safety meant more than her need to have this last exchange.

"You have to go. Now."

"I love you."

The words sent her reeling. Did Aimee mean them or were they parting gifts? She denied herself their pleasure because to bask in the revelation would ensure none of them would make it out of there.

"Go. Now."

Aimee didn't hesitate this time. She pulled Nicki with her and ran for the path. Skye kept careful watch until they were out of sight.

Seconds later, she was surrounded. As she knelt on the ground with her hands on her head, she finally allowed herself a moment to savor Aimee's words and the truth behind them. Aimee was on her way back to her respectable life. She was on her way to jail. Aimee would forget what she'd said in the heat of the moment, but Skye would feed on the memory for the rest of her life.

CHAPTER TWENTY-THREE

Aimee jammed the key into the ignition of the pickup and the engine roared to life. Beside her, Nicki twisted back and forth in her seat. "Is anyone coming?"

"No, no one. Aimee, we need to get out of here."

"I'm not leaving Skye." Aimee stared down Nicki's fear. Nicki returned the look with a puzzled expression, and Aimee realized she didn't know what she was talking about. "I mean Samantha. Her real name is Skye. If it wasn't for her, we never would have found you. You're in serious trouble, and I don't care what you believe, but I couldn't let them arrest you and throw you in prison." She stopped abruptly when she realized she was babbling.

Nicki reached across the console and gave her a quick hug. "I'm sorry. It's not what you think. I didn't realize what I was getting myself into. I'll explain everything, but seriously, we need to get out of here."

...count to twenty. If I'm not there by then, get the hell out of here.

Aimee considered her options. The fact that Skye hadn't appeared meant she was either in custody or hiding. If the latter was true, she didn't have the time or skill to find her. If she'd been arrested, the only people who could help were Morgan and Parker.

...call Morgan. She'll know what to do.

Aimee slammed the truck in gear and smashed the accelerator. No way was that quick kiss they'd shared going to be a final embrace. Her declaration of love was meant to signal a beginning, not an end. It was time to call in the cavalry to rescue the woman she loved.

❖

Skye didn't bother testing her restraints. Her body was bruised and sore from the rough take down, and her wrists and ankles were cuffed and linked by a length of chain fastened to a bolt in the floor of the van. She was seated on a bench along with a dozen other women whose faces she recognized from the coalition members back at the compound. Their captors were federal agents. She searched her memory for clues about where they might be headed.

She'd worked with the feds on several occasions when she was a cop, but not in this district. She didn't know exactly where they housed female prisoners, but she figured it would be one of the county jails nearby.

Today was Saturday. Unlikely they would see a judge until Monday. Not that it mattered. She'd been arrested in the company of people the government considered to be terrorists, a threat to homeland security, which meant there was no chance of bond, even if she could afford it. She forced herself not to think about her own fate, and instead focused her energy on Aimee and Nicki. *Please let them get away.* Morgan and Parker would take care of Nicki, and Aimee would eventually put this adventure behind her.

I love you.

Skye believed Aimee's words in the moment they were spoken, and that would be enough to get her through whatever came next. Her only regret was that she hadn't said, "I love you too."

❖

Despite Nicki's pleas for her to "step on it," Aimee followed Skye's instructions exactly. She hadn't violated a single traffic law. To distract herself from the interminable drive, she made Nicki tell her everything she knew about the coalition. Nicki explained how she met Earl Junior in Professor Latamore's class. At first, his constant bragging about being involved with a militia group was annoying, but when she realized his zeal was based in fact, she decided to capitalize on his craziness. Undeterred by her journalism professor's apathy about her story idea, she played along with Earl Junior's rhetoric until she convinced him she was a true believer. His father was part of the leadership of the coalition, and once Earl Junior vouched for her, she had access to the inner circle. She'd actually enjoyed playing the role until reality struck in the form of federal agents raiding the original Wimberley compound. As shots rang out, coalition members scattered and she wound up running for her life in the company of Earl Junior and the Supreme Leader himself.

While she was relieved to learn Nicki hadn't really bought into their extremist ideas, she was appalled that Nicki had carelessly endangered her own life in an attempt to score a journalistic coup and she told her so.

"After the raid, I had to keep playing along. Gale is certifiable. That's not even his real name. It's the name of one of the guys who started this whole Christian Identity movement. He decided since I was from a pure Caucasian strain, we'd make a perfect couple—him as the leader, me as his baby slash soldier maker."

"Did he…did you…?"

"No, he was waiting for later this afternoon. We were supposed to be 'married under the laws of the coalition' and have our little honeymoon at the new compound."

Nicki fell silent for a few moments. When she spoke again, she did so between sobs. "He killed Earl." She rocked back and forth in the seat. "I only dated Earl to get access to these people. He really believed in all this crap. When Gale decided he wanted me, Earl was a threat to him. He shot him and left him in the woods."

"Oh, honey, I know. We found his body." Aimee could no longer hold back her own tears. "I was sick when I saw him. I was certain you'd been murdered too."

"I don't know what I would have done if you and your friend hadn't shown up when you did."

"Skye's an investigator." Aimee tightened her grip on the steering wheel. "I hired attorneys when I found out you were in trouble. They hired her to find you."

Nicki's tears subsided and she offered a knowing smile. "Investigator, huh? Do you let all the help kiss you on the lips, or just the sizzlin' hot investigator types? I got the distinct impression she cares deeply, and not just about her job."

"Oh yeah?" Aimee resisted the desire to smack her impertinent niece. This was the Nicki she remembered. Sharp and sassy. "Well, I care about her too. Deeply. As soon as we get where we're going, I'll need your help to get her out of whatever mess we left her in. You on board?"

"Absolutely."

❖

Aimee struggled to remain calm, but her words tumbled out in a frantic rush. "Morgan, I'm at your parents' house. I have Nicki, but Skye's in trouble. I think she may have been arrested by the FBI. I need to know how I bond her out. Can you get down here right away? I'll pay whatever it takes."

Morgan urged her to take a deep breath and then asked her a series of questions. Where and when did she last see Skye? Who were they with? Was she sure the raid was conducted by federal agents? After she heard Aimee's answers, she told her to hold tight, she would call back shortly with more information.

During the intervening hour, Aimee stood guard over the phone. When it finally rang, the sound nearly gave her heart failure, but she forced herself to be calm. "Yes?"

Morgan reached her contact with the marshal's service. He told her female federal prisoners were usually taken to the Caldwell County jail. She'd already phoned there and received confirmation of Skye being booked in.

"I left a message for the prosecutor, but since it's Saturday, I don't know if she'll check her voice mail. The usual procedure is that Skye will be taken before a federal magistrate judge for an initial appearance on Monday morning. If the government wants to detain her, they'll file a motion with the court at that time, and we can have a hearing then or set it off a few days to give us time to put together a response."

"Monday's two days from now. We can't leave her in there until then." Aimee dug through her wallet and pulled out the phone number her childhood friend and pilot Ken Gains had given her. "Can you come here now? I can arrange for you to fly on a private plane in the next hour." She paused to quell the panic running through her. "I know I'm asking a lot, but it's my fault she's in trouble. Please."

Morgan asked her to hold the line for a moment. Aimee heard muffled voices and decided she was discussing the issue with Parker. Imagining the two of them, heads together, partners in life and their profession only made her more desperate to free Skye. By the time Morgan came back on the line, she was ready to burst.

"Aimee, let me talk to my dad, but go ahead and arrange for the plane and text me the details. Parker's coming with me. We'll be at the airport in an hour."

Aimee handed the phone to John, and sank into a nearby chair. She'd done everything she could for now.

❖

"Hey, sunshine, you have a visitor."

Skye looked at the female jailor dangling a slip of paper through the bars. She considered ignoring her. She didn't want anyone she knew seeing her in black and white stripes. The last twenty-four hours had been thoroughly humiliating, from the overly thorough body search to the disdainful taunts of the jailors, but the loneliness was the worst. For all her years in the law-and-order profession, she didn't have a clue about this part of the process. Her cellmates were happy to bring her up to speed on the ins and outs of the system, but she wasn't interested in making friends with convicts. Eventually, they muttered remarks about the "stuck-up bitch" and left her alone.

"I'm not waiting here all day. Sign or I'm leaving."

What the hell. Skye grabbed the form and signed her consent to the visit. She turned and stuck her wrists through the tray slot opening in the bars and waited to be handcuffed. She walked in front of the jailor who directed her to the door of a small room filled with people.

Morgan was the first face she saw, and she offered an encouraging smile. The jailor turned to leave, but before she reached the door, a tall, imposing woman next to Morgan ordered her back. "Remove the cuffs."

The surly jailor obeyed and then left in a huff. Morgan motioned for Skye to sit next to her, then introduced the other people in the room, beginning with the woman who'd casually bossed the jailor into submission.

"Skye, meet Lily Berek. She's the criminal chief for the U.S. Attorney's office in the Western District." Morgan pointed at the other two. "Special Agent Nancy Morrison and Special Agent Kevin Neely. Ms. Berek has something she wants to say to you and then she'll give us a moment alone to talk before we go any further."

Berek stared at her for a full minute before she started talking. Skye recognized the maneuver as an impromptu polygraph, and she stared back, never wavering. Finally, Berek cleared her throat and started talking. Her first remark took Skye by surprise.

"Girl, you have a lot of friends. I've been on the phone all day with various folks reaming me out for keeping you locked up. Ruined my damn dinner.

"Bottom line, I got a couple dozen gun-toting homeland terrorists locked up and I'm told by some pretty credible sources that you're not one of them. You have a right to remain silent, and seeing as how you were a cop, I imagine you're well aware of that right and likely to take advantage. You do that, and I'll leave now and I won't be back. You can show up in court and your fancy lawyer, here"—she jerked her head toward Morgan—"can do all that expensive stuff she does to try to convince a jury you were in the wrong place at the wrong time.

"Or you can talk to me now. Tell me everything you know. I won't use it against you unless I find out you lied to me. If I like what you have to say, I'll void the arrest, and Morgan can spring you in time for supper. What'll it be?"

Skye wasn't sure what to say. "I—"

Morgan cut her off. "Lily, we'd like that moment alone now."

The moment the door shut behind them, Skye found words and the questions tumbled out. "Are Aimee and Nicki okay? How did you find me? What are you doing here?"

"Aimee's fine. So is Nicki. Aimee figured you were arrested, and a few well-placed phone calls got us your location. I'm here to represent you, if you want me to."

Skye's head spun. She churned through Morgan's words and tried to make sense of her situation, but the only important piece was: "Aimee's fine." A wave of relief washed over her. She could stand all of this as long as she knew Aimee was out of harm's way. She closed her eyes to regain her focus.

After a few seconds, she was ready to talk. "But you're Nicki's lawyer."

"Technically, no. Nicki never hired us. Aimee did. Now Aimee wants us to represent you. We've located another very reputable lawyer to represent Nicki."

"What's going to happen to her?"

"She's a very important witness in a high-profile federal case. She's going to have a lot of explaining to do about her involvement with the coalition, but I can't imagine they are going to send a young, charming key witness to prison. She may never get a Pulitzer for her efforts, but she'll have her freedom." Morgan cocked her head. "Don't get me wrong, but I figured you would be a hell of lot more concerned about your own fate than that of a girl you never met until yesterday."

Skye wasn't sure what to say. Morgan had her pegged. She'd spent most of her life only concerned about her own needs, and the job and freedom to fuck around had topped the list. She lost the job, and she didn't care about fucking around anymore. How could she explain that she cared what happened to Nicki because she cared about Aimee? More than cared about her, she loved her. She'd lost everything that had once defined her, but she was ready to redefine herself. Was she only dreaming to hope that Aimee would be part of her new life?

She shook her head. She couldn't explain her feelings to Morgan. She'd suffered enough embarrassment, but at least it had been limited to her professional failure. She wasn't about to lay bare her personal wounds as well.

She didn't have to. Morgan could apparently read her mind. "Skye, you've been through a lot lately. Accept my help. Talk to Berek. I trust her not to screw you." Morgan smiled. "Besides, there's a very agitated woman waiting for us at my parents' house. If I don't have you home tonight, I'm the one who's going to be screwed."

Skye tried to mask a hopeful expression, but Morgan's next words told her it was no use. "Love heals. Let's get you out of here so you can experience that for yourself." She walked toward the door and knocked to signal to the others Skye was ready to talk, but before they entered she said, "Oh, and next time I need an investigator, you're the first person I'll call."

CHAPTER TWENTY-FOUR

Aimee sat on the Bradleys' porch completely unconcerned about the dark sky and the falling temperatures. Morgan had called a few minutes ago to say she had obtained Skye's release. Aimee had consulted her GPS app, synchronized her watch, and planted herself on the porch to wait out the fifty minutes it should take for Morgan to bring Skye back to her.

She should use the time to plan the perfect words to declare her feelings. The simple "I love you" in the thick of danger had fallen far short of her intentions. In the day since they'd been separated, she considered dozens of scenarios, all variations on the same theme—a lifetime with Skye. If Skye didn't like her Highland Park home, they would find another. If Skye had issues with their disparate incomes, then she'd scale back her extravagant lifestyle. After witnessing the sacrifice Skye had made to ensure that she remained safe, she would happily offer anything she had to get the love she wanted, to deliver the love she felt.

The moment the sedan turned into the drive, her heart began to race. The car pulled to a stop. Skye stepped out and began walking toward the porch. Her gait was slow, careful, not the cocky, sure strides she'd come to know. Aimee hesitated, unsure. She'd imagined this moment differently. Two lovers running into each other's arms, reunited at last. Skye had just spent the last twenty-four hours locked in a cell. Was it possible that she blamed Aimee for her incarceration? If so, she might not want to see her at all. If

Skye would only look up, if she could just see her eyes, she could read her future.

Her thought was barely complete before Skye lifted her head and their eyes connected. She witnessed a swirl of emotion, and in the spin she saw her love reflected back. She ran down the steps and swept Skye into her arms.

❖

Hours later, Aimee closed the door to the Bradleys' guestroom, thankful Morgan and Parker had graciously agreed to bunk in the study downstairs. Dinner and the subsequent debrief had lasted an eternity, but she hadn't felt she could deny their friends the opportunity to hear the complete story of Nicki's rescue told from both her and Skye's perspectives.

Her brother was flying in the next day to pick up Nicki, who was fast asleep on the couch in the living room. At her request, Morgan had located a reputable local attorney who would guide Nicki through the hours of government debriefing ahead. She loved her niece dearly, but she'd done all she could do for her. It was time for her parents to take a more active role. She'd had a long talk with Neil, and he promised he would be more involved in his daughter's life. She vowed to hold him to his promise.

In the meantime, she had pledges of her own to keep. She'd barely had two minutes alone with Skye. She'd headed straight for the shower upon her arrival and she was back there now. She considered joining her, but she hadn't been invited in.

She's not avoiding you. Skye had spent the last day locked up in a cell with three other women. Of course she'd want a few minutes alone. The water stopped, and Aimee chided herself for taking Skye's actions personally. She'd take a towel to her now. Wrap Skye tight in her arms, and declare her love again.

She rapped once, then opened the door slowly and gasped.

She'd expected Skye's body to be breathtaking, and it was, especially now slicked from the shower. Full, perfect breasts; tight, round ass; lean, athletic legs, all beautiful features marred with angry bruises. Aimee bit back a cry. She moved toward Skye, but Skye stepped back.

Aimee handed Skye a towel and averted her eyes until she had a chance to cover herself.

Skye offered a mirthless smile. "I keep trying to wash them off."

"Oh, baby. I'm so sorry."

"Don't be."

"If I hadn't left you—"

"We'd both be sitting in a cell right now. If it wasn't for you, I'd still be there." Skye pulled her close. She stroked her head. "You're amazing. Thank you for everything."

Aimee leaned back so she could see Skye's face. Her eyes reflected the love she'd seen earlier, but mixed with pain. "Hey, you sound like you're saying good-bye."

"We have to eventually."

"Who says?"

"You did."

Let's find Nicki, and then you can go back to your life and I'll go back to mine. Dammit. She'd spoken the words casually, a defense against Skye's rejection. To have the words used against her now was cruel irony. *Tell her you didn't mean it. Tell her you want to spend the rest of your life with her, on terms you both agree on. Don't you let her say good-bye.*

"I didn't mean it. I don't want us to go back to separate lives."

Skye took a moment to repeat Aimee's announcement silently to herself. When she was sure she'd heard her correctly, she spoke. "I don't want that either."

"I hear a 'but.'"

She'd tried to hide her hesitation, but it loomed large. She cast about for the right words to let Aimee know her wavering was all about herself, and her own insecurities. Redefining herself wasn't going to be easy, but she could at least start with being honest about her feelings, no matter what the cost. Before she could find her voice, Aimee cut to the chase.

"I love you. Do you love me?"

A simple question, beautiful in its directness. "Yes. Absolutely."

"Then let everything else go for now and make love to me." Aimee took her by the hand and led her to the bed. She sank into the covers and waited. Skye took a deep breath. In this moment, their needs and wants were the same, and she gave hers free rein.

"I'm going to undress you."

"Yes, please." Aimee unfastened her jeans, and started to push them down, but Skye stilled her hand. "*I'm* going to undress you." She leaned in and lightly kissed the flesh Aimee had exposed, then ran her tongue along the rim of her panties. Without breaking contact, she unzipped her fly, and trailed her hands down into Aimee's jeans and massaged her thighs. Aimee groaned in response to the measured touching. Skye groaned with her. She longed to go slowly, but a fierce need threatened to consume her if she couldn't feel Aimee's skin along the length of her soon. Aimee must have sensed her urgency. She raised her hips and Skye quickly shucked away the denim and the silk panties underneath.

Skye slid between Aimee's legs, placing Aimee's legs over hers and pulling her forward until they were sitting face-to-face, center-to-center. As the heat burned between them, she drew Aimee into a deep, lasting kiss, the passionate embrace she'd wanted in the forest. The one she'd dreamed about ever since. As they broke to breathe, Aimee grinned and yanked her sweater over her head, as if daring Skye to stop her.

She didn't, but she did dive between the luscious breasts, selecting first one nipple then the other to tease with her tongue. Aimee cried out and rocked against her. Skye felt Aimee's hands on her breasts, and she arched into her touch. Aimee responded by pinching her nipples in alternately hard and gentle twists that caused a wet rush between her legs.

She ached for more. All her life she'd ached for more, but she'd never realized the depth of her need until now. She'd lived life along the edges, never crossing the rigid boundaries she used to define herself. She was a cop from a long line of cops, groomed to rise through the ranks, skipping steps if necessary to achieve success. She was a loner who satisfied her physical needs, but avoided emotional connection as a weakness designed to distract her from the job. She'd embraced these traits, even taken comfort from them, but now she knew they were chains, locking her away from the discovery of her own definition of happiness. She looked deep into Aimee's eyes, half-lidded with desire, and she saw a reflection of what she could be, what she wanted for herself. Aimee's look conveyed admiration, passion, love. She knew in the deepest part of her soul that being worthy of those sentiments was the true measure of success, and she silently dedicated herself to achieving it. She gently grasped one of Aimee's hands and urged it lower, as she reached for Aimee's sex with her own. They settled into a simultaneous rhythm that lasted only seconds before the pressure became a frenzy that overtook them. Skye surrendered to the pace, but didn't allow the increasing excitement to break the emotional connection between them. She locked eyes with Aimee and the strength of the passionate intensity they exchanged drove them closer. Sharing this climax with Aimee, fast and hard, felt like the most important thing in the world. They'd save slow for later.

Later. As waves of pleasure swept them both into orgasm, Skye cried out with pleasure, and she knew in her heart there would be a later.

❖

Aimee curled up against Skye's naked body and sighed. After hours of lovemaking, she yearned for more, and she was certain she would never grow tired of Skye's touch. Skye was a perfect blend of tender and aggressive.

She'd told Skye they could let everything else go and make love, but now that they had, she knew she couldn't keep her word. She couldn't let Skye go.

"What are you thinking?"

Aimee looked over and saw Skye's wide-open eyes assessing her. She answered honestly. "I'm plotting."

Skye arched her eyebrow. "Is that so?"

"Yep."

"Care to tell me what you're plotting?"

"A defense."

"Really. Planning on some trouble with the law?"

"Not with the law. With you."

"Me?"

"I'm lying here, basking in the memory of several amazing orgasms, and waiting for you to say good-bye, tell me that our lives are too different, that we'll never be able to make a relationship work. I'm working out my arguments before you even open your mouth. The best defense is a good offense."

"Gee, sounds like you're expending a lot of energy." Skye rolled over and pinned her to the bed. "Why don't you give up your offensive and kiss me?"

Aimee mock struggled. "Only if you tell me you'll spend the rest of your life with me."

"I'll spend the rest of my life with you."

Aimee jerked out of Skye's grasp and sat up. "Say it again."

Skye's expression was sincere and she delivered each word with emphasis. "I will spend the rest of my life with you."

"What made you change your mind?" She wouldn't believe the pledge until she knew its foundation was strong.

Skye laughed. "You mean besides five mind-bending orgasms?" She stared into Aimee's eyes and quickly realized her attempt at levity detracted from her declaration of commitment. She assumed a serious expression. "It was what you said about letting everything else go. I've been so focused on what I've lost, I haven't paid attention to everything I've gained. I'll never be a cop again, but I can have a new career as a P.I., where I pick the cases I want to work on, where I call the shots.

"And then there's you. You've broken through all my barriers, and I love you for your tenacity. I love you for how dedicated and loyal you are to the people you love, and I want to be the one you love the most. You make me want to be a better person. For me, for us." She ducked her head and her voice was shy. "So, Aimee, will you spend the rest of your life with me?"

Aimee swept Skye into her arms. "With pleasure."

THE END

About the Author

Carsen Taite works by day (and sometimes night) as a criminal defense attorney in Dallas, Texas. Her goal as an author is to spin plot lines as interesting as the cases she encounters in her practice. She is the author of four previously released novels, *truelesbianlove.com*, *It Should be a Crime* (a Lambda Literary Award finalist and winner of a Lavender Certificate award from the Alice B. Readers), *Do Not Disturb*, and *Nothing but the Truth*. She is currently working on her sixth novel, *Slingshot*, which, like several of her prior works, contains a heavy dose of crime. Learn more at www.carsentaite.com.

Books Available From Bold Strokes Books

Firestorm by Radclyffe. Firefighter paramedic Mallory "Ice" James isn't happy when the undisciplined Jac Russo joins her command, but lust isn't something either can control—and they soon discover ice burns as fiercely as flame. (978-1-60282-232-0)

The Best Defense by Carsen Taite. When socialite Aimee Howard hires former homicide detective Skye Keaton to find her missing niece, she vows not to mix business with pleasure, but she soon finds Skye hard to resist. (978-1-60282-233-7)

After the Fall by Robin Summers. When the plague destroys most of humanity, Taylor Stone thinks there's nothing left to live for, until she meets Kate, a woman who makes her realize love is still alive and makes her dream of a future she thought was no longer possible. (978-1-60282-234-4)

Accidents Never Happen by David-Matthew Barnes. From the moment Albert and Joey meet by chance beneath a train track on a street in Chicago, a domino effect is triggered, setting off a chain reaction of murder and tragedy. (978-1-60282-235-1)

In Plain View by Shane Allison. Best-selling gay erotica authors create the stories of sex and desire modern readers crave. (978-1-60282-236-8)

Wild by Meghan O'Brien. Shapeshifter Selene Rhodes dreads the full moon and the loss of control it brings, but when she rescues forensic pathologist Eve Thomas from a vicious attack by a masked man, she discovers she isn't the scariest monster in San Francisco. (978-1-60282-227-6)

Reluctant Hope by Erin Dutton. Cancer survivor Addison Hunt knows she can't offer any guarantees, in love or in life, and after experiencing a loss of her own, Brooke Donahue isn't willing to risk her heart. (978-1-60282-228-3)

Conquest by Ronica Black. When Mary Brunelle stumbles into the arms of Jude Jaeger, a gorgeous dominatrix at a private nightclub, she is smitten, but she soon finds out Jude is her professor, and Professor Jaeger doesn't date her students...or her conquests. (978-1-60282-229-0)

The Affair of the Porcelain Dog by Jess Faraday. What darkness stalks the London streets at night? Ira Adler, present plaything of crime lord Cain Goddard, will soon find out. (978-1-60282-230-6)

365 Days by K.E. Payne. Life sucks when you're seventeen years old and confused about your sexuality, and the girl of your dreams doesn't even know you exist. Then in walks sexy new emo girl, Hannah Harrison. Clemmie Atkins has exactly 365 days to discover herself, and she's going to have a blast doing it! (978-1-60282-540-6)

Darkness Embraced by Winter Pennington. Surrounded by harsh vampire politics and secret ambitions, Epiphany learns that an old enemy is plotting treason against the woman she once loved, and to save all she holds dear, she must embrace and form an alliance with the dark. (978-1-60282-221-4)

78 Keys by Kristin Marra. When the cosmic powers choose Devorah Rosten to be their next gladiator, she must use her unique skills to try to save her lover, herself, and even humankind. (978-1-60282-222-1)

Playing Passion's Game by Lesley Davis. Trent Williams's only passion in life is gaming—until Juliet Sullivan makes her realize that love can be a whole different game to play. (978-1-60282-223-8)

Retirement Plan by Martha Miller. A modern morality tale of justice, retribution, and women who refuse to be politely invisible. (978-1-60282-224-5)

Who Dat Whodunnit by Greg Herren. Popular New Orleans detective Scotty Bradley investigates the murder of a dethroned beauty queen to clear the name of his pro football–playing cousin. (978-1-60282-225-2)

The Company He Keeps by Dale Chase. A riotously erotic collection of stories set in the sexually repressed and therefore sexually rampant Victorian era. (978-1-60282-226-9)

Cursebusters! by Julie Smith. Budding-psychic Reeno is the most accomplished teenage burglar in California, but one tiny screw-up and poof!—she's sentenced to Bad Girl School. And that isn't even her worst problem. Her sister Haley's dying of an illness no one can diagnose, and now she can't even help. (978-1-60282-559-8)

True Confessions by PJ Trebelhorn. Lynn Patrick finally has a chance with the only woman she's ever loved, her lifelong friend Jessica Greenfield, but Jessie is still tormented by an abusive past. (978-1-60282-216-0)

Ghosts of Winter by Rebecca S. Buck. Can Ros Wynne, who has lost everything she thought defined her, find her true life—and her true love—surrounded by the lingering history of the once-grand Winter Manor? (978-1-60282-219-1)

Blood Hunt by L.L. Raand. In the second Midnight Hunters Novel, Detective Jody Gates, heir to a powerful Vampire clan, forges an uneasy alliance with Sylvan, the Wolf Were Alpha, to battle a shadow army of humans and rogue Weres, while fighting her growing hunger for human reporter Becca Land. (978-1-60282-209-2)